DINOSAUR PLANET

A bat-winged darkness clawed over the top of the wooden posts: a banshee, a hell-creature. The thing shrieked, cupped air in wings like great leather sails, and fell on them. Jennifer had only a glimpse of the creature: taloned fingers set on the forward edge of the wings; a long and narrow head at the end of a thin neck; a beak fenced with needled teeth; short, muscular legs and clawed feet that gouged chips from the logs as it launched itself at them; a wingspan that was easily ten feet or more.

RAY BRADBURY

P R E S E N T S

DINOSAUR PLANET

A NOVEL BY

STEPHEN LEIGH

Illustrated by John Paul Genzo

A Byron Preiss Book

AVON BOOKS • NEW YORK

RAY BRADBURY PRESENTS DINOSAUR PLANET is an original publication of Avon Books. This work has never before appeared in book form. This work is a novel. Any similarity to actual persons or events is purely coincidental.

AVON BOOKS
A division of
The Hearst Corporation
1350 Avenue of the Americas
New York, New York 10019

Copyright © 1993 by Byron Preiss Visual Publications, Inc.
Cover illustration by Wayne Barlowe
Illustrations by John-Paul Genzo
Published by arrangement with Byron Preiss Visual Publications, Inc.
Library of Congress Catalog Card Number: 92-90441
ISBN: 0-380-76278-1

First AvoNova Printing: February 1993

AVONOVA TRADEMARK REG. U.S. PAT. OFF. AND IN OTHER COUNTRIES, MARCA REGISTRADA, HECHO EN U.S.A.

Printed in the U.S.A.

RA 10 9 8 7 6 5 4 3 2 1

For Devon
With whom I travel back in time
to my own childhood . . .
and who sometimes has the temperament
of a T-rex

CONTENTS

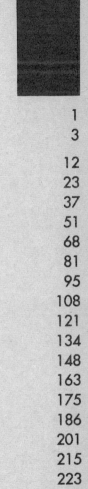

INTRODUCTION

Imitation, they say, is the sincerest form of flattery.

There are all kinds of imitations, of course. The Russians have been borrowing my ideas and stories for forty years and not paying for them. That is neither imitation nor flattery. Jack Finney, the fantasy author, asked permission many years ago to do a sort of takeoff on one of my Time Travel Stories. Flattered, I said yes. School children, constantly reading my Travel in Time stories, send me new endings for these tales. All quite wonderful and superb.

And then we have this new series of novels here by Stephen Leigh. Where did *it* come from?

The best answer is in the story found in the appendix. My tale was written way back in 1951 and appeared in *Collier's*, magazine: "A Sound of Thunder." I was amazed to see that after it appeared it caused quite a stir. Since then it has appeared in more then sixty anthologies of short stories and school textbooks. Ecologists, coming on the scene in the past decade, have adopted it as part of their propaganda concerning possible (or impossible) futures based on what was done in the past.

Mr. Leigh, has taken my tale backwards, forwards, forwards, backwards like the proverbial *Lobster Quadrille* in *Alice in Wonderland*. He has salted it and basted it, grounded it and flown it in various Time Channels where events and people pass each other like the richocheting inhabitants of a Mirror Maze. Along the way, I told him I liked his pterodactyls, but couldn't we have more of these incredible aerial beasts. He flew me a few more ancient kites. I have behaved like a proper parent watching his kid out there on the literary lot, batting as well as catching his own flies. I hope you will enjoy "A Sound of Thunder" and its precipitous sequels. *I* did.

Ray Bradbury

PROLOGUE—
A SYNOPSIS OF
BOOK ONE

Aaron Cofield and Jennifer Mason are sitting on the hill behind Aaron's house in Green Town, Illinois, enjoying the summer afternoon and lamenting the coming school year. Their affectionate talk is suddenly interrupted by a loud commotion in the woods below and a glimpse of something huge just beyond the line of trees. Whatever it was is gone as quickly as it had come. Goading each other, Jennifer and Aaron go to investigate. Rather than the expected bear, they find a clutch of very large and very odd eggs, evidently newly laid. The two call their friend Peter Finnigan to help document the strange find; but as they are photographing the eggs, they are suddenly hit from behind by a running, badly injured man.

Before any of them can move, the reason for the man's wild flight becomes painfully obvious—a charging, angry allosaurus crashes wildly through the trees. The stranger manages to kill the beast with his rifle. As the dinosaur crumples, so does the stranger.

The trio take the man back to Aaron's house, and there confer with Aaron's grandfather Carl. While Carl walks back into the woods to view the dinosaur's body, the stranger—Travis—regains consciousness long enough to tell the three teenagers his story.

Travis tells them that he is a time safari guide from two hundred years or so in the future. While shepherding a group of hunters through the Mesozoic era in order to kill a *Tyrannosaurus rex*, there was an accident: one of the hunters, a man named Eckels, went blundering off the special path laid down by Travis so that the past would not be disturbed. On their return home, the time travelers found history changed—for the worse. When Travis attacked Eckels in a rage, Eckels fled for his life in the time machine, returning to the preset time. Unfortunately, the time machine met itself in the Mesozoic, and the resulting paradox caused the explosion of Eckels's machine *and* the destruction of the floating path.

Travis, in pursuit of Eckels in another machine, came upon the wreckage. Infuriated and despairing, Travis was about to return to his own time when the allosaurus attacked. Running from the beast through the jungle, Travis came across a piece of the path still floating a few inches above the ground. Instinctively, he leapt upon it—and landed in the Green Town woods with the allosaurus close behind.

Travis lapses again into unconsciousness after this lengthy and strange tale, and the trio retires to the kitchen to eat lunch and talk. Grandpa Carl returns at the same time, bearing with him the clutch of dinosaur eggs. These lend credence to the wild, improbable story; Carl may not entirely believe the tale, but it's obvious there is something strange happening. A few minutes later, Jennifer goes back to check on Travis but finds the man gone—slipped out of the open window. A quick search doesn't locate him.

As they sit in the kitchen wondering what to do next, Aaron spies a triceratops nibbling on the grass at the edge of the incline. In a second, the three are up and out of their chairs; the triceratops snorts in surprise and fear and makes for the cover of the trees with the teenagers in close pursuit. Grandpa Carl hollers at them to be careful, but he can't stop them.

Aaron, Jennifer, and Peter go streaking across the lawn in pursuit. Once in the woods, the three are separated: Aaron, out ahead, literally falls on a section of the broken path—and finds himself with Travis and the body of the dead T-rex in the Mesozoic.

At the same time, Jennifer and Peter, growing more concerned at Aaron's refusal to answer their calls, have found a section of the path themselves—another section entirely. Jennifer insists that they step onto the path. She's certain that Aaron must have done the same. Despite Peter's reluctance, they do so . . .

. . . and enter a world they have never seen before, lush with primitive plants and strange reptilian life. Jennifer is excited—certainly this is the Mesozoic that Travis was talking about. They explore and find footprints leading into a cave. Entering, they are ambushed by Eckels. The man is raving about talking dinosaurs, rambling on and on about things that make no sense to the two. He eventually ties them up and leaves the cave, saying that he's going to offer the two teenagers to the dinosaurs. While Eckels is away, Jennifer and Peter manage to escape.

They are trying to return to the section of path when they are captured once more—this time by a group of sentient man-sized dinosaurs armed with spears.

After their capture by the dinosaurs, Peter and Jennifer's feet are hobbled with vines. They are herded down from the hills toward the valley. On the way, their little group is set upon by a small band of what seemed to be medieval samurai warriors. The dinosaurs, after dealing quickly and violently with that threat, bring Jennifer and Peter to their own encampment. The two are placed within a barricaded compound. The dinosaur placed in charge of them, Jennifer learns, is a female named Struth.

Over the next several days, Jennifer attempts to learn at least a few words of the dinosaur language, though it is extremely difficult for her human throat to reproduce the various honks, trills, and bleats with which the words are sprinkled.

Jennifer and Peter learn that the Mutata (as the dinosaur tribe is called) are one of two sentient species of dinosaur, that they have been troubled recently by invasions from what they called Floating Stones (which the two teenagers know must be portions of Travis's path), and someone they name the Far-Killer. The Gairk, a tribe of warlike carnivores, are also upset by the changes within their valley, and the Gairk are also searching for this Far-Killer.

It also becomes obvious that Struth is not exactly in the best graces of the dinosaur called the OColi—the Eldest—who is the head of this Mutata tribe.

Struth manages to capture the Far-Killer and bring him back to the encampment, where Jennifer and Peter discover that the Far-Killer is in fact Eckels. Eckels claims not to remember abducting the two of them. In fact, he gives a very different telling of Travis's tale, in which Travis, not Eckels, is ultimately responsible for the destruction of the path and the timestream. The explosion of the time machine knocked Eckels here, where he wandered confused and perhaps a little mad for a time—that, he says, is why he can't remember their first meeting. He asks for their forgiveness. Peter shrugs; Jennifer is not quite so inclined to believe him.

The three plot to escape, though Jennifer holds back, not wanting to do anything which might hurt Struth, with whom she is beginning to share a friendship.

There are other forces at work, however. Struth is under pressure from the OColi. In particular, Frraghi (or 'Fergie,' as the humans call him), the OColi's second-in-command, is pressuring Struth to dispose of the humans. Many of the Mutata blame the humans for the strange visitations and attacks coming from the Floating Stones. The Mutata are set in their ways, following a half-instinctive set of rules called the OColihi, or Ancient Path. The recent disruptions have threatened these old ways. Complicating this is the fact that Struth's mentor, Raajek, once attempted to upset the outmoded and constricting Ancient Path. Raajek wanted to lead the Mutata on the OChiihi, or New Path. Her attempt failed, however, and Raajek left the Mutata, exiling herself.

The OColi gives Struth one boon—if Jennifer can show that she is 'intelligent' (and thus knows the Ancient Path), he will allow the humans to live. If not . . .

Eckels had killed one of the Mutata during his capture. The OColi insists that Jennifer be brought in to perform a part of the ceremony, though Struth is instructed not to teach her any of the rites or even to speak of it. Jennifer will succeed or fail entirely on her own.

Confronted with a ceremony she doesn't understand, Jennifer manages at last to stumble through well enough to impress the OColi. Peter, on the other hand, has not been so fortunate. Eckels and Jennifer can live, the OColi rules, but Peter is to be killed and his body shown to the Gairk as proof that the Mutata have done something about the Floating Stones.

In the Mesozoic, Aaron has been dealing with a badly-hurt and rather unstable Travis. In a rage, Travis orders Aaron into his time machine and they return to Travis's 'present,' there to find only a desolate, cold waste utterly devoid of anything human at all. Travis goes mad, shouting that Eckels has destroyed known history entirely; Aaron is also shocked, wanting to disbelieve all of this since it also means the end of his own time. When Travis is nearly killed by the plant life of this odd future, Aaron convinces the man to take the time machine to *Aaron's* Home Time. Aaron is certain that there he will find Jennifer, Peter, his family, and Green Town all intact. He must.

But he doesn't. This world is far too much like the world they have just left. Aaron's world is shattered. His entire past is gone, all of it. Eckels has destroyed the timestream entirely, changed the past so much that nothing is the same as it once was. Aaron's family has never lived, nor Jennifer, nor any human at all. . . .

As the two, despondent, are about to return to the Mesozoic, where at least things are familiar, a whirlwind attacks them, changing shape as it comes. Worse, there is no sign of the time machine—it has disappeared.

In defiance, Aaron strikes at the whirlwind, which dissolves and changes shape, turning first into an image of Jennifer and finally into a fantasy-cover wizard. The creature—whom they address as Mundo, though it actually has no name—is an extension of the World-Mind, a consciousness that encompasses all living creatures. Mundo doesn't understand much of what Aaron and Travis are worrying about, doesn't understand their 'aloneness' at all, and certainly doesn't share their concerns. Mundo refuses to deal with them at all, dissolves back into the wind-shape, and disappears.

Struth is unable to conceive of disobeying the OColi. She has only one option—to allow Jennifer and the others to escape, even though that will mean her own death. Struth makes that decision, but before she can put the plan in action, they are interrupted. The Gairk have sent an emissary who insists on seeing the humans. They are presented to him, but before the Gairk can act, a strange lightning storm begins. Devoid of rain, coming upon them with no warning, the lightning flashes display shifting patches of other realities, both familiar and unknown. One of these small worlds happens to appear where the Gairk is standing, killing the creature, as half of him simply disappears. The storm passes; fearful, Fergie orders the humans killed.

Struth, in desperation, seeks out Raajek, who, though blind, has sensed the omens. Raajek agrees to return to the Mutata to help Struth. In a confrontation with the OColi, Raajek uses a deception to save the humans.

If only for the time being . . .

Aaron is desperately digging, hoping to find the time machine that he suspects Mundo has buried. Travis watches, too hurt and despondent to help. This world is frigid, and they realize that without shelter and food, they are both going to die.

Mundo reappears, and Aaron convinces the being to return with them to the Mesozoic—since if they *don't* do that and Eckels is still alive back there, then Eckels will change history yet again and destroy Mundo in the process. Aaron convinces Mundo there's no danger, since not only can they return him via the time machine, but the section of path that leads from the Mesozoic to Green Town now must connect to *Mundo's* present, not Aaron's.

The strange trio returns to the past, but the trip is very disturbing to Mundo, who goes into a shrieking fit as this part of him is suddenly disconnected from his greater whole. Aaron calms him, and they go off to find the pathway. Before they can do that, however, a time storm much like the one witnessed by Jennifer and the others assails them. When it passes at last, Aaron—more desperate than ever now—sets off with Mundo. They find the section of broken path and step onto it.

It's with incredible surprise that Aaron finds himself in the Green Town forest once more. Mundo, angered, bolts and runs, cursing Aaron for having tricked him. Aaron starts to go back to get Travis, then stops. He's home now. If he goes back through, he may find himself trapped once more.

Instead, Aaron moves through the familiar, comfortable forest toward his house. He spies Grandpa Carl on the porch. Waving, shouting, Aaron goes to greet him.

A FAMILIAR FACE

1

"Hey!" Aaron shouted. "Grandpa! You're never going to believe this!"

The figure on the porch turned and waved back. Aaron, laughing, ran toward him. But the laughter lasted no longer than a moment—a gasp, a sigh. Aaron knew something was very, very wrong even as he slowed to a trot.

The house . . . Paint peeled from the rear of the building in great, leprous patches, and what patches of color remained were a slate-colored gray-blue that Aaron had never seen before. The shutters his father had so carefully nailed in place in May, only three months before, now hung askew like falling men clinging to a cliff with desperate fingers. The screening on the back porch door was rusty and torn, crudely patched with newer, bright pieces of screening. The steps to the back porch sagged as if crippled by the booted feet of a giant.

To one side of the house a huge, irregular clump of boulders was piled, as if a giant's child had been playing with stones. Closer to the house, the heap rose in a steep incline, reaching nearly the height of a three-story roof. Ten feet from the side of the house, the pile suddenly stopped, looking as if it been sheared off the side of some mountain with a divine knife. The edge was perfectly smooth, curving outward in a semicircle. Aaron wondered whether it was some kind of abstract sculpture—whatever it was, it hadn't been there yesterday. He couldn't imagine his parents allowing it to be built—his mom went in more for the concrete goose type of lawn decoration.

Aaron's grandpa Carl was gripping the railing with fingers gone white with tension. Aaron heard the older man breathe his name—"Aaron . . ."— then Carl leapt over the wobbly length of oak and to the ground like a child himself. That graceful movement startled Aaron more than the appearance of the house or the baby mountain of rocks. He hadn't seen his grandfather move that way since his arthritis got bad over a decade ago, back when Aaron was still in grade school.

"Aaron!" Grandpa Carl shouted now, running as Aaron jerked back into a headlong rush himself. In a tangle of arms, the two came together in the middle of the yard. They hugged each other, Carl cradling Aaron's head to his shoulder. "Aaron, oh my God, Aaron . . ."

Aaron pulled himself back so that he could look at his grandfather's eyes. The old man was weeping unashamedly, tears running like a floodstream in the weathered channels of his face. "Grandpa, it's only been . . . what, eleven, twelve hours? Twenty at the most. What's going on? What happened to the house? What's with the rocks?"

"Hours?" Carl tried to laugh and sob at the same time. "Aaron . . . son . . . it's been a dozen *years*, boy, a long and lonely crowd of days. And you . . . you . . ."

Carl held Aaron at arm's length. His fingers dug like steel claws into Aaron's biceps. Something changed behind Carl's eyes suddenly, like a sheer curtain being pulled across a picture window. The tears still pooled at the bottoms of his eyes, but the flow had stopped and the warmth in his eyes had cooled as the lines of his face deepened.

"You haven't *aged*, son," he continued. "You ain't grown a year in that time. You ain't changed at all . . . It's one of them storms, isn't it? You've stepped out from the middle of a lightning bolt."

"Storms? Lightning? Grandpa, what's going on? The house, that rock pile . . . Where are Mom and Dad? Jennifer, Peter—what happened to them? Since when did you start running and jumping like that again? My God, twelve *years* . . ." A fist seemed to twist Aaron's insides at that moment. He couldn't breathe. "Jennifer . . ."

His grandfather's fingers dug deeper into Aaron's arms, as if the man were afraid that if he let go, Aaron might disappear like some dream-phantom. "Come in the house, son," he said. "We got a lot to figure out."

"I waited until it was nearly dark to call Sheriff Tate that night. I remember it so well . . . I told Sheriff Tate that you'd all gone off, the three of you, that I'd expected you back for supper but you hadn't shown. I didn't mention Travis or those dinosaurs, of course—not then, anyway. Tate wouldn't do anything when I called. He said he couldn't, not until you were gone for twenty-four hours. He tried to tell me that you were probably off at some party and had forgotten to call.

'Kids do that all the time,' he said. 'They'll probably be back around midnight, wondering why you're mad at 'em. Give 'em some time, Carl,' he said. 'Give 'em some time.' " Carl stopped and took a deep, shuddering breath. "But I knew . . . After all, I'd seen the dinosaur. I was afraid . . ."

"Gran'pa," Aaron said. He laid his own hand on top of the wrinkled one on the battered kitchen table, patting the dry skin. "I'm sorry you were put through all that. But from *my* point of view it's only been a few hours. Really. Time must run at radically different speeds on the two sides of the portal. Grandpa, Jennifer and Peter didn't follow me through. They *must* have stayed here. I never saw them in the Mesozoic. I'd have heard them or seen them if they'd been there."

Carl only shook his head. His eyes had a rheumy mistiness that Aaron didn't recall. The webbing of skin around the pupils had grown deeper, the folds of his eyelids drooping. The age-spots on his forearms, hands and face had grown darker and more pronounced. The head shivered with a faint trembling that had never been there before. To Aaron, the symptoms were a strange combination, as if his grandfather had aged a decade overnight, yet somehow been cured of the crippling arthritis at the same time. He'd traded stiff, aching joints for a palsy.

"I went out that night after Tate hung up," Carl continued. "I took a flashlight and went down in the woods, hollering your names. I couldn't find any of you. I called until my throat was hoarse. The woods would go silent for a few seconds every time I shouted; you'd've thought that the crickets and frogs and the rest resented my being there. I'd listen for you but there wasn't ever any answer to my calls—at least nothing beyond birds fluttering up in the trees or a raccoon's eyes glaring like a demon's in the flashlight beam. I guess . . . I guess I really didn't expect you to answer. I figured I knew what had happened: you'd found that pathway Travis had been raving about, the one the dinosaurs had come from, and you'd gone through. I couldn't even blame you, because I knew what *I'd* have done had that temptation been put in front of me at your age—heck, maybe even now. That's what *I* was looking for, Travis's grand floating roadway to the past. Well, I couldn't find it.

"Jenny and Peter's folks came by the next day, and we all went through the tangle of brush and the deeper woods. The neighbors helped, your friends. I called your folks that second night. They . . . they . . . "

Carl stopped. The bleak despair in his eyes spoke more than any words.

"Grandpa?"

"I'm sorry, boy, I truly am. I *told* them not to rush home, told them that it wouldn't matter. Take your time, wait until morning I said, but they didn't. It was late at night, and there was a nasty thunderstorm coming down from Chicago off the lake. Their train derailed before it even made it out of the city. It was a bad wreck, and two of the cars . . . well, Gary and Mary Lynn were just sitting in the wrong place. Aaron—"

"Why didn't they drive back?" Aaron asked. *What a stupid question . . . Gran'pa says they're dead and you ask why they didn't drive? . . .* Aaron felt numb. A part of him wanted to scream, to react in grief and anguish, but denial clamped down on his emotion like a vise. "Why in the world would they take a *train?*"

"Car?" Carl said. "Boy, don't you remember? We've never owned a car—you think we're filthy rich or something? They took the regular Saturday train into Chicago. How else were they going to get back?"

"Gran'pa . . ." Aaron stopped, his voice choking. *No car?* he wanted to say. *What in the world are you saying? Of course they had a car. Everyone has a car . . .* Aaron swallowed and tried to start over.

He couldn't—in that moment, the full impact of what his grandfather had said struck him. The room darkened and seemed to whirl once around him.

This world's been changed, the same way Travis's was—it's not just the lost years, it's everything.

"I'll never *see* them again?" Aaron cried, half in question and half in desperation. "You're telling me that they're *gone,* just like that, that I'm never going to talk to them or help Dad bring in the corn or—" Aaron stopped. He had to breathe, had to force the hysteria back down. "Gran'pa, I wasn't even gone a whole *day.*"

"You've been gone a dozen years," Carl said solemnly and frighteningly. "It's been a damned long time, Aaron. A damned long time. It's not been a pleasant time, either. With all—"

Aaron felt the touch of his grandfather's fingers on his cheek. He hadn't realized that he was crying, but Carl was crying, too. After a few minutes, Aaron sniffed, trying to dam up the sorrow. After all the strangeness of the last day, this was too cruel a blow. He wondered if he could even believe it.

The phone rang, interrupting his next question. The look Carl gave the phone was very odd, and the old man's face dissolved from grief to suspicion in an instant. The tears were suddenly out of place in that grim expression.

"You be quiet, Aaron. You understand? Don't say anything."

With that strange admonition, Carl shoved his chair back from the table with a scraping of linoleum and shuffled to the wall phone. He let it ring twice more, his hand hovering over the receiver in indecision. Then Carl plucked the receiver from its cradle as though it were hot. " 'Lo?" he grated out. "Yeah . . . I know. I heard about it. Well, you can tell them that I didn't have anything to do with it . . . I don't *care* what they found here and I don't care what anyone's saying . . . No, don't worry about me. I've been taking care of myself for a long time now and I don't intend to stop now. Uh-huh . . . Listen, you just tell him for me that he can stuff his regulations and court injunctions. And be sure you use exactly those words."

Carl slammed the phone back onto the receiver, the bell chiming in protest. The back of his neck was flushed.

Aaron barely noticed. He sagged in his chair. It was too much—after all that had happened in what for him had been only a few hours, this was simply too much. He couldn't believe it; he *wouldn't* believe it.

"Gran'pa, what's going on? I'm really confused right now."

"Nothing's going on," Carl spat out. "I shouldn't have answered the phone—every time I do they make me angry. But if I hadn't, they'd've had an excuse. The Committee would have been over here the next day, nosing around, or they'd've sent over one of the 'suits' from the Compound. Just to see if I was 'all right' or some such excuse. Just an excuse to go prowling around. I've about had it with this National Emergency Regulations garbage, I can tell you that."

"Committee? Compound? National Emergency? I don't know what you're talking about."

"The General and his cronies . . ." Carl blinked. He was looking at Aaron now in the same way he'd looked at the phone. When Carl spoke again, his voice was strangely soft. "Tell me, boy: when you and I used to go down to Twin Lakes to fish for crappies and bluegill, what'd we use for bait?"

"Bait? Fishing? Gran'pa . . ."

"You heard me, boy. Just answer the question."

"Gran'pa, we never *used* live bait—you always told me you didn't have the patience to just 'twiddle my thumbs and stare at a bobber.' So we used lures: L'il Skunks, usually."

Aaron tried to smile at the memories fishing brought back. He couldn't manage it, not in the face of the rest. "Gran'pa, your asking questions like that makes me wonder if you don't believe I'm Aaron. You sound paranoid, like you think someone's out to get you. You sound—"

Aaron choked off the rest . . . . *You sound crazy, Grandpa, You sound utterly loony . . .*

His grandfather's face hadn't relaxed. Carl nodded, grim-faced. "So that's what it sounds like to you, does it?"

"Gran'pa, what's going on? Why'd the phone call upset you so much? Why are you so suspicious?"

Carl only shrugged. The hardness in his face remained. "Twelve years change a heck of a lot of things," he said. "I never thought Aaron—*you*, I mean—were dead. I tried to follow you in my mind, boy. Each year I'd add a wrinkle or two to the portrait of you I carry around in my head, brush in the lines of maturity and the furrows of wisdom. I made sure that you aged with the seasons. I did that so when I saw you again, I'd recognize you. You should be *thirty*, Aaron, thirty years old and looking almost like your father. But I see you sitting there and I'm looking at a memory or a photograph from over a decade ago. I'm not seeing a reality."

"I hear what you're saying. I don't understand it myself. But I'm me, Grandpa. Really. I'm Aaron. And this is all as hard on me as it is on you. I've lost my *parents* . . ." Aaron couldn't go any further. He took a deep breath, clenching his hands together on the kitchen table.

His grandfather nodded, but now there was nothing friendly in his eyes at all. The phone call had driven it all away. *He never used to be like this*, Aaron thought. *Never these kinds of quicksilver changes of mood. He's different.*

"I'm tired," Carl said abruptly. He nodded more enthusiastically now. "Yes, I'm very tired. I think we ought to call it a day, boy."

"Gran'pa, the sun's just going down. I want to know what's happened and why everything's so different. It's barely dark. We'll just turn on . . ." Aaron stopped.

He'd begun to gesture at the big overhead light and fan that had always been above the kitchen table. Only now they weren't there. The ceiling was empty—a barren field of plaster, not even a sign of the old socket. Puzzled, Aaron looked more closely at the room. The switch for the light was gone, too, and the plug by the counter where his mother's battered old toaster usually sat. The refrigerator looked odd also. It was smaller, boxier, and it didn't hum. A kerosene lantern sat on a shelf above the device; the glass was soot-smeared with use.

Carl was looking at him expectantly, like this was some weeknight back when Aaron was in grade school and had to get to bed early. *Gran'pa,* he wanted to say, *I've been on an emotional roller coaster myself, I thought for a little while that I'd lost my whole world, but this is worse. You just told me that I've lost twelve years, that my parents are dead, and my two best friends never came back. I don't need sleep; I need information. I need to try to make some sense of this, and this world doesn't match my memories. I'm afraid to go to sleep because at this point I don't know what I'll find when I wake up.*

The room was threatening to begin spinning around him. Aaron closed his mind to the thoughts, swallowing hard.

"Look, Gran'pa, umm . . . if you're tired, why don't you just go on to bed? I've got a lot to think about. I'll stay up, maybe watch TV or listen to the radio—"

Aaron stopped. Carl's face and demeanor had shifted again, the eyes narrowing and furrows deepening in his brow. "You'll watch *what*?"

Something in the old man's tone made Aaron hesitate. He very much suspected that the television in the front room wasn't going to be there. "Nothing, Gran'pa. I'm just not sleepy yet. I think I'll sit out on the porch. Watch for shooting stars."

Slowly, Carl's face relaxed. He smiled and patted Aaron's shoulder. "Great." he said. "See you in the morning, son. And son . . ."

"Gran'pa?"

"I'm glad you're back. Believe me. I'm very glad." With that, he left the kitchen. Aaron listened to him moving through the house and up the stairs. After a while, when he heard the creaking of bedsprings, Aaron got up and walked through the downstairs rooms.

Much of it was as he remembered. Yet . . .there was no television set in the corner of the living room, no stereo system, no radio—in fact, there were no electrical outlets at all. He might have been looking at a nineteenth century parlor.

"Things have certainly changed," Aaron said softly. "What in the world is going on?"

ATTACK FROM
THE SKIES

"No, Jhenini," Raajek said patiently. "The word for a precious item is 'ghiora'—you must add the full roar and you should also incline your head just so, or it becomes 'ghiara,' which means an ordinary item, a tool you might use to work with. You should also change your scent to a faint sweetness to accentuate the change. I know you can't do that, but this means that the sound and the stance are much more important. Do you see and hear the difference?"

"No, OTsio Raajek," Jennifer answered truthfully, trying to add the double roar to the dinosaur's title and the middle snort to the name, as well as raising her chin just *so* to indicate her respect. Jennifer suspected that she didn't do either very well. The intricate body-dance of the Mutata language was hard enough. As for what Peter called the "animal grunts and hoots and hollers," well, it was much easier to simply drop that component—that tendency on her part was what had started this lecture in the first place. "Well, I mean I have an idea of what you mean, OTsio, but it's very hard for me."

Raajek gave the wide grin that was the Mutata smile. Her blind eyes, a startling and empty milky-white, gazed past Jennifer into unseen landscapes.

"Actually, you do better than I would have expected, Jhenini. But you must always realize that our language has *three* components, not just one: the sound, the language of the body, and also smell. Since you humans cannot control the last, you must work very hard on the rest. A little difference in inflection or stance can change meanings, especially when there is no smell."

Raajek snorted to emphasize the sentence, then lowered her body slightly until the tip of her heavy tail rested on the ground. Her massive head inclined down toward Jennifer affectionately, and Jennifer reached out to stroke the sagging folds under the elderly dinosaur's snout. Raajek sniffed contentedly; Jennifer caught the scent of decay from the ulcerated sores along the dinosaur's spinal crest, but she just wrinkled her nose and ignored the smell.

"That feels good," Raajek said. "Thank you, Jhenini. You have learned much in a very short time. You should be satisfied with your progress."

"I'm not."

"I wish your companions would take even half of your interest," Raajek said. She lifted her snout, her nostrils flaring as she scented Peter and Eckels. Jennifer and Raajek were sitting near the entrance to the humans' enclosure within the Mutata settlement. Peter and Eckels were near the rear, as far away from the dinosaur as they could get as they talked with each other. Hunkered down in a patch of sun, one of the Mutata guard-lizards watched them. It would be evening soon, the time when the dinosaurs' metabolism slowed and they retired to their dwellings for the night.

"They don't," Jennifer answered. "I've tried, but Peter refuses and Eckels simply doesn't seem interested. They both—" Jennifer stopped.

"They both believe they will escape," Raajek finished for her.

"Yes."

"That would be a mistake—" Raajek began. Stopped. She rose up again to her full height. "SStragh is coming."

"How do you know that?"

"I can hear her and smell her . . ." Raajek lifted her snout. Her nostrils widened, wrinkled. "Something is wrong."

The gate to the enclosure crashed open at that moment, and SStragh rushed in. Two more of the guard-lizards were with her; they ran obediently to cover each side of the entrance. The younger Mutata had her spear in her right hand and clutched several more in her left. She threw them down in middle of the enclosure.

"Jhenini, Peeitah, Eikels! Take the weapons! Now!" SStragh shouted. As the three humans scrambled to obey, SStragh moved directly in front of Raajek. "SStragh, what is—?"

Raajek got no further. At that moment, a moving shadow fell over the enclosure. A bat-winged darkness clawed over the top of the wooden posts: a banshee, a hell-creature. The thing shrieked, cupped air in wings like great leather sails, and fell on them. Jennifer had only a glimpse of the creature: taloned fingers set on the forward edge of the wings; a long and narrow head at the end of a thin neck; a beak fenced with needled teeth; short, muscular legs and clawed feet that gouged chips from the logs as it launched itself at them;

a wingspan that was easily ten feet or more.

Jennifer ducked—one wing caught her and sent her tumbling. The rough surface of the creature's skin opened a long, shallow cut on her forehead that sent blood running down, half-blinding her. Jennifer cried out with the pain; it felt like someone had taken a grinder to her head, and for a moment she felt dizzy and nauseous. On her knees, she wiped at her eyes with the back of one hand as the creature swooped up and over the other side of the compound. With great lazy sweeps of its wings it rose high above them.

"What *is* that?" Jennifer yelled at SStragh, trying to ignore the pounding of her head. She'd seen something similar in Aaron's books on dinosaurs, with one of those unpronounceable names underneath it.

"I don't know," SStragh hollered back, her gaze still on the sky. "Some type of saorod, maybe, but bigger—"

SStragh had no time to speculate further. The beast had banked and turned, diving back down at the group. Another saorod joined it, both creatures wheeling down from the sky like twin, screeching dive-bombers, their deadly mouths gaping and snapping. They cleared the fence with scant inches to spare, barreling in.

The guard-lizards leapt for the neck of one of the saorods as it soared past; a flip of the flying creature's head sent the smaller dinosaurs tumbling The other saorod came at Peter and Eckels, who jabbed at the thing with their spears and then rain; its companion arrowed in toward SStragh, Jenny, and Raajek. SStragh put herself between Raajek and the attacker, thrusting at the saorod with her spear. It shrilled once more, beating at the air with its wings so that the hurricane blast buffeted all of them, and lifted away again to perform another acrobatic rise, turn, and dive.

"Peter!"

Jennifer had a moment to glance around for her friend. Peter and Eckels were scrambling for the enclosure's 'house,' a roofed shelter the three of them had built in their first week here. The two reached it seconds before the other beast's feet dug ragged furrows in the ground where they'd been.

The saorod lifted its beak and screamed in frustration. A kick sent one of the walls tumbling. The saorod began to tear at the thatched roof of the shelter, digging for Peter and Eckels as its wings flapped angrily and one of the guard-lizards rushed it, snarling. Through the shattered walls, Jennifer could see the two men trying to fend off the creature with their spears.

Jennifer had no time to watch or go to help her companions. Once more, the other saorod was on them. SStragh had planted the end of her spear in the ground, angling the sharp tip upward as the flying creature rushed toward them.

The impact was jarring. The onrushing beast impaled itself on the spear, the momentum causing the tip to tear through muscle and bone and lodge deep in its chest. The saorod hissed and shrilled, beating at SStragh with wings and claws. Its struggles cracked the wooden shaft of the spear, splitting it in half and sending SStragh sprawling. The injured saorod lunged toward SStragh and Raajek, staggered and missed, then gathered itself again. Blood streamed down its chest, pulsing around the broken spear.

"No!" Jennifer screamed. She picked up the last of the spears SStragh had tossed down and charged the saorod herself. The beast heard her, turning to face Jennifer as she thrust the weapon into its body. It snapped at her as she tried to hold it away with the shaft; the gales from its wings tore at her as it flapped and hopped and squealed.

"No!" Jennifer screamed again, grunting as she shoved the spear in deeper. She felt something break inside the saorod; it shrieked in agony. A leg kicked out and reopened the just-healing cut Jennifer had inflicted on herself a few weeks before, during the Giving ceremony. Blood made the wood slick under her fingers. The injured arm, already weak, threatened to give way entirely. The saorod, sensing that it was about to break free, redoubled its efforts.

"No!" Jennifer hung on desperately as the wings beat at her, as the fingers dug into her shoulder and the sawtooth mouth snagged her shirt.

"Jhenini!" SStragh was suddenly alongside her, with the remnant of her spear in her hands; the Mutata plunged the weapon into the saorod again and again. The creature quivered in agony, its head arcing back in pain, now trying to back away from its tormentors. The saorod rammed backward into the enclosure's fence. Jennifer was pulled along with it as she held onto her embedded spear, SStragh pursuing. Pinned against the logs, the beast shuddered. The wings flapped convulsively, and its mouth opened in a silent cry. As SStragh plunged the spear in one last time, the creature collapsed, tearing the spear from Jennifer's hands.

The dying saorod shivered, thrashed at the ground once with its wings, and went still.

"OTsio Raajek!" SStragh called. Jennifer turned her head away from the gory scene in front of her. The second saorod had abandoned Peter and Eckels for easier prey. Peter and Eckels were standing in the shambles of the enclosure, either too stunned or not caring to pursue. Raajek had not moved, her ancient, blind head cocked as she listened to the sounds of the struggle. The saorod came right at her, guard-lizards snapping at its legs as the creature half ran, half flew across the enclosure.

SStragh, weaponless, slammed her own body into the saorod, knocking it aside as the wings battered at Raajek. The old Mutata fell, crying out as she tumbled sideways. The impact caused both SStragh and the saorod to go sprawling. The saorod was up almost instantly, one wingbone bent and broken, its eyes flashing in fury.

Panting, Jennifer yanked her spear from the saorod she and SStragh had killed. She glanced quickly at Peter and Eckels. They were standing, just watching—as the saorod gathered itself up again, as SStragh pulled herself groggily to her feet, as Raajek shook her head in confusion and hurt.

"Peter!" Jennifer called. "Help me!"

Jennifer could see Peter looking at her, but he didn't move.

She could waste no more time. With a sound that was half-sob and half-grunt, she flung the broken spear at the saorod. The spear went flying end over end, striking the saorod in the head with the butt end and then falling to the ground. The creature snarled at her. Then the guard-lizards hit it in concert, tearing at its neck and wings with massive, powerful jaws. The saorod hissed and wriggled, flinging them loose only to have them come at it again. The attack gave SStragh and Jennifer time to get to Raajek and lift her up.

"Chodoe!"

The call came from the gate: *Follow me!* Frraghi and several other Mutata rushed through. As the saorod tried to react to this latest threat, they quickly encircled the creature, their spears ready.

The saorod seemed to have no fear of its imminent death. It screeched a wordless, primal challenge at the Mutata surrounding it; then it charged, its short legs churning. The long beak snapped in two the first spear to jab at it, and then another quick bite tore open the shoulder of the unlucky dinosaur in front. But the saorod had no chance to follow up its fleeting advantage. Frraghi and the others closed quickly, stabbing again and again at the beast until at last it hissed and crumpled to its side, the wings giving one last, futile flap.

Frraghi let out a whistling hoot of triumph, then came over to where Jennifer and SStragh were attending to Raajek. Frraghi slammed the end of his spear down on the ground in front of Raajek.

"Elder," he said, and even Jennifer could smell the scent of disrespect in him. "I hope you're not hurt."

"No, Frraghi," Raajek answered. Jennifer noted that Raajek's head was inclined downward and she did not even bother to turn her unseeing eyes toward Frraghi. The blatant disrespect in that gesture added an undertone of mockery to her words. "I'm fine. I'm certain both you and the OColi will be most relieved to hear that."

Frraghi snorted, then recovered his politeness. "Yes, I'm certain he will." Frraghi glanced at Jennifer then. "The human is hurt."

"I will live, Frraghi," Jennifer answered him. She also refused to look at him, glancing instead at the gory carnage around her. She deliberately used her injured arm to wipe away the blood still streaming from the forehead cut. "The OColi will be glad to hear that also, yes?"

Another snort. Frraghi glanced around at the wreckage of the enclosure, then noticed Peter and Eckels. His eyes widened and the crest rose on his spine as he shifted his spear from his right hand to his left. "The human males have weapons," he said. "That is not allowed."

Frraghi started toward Peter and Eckels. There was no mistaking the grim satisfaction in his voice.

"Peter," Jennifer called. "Drop your spear. Now!"

Peter hesitated. Now several of the other Mutata began to follow Frraghi toward the two. Peter brought his spear up in both hands, threateningly. "Keep back, you ugly lizard!" he said to Frraghi.

Peter spoke nothing of Mutata; Frraghi, like the rest of the dinosaurs, spoke no English. The insult went unnoticed. That hardly mattered; it was apparent that Frraghi intended to end this perceived threat as he had that of the saorod. He and his group continued to advance on Peter and Eckels.

"Peter, Eckels, they'll kill both of you," Jennifer shouted desperately. "You can't fight all of them! Please!"

Peter scowled. "No!" he said.

"There are too *many* of them. Frraghi will kill you, Peter. You know that—all he needs is the excuse."

For a moment, Jennifer thought that Peter wasn't going to listen. Eckels, behind Peter, had tossed his spear down the moment Frraghi had started toward them. Peter, his face twisted in disgust, took a step backward and threw down the spear. Frraghi plucked both weapons from the ground with a contemptuous sniff, handing them to his entourage and then turning his back on Peter and Eckels as if they no longer mattered.

He came back toward the gate, glared once at the bodies of the saorods, then looked at Raajek. "This is what comes of your OChiihi, your New Path, Raajek: death and destruction. Five of these horrors attacked us; more were seen in the direction of the Gairk. Three Mutata died today because the Floating Stones are still open. You have said that the humans can help us close them, and they have not. The OColi will not tolerate you or your *pets* very much longer."

"Then the OColi is not as wise as I believed him to be," Raajek answered. "The OColi has let them live so far. So perhaps the OColi does not listen to you as much as you think, Speaker."

Frraghi glared at the remark. For a moment, Jennifer was certain that the younger Mutata would respond in kind and Raajek and he would become locked in a battle of words that—as Jennifer had seen—sometimes led to a more physical confrontation with the Mutata.

"The OColi listens longer and more intently each day, Elder," Frraghi said slowly. "There will soon be a time that it won't matter that you have used your OChiihi tricks on the OColi. Soon, Raajek. Soon."

With that, Frraghi gave a shrug and stalked out of the enclosure, the Mutata with him following. As the gate closed behind them, Jennifer sat down abruptly. "Jhenini?" SStragh hurried over to her. Peter started forward, then stopped after a warning glance from SStragh.

"I'm fine," she told the Mutata. "Just a little weak, still. The blood . . . I need to clean the cuts, bandage them . . ." She sighed, looking at the saorod that lay directly in front of her. "SStragh, did those things come from one of the Floating Stones?"

"They must have, Jhenini. We've never seen anything like them before. I saw them across the valley, a flock of them. They split into two units, the smaller coming here, the other flying fast toward the Gairk village, as if they knew exactly where they were going. . . ."

Raajek went to the body. The ancient Mutata gently explored the body of the creature with her hands. "Look," she said. She held up one of the 'fingers' of the wingbone.

They all saw the band of carved, polished stone behind the saorod's knuckle. "Ghiora," she said.

"Animals do not wear jewelry." Her smell was tart, astringent. "Like you, Jhenini, these saorod are nothing known in the OColihi."

"They're nothing I know, Raajek. They're not from my world, either. They must have come through another Floating Stone, one you haven't found yet."

Raajek gave a loud exhalation. "Frraghi is right. The OColi will be wondering whether he has done the wise thing in listening to me at all. The Gairk OColi will be furious at this attack and will be blaming Mutata for this as well as everything else that has happened."

Raajek's scent changed. She dropped the saorod's wing and turned her head in Jennifer's direction. "Jhenini," she said. "I have not asked you to tell me everything. I have not tried to force you to say more than you wish to say."

"I know. I have appreciated that, OTsio Raajek."

Raajek straightened with a groan. "But we must have that talk, Jhenini. We must have it soon, and you must tell me *all* you know. You must tell me so that I can convince the OColi of your worth."

"OTsio—"

Raajek raised her arm, the long, agile fingers flexing as the color of her crest changed from emerald to aquamarine. "Later," she said. "For now, I want to soak my bones in the Hot Pit, and you must care for yourselves. I will send in some younglings to dispose of these saorod and to help you repair the damage to your dwelling. SStragh . . ."

Without another word, Raajek turned and left the enclosure. SStragh looked at Jennifer. "Go on,

SStragh," Jennifer said. "Peter will help me."

SStragh snorted and her smell was sour, but she nodded. SStragh followed Raajek out, closing and locking the gate behind her. Jennifer huddled on the ground, clasping her wounded arm and trying to ignore the stench of the saorod. After the Mutata had left, Peter approached her, crouching down beside her while Eckels stood a few feet away.

"What were the lizards saying?" Peter asked. "What'd you tell them? Jenny, you know we gotta be careful what we tell them—"

Peter stopped at her glare. "You just *stood* there," Jennifer spat out. "Both of you. That thing was coming right at poor Raajek."

"Yeah. So?"

" 'So?' You can't really mean that, Peter."

"If it had been you, we wouldn't have hesitated, Jenny," Eckels broke in. "But hey, it was only Old Blind Eyes." He grinned, the expression just touching the lips, as if they were trying it on for size.

Peter laughed with Eckels's comment, then his expression sobered. "We were thinking that maybe this was our chance to get out of here. The gate was unlocked; we had spears, and if we could find the piece of roadway we came in on . . ." Peter stopped, looking at Jennifer's expression. "Or maybe you just prefer it here with your scaly friends and their snorting and hooting," he said.

"SStragh and Raajek are the only reason we're still alive," Jennifer told them. The pain from her arm and her irritation lent the words heat. "I shouldn't need to remind you two of that. Between the Gairk and Frraghi and the OColi—"

"What you don't need to remind me of is that we've been here for almost a month and a half now, Jenny," Peter interrupted. "It's time we took our fate into our own hands."

"You know something, Peter, you're beginning to sound just like Eckels."

Eckels raised his eyebrows at that remark. Jennifer ignored him, continuing. "Peter, we don't know *where* our piece of the roadway is. The Mutata and Gairk both keep patrols out in the valley, not to mention the wild creatures out there or the things from the Floating Stones or the Dreaming Storms. If we escape, we're fair game for everyone: the Mutata, the Gairk, and anything out there that's hungry. We don't have weapons, we don't have protection, we're not as fast or as big or as agile as half the things out there. Here we're at least protected. It's only been a month. If we work with Raajek and SStragh, we'll get back. I'm sure of that. If we do what *Eckels* wants, even if we *do* get out of here, we'll have nothing. Nothing to eat, nothing to protect ourselves with, no shelter, and only the vaguest idea where the path might be."

Jennifer started to stand and grimaced as the movement caused the cut on her forehead to begin bleeding again.

"C'mon, Jenny, let me help you," Peter said. "Let us *both* help you."

"I really don't want you to help me, Peter," she answered. "With the kind of advice you've been giving lately, I'm afraid I might die following it."

With as much dignity as she could manage, Jennifer pushed past the two men and went to the ruins of their house.

SCRAMBLED WORLD FOR BREAKFAST

Outside, an electrical storm was raging. Through the stroboscopic lightning flashes, Aaron could see brontosaurs moving like black hills against the horizon, a long mounded line of them trailing into the distance. With each lightning flash, the landscape beyond his window changed. First, broken cliffs leaned over a thrashing sea. Then came a flat plain of waving grass, rolling hills lost in wreaths of mist, a green mountain on whose slopes he could see a peaceful Buddhist temple. Through all the changes, Aaron was in the same room—*his* room, in his familiar house. Thunder snarled and lightning stretched forth wild fingers, but he was safe inside.

"Aaron?" His mother's voice sounded from downstairs. "Are you all right?"

"Mom!" he cried. "I knew you weren't—" *Dead*. He couldn't say the word. "Mom! Dad!" He started to fling the covers aside, ready to run out of his room and down the steps to find her.

But then there was a crash that was not the storm but something closer and more terrifying. Mundo was at Aaron's bedroom window, glaring in with glowing red eyes like some Hollywood monster, shaking the frame with his apelike hands and gibbering with animal shrieks. The storm raged

behind him and the clouds were like the head
of a T-rex, the lightning its teeth, the thunder
its roar, the wind its carrion breath. Aaron huddled as far away from Mundo and the threatening
storm-creature as he could.

"Go away, Mundo!" Aaron shouted. "Leave
me alone! I didn't mean to leave you stranded
here, I didn't! I really thought that I was taking
you home."

Mundo hissed in rage. He drew a fist back to
break the glass, and the storm-beast behind him
gathered itself to leap in at Aaron . . .

"You go away, you hear me! Get off my property!"

The distant shouting shredded the dream,
swept away the nightmare storm and dragged
Aaron from a long, exhausted sleep. He groaned
his way from the bed, knuckling his eyes at the
unexpected sunlight with one hand and pulling
at the waist of the pajama bottoms he'd borrowed
from his grandfather with the other. Aaron peered
through the slats of the dusty blinds. The roof of
the front porch obscured Aaron's view, though he
could make out the top of a man's head as he stood
at the foot of the steps, a swirl of wispy dark hair
over a bald scalp and a gray tweed suit coat that
looked two sizes too big in the shoulders. The man
seemed to be arguing softly with Aaron's grandfather, who was either at the door or on the porch
itself. Aaron could hear the tone of the stranger's
voice, though not the words themselves.

"Get out or I'll run you off!" Carl shouted in
answer.

Downstairs, the screen door slammed, followed
by the heftier *tchunk*! of the front door. The man

seemed to shrug, then waved his hands at the house in a gesture of disgust before walking away. Aaron's gaze followed the man's gray suit as he headed down the long walk toward the lane—the pants were as loose and ill-fitting as the coat, the thin fabric flapping in the breeze. Whoever he was, he looked like a kid playing dress-up. Aaron wondered whether that was the current style or just poor tailoring.

Aaron's brow suddenly furrowed. His nagging sense of unease intensified. The scene was wrong, little details out of place. The lane leading down to Mill Creek Road was missing the blacktop that Aaron, his father, and grandfather had laid down three hot summers ago—*no, it was fifteen years ago*, he reminded himself. The Cofield driveway was rutted gravel, as if the blacktop had never been there at all. The car that Baggy Suit climbed into was odd, as well. The lines were hardly aerodynamic: a plain ebony box on overlarge, spoked wheels. Rust was chewing large holes along the edges of the doors and around the fenders. The engine seemed to be in the rear, and greasy, black smoke poured from the exhaust when the starter churned and the cylinders fired. The machine bounded down their lane as though the entire suspension was just a set of springs, the body lurching right and left as it negotiated the potholes.

Aaron watched the car until it disappeared behind the old sycamores that walled in the entrance to their land, then looked back at the landscape outside his window. The image still wasn't right. The green ramparts of the woods across the field looked as he remembered, the yard was the same . . .

The electrical pole's missing, the one where Peter and I hung the basket back when we were kids. There weren't any wires running from the house at all, though Aaron knew that the phone was hooked up somehow, maybe underground.

No electricity. No television or radio. Cars that looked like Detroit had decided to return to the Bad Old Days. Commissions and Regulators. A mound of boulders sitting next to the house, and blacktop missing from the driveway.

Aaron's stomach knotted. He felt disoriented and lost. Nothing seemed solid anymore, and the residue of everything that had happened to him only (for him) the day before burned in his throat like acid. Reality was stretched and distorted like an image in a fun house mirror, like Mundo's magical changes of body, like the lightning-stroke glimmerings of a dozen histories in the strange storm he'd witnessed back in the Mesozoic.

This world was no better than Aaron's nightmare or the barren vision of the future that he'd seen with Travis. In fact, the near-familiarity of this place made the differences more stark and upsetting. This was a history where his parents were dead and his grandfather seemed more and more to be a crazy, maybe even dangerous, old recluse.

Aaron pounded his fist on the sill of the window. It seemed solid enough—and the pain was definitely genuine. He grimaced and shook his hand.

"I want everything back the way it was," he whispered. "I want Jenny and Peter and the end of summer and Mom and Dad on their way back from Chicago."

But nothing changed. This was no dream from which he could awaken.

"Aaron!" his grandfather called from the foot of the stairs.

The odor of frying bacon wafted into the bedroom. The growling in his stomach reminded Aaron that he hadn't eaten since yesterday afternoon, lunch with Jennifer and his grandfather on the back porch. A yesterday that had taken over a decade.

"Twelve years is a long time between meals," Aaron told his faint image in the glass. He didn't want to put on his old clothes—they were torn and filthy, and a long bath the night before had made him feel at least partially clean again. He rummaged through the closet and found a robe. Lacing it around himself, he went downstairs.

His grandfather was in a grimly jolly mood. His smile was brittle and stiff, and anger smoldered under his thick, gray lashes. "Thought the smell'd finally wake you up," he said as Aaron entered the kitchen, running fingers through his sleep-tousled hair. Carl's voice had all the heartiness of a used car salesman's greeting. He reached under the stove and turned off a spigot: propane, Aaron realized. Not natural gas. Carl slid several pieces of bacon onto a plate, scooped a mound of scrambled eggs from the pan, and ladled them onto the plate.

"You want some coffee, boy?" he asked as Aaron sat down. "I'll make a pot."

"I don't drink coffee, Grandpa."

"Since when? You started having coffee in the morning when you were fourteen—thought it made you more 'adult.' Cream, no sugar. I remember." That didn't seem to be worth arguing about.

"Grandpa," Aaron said slowly, "I heard you arguing with the guy in the baggy suit."

The plate clattered as Carl set it down too fast. Bacon slid up and over the edge; the fork nearly went to the floor. For a second, Carl's face went blotchy with anger, then Carl shook his head like a dog shaking water from its fur. The leering smile returned.

"Paper's there on the table," Carl commented as if Aaron had said nothing at all. "Picked one up yesterday in town." He went back to the stove, fixing a plate for himself.

Okay, fine, We're not going to talk about it. Great. Aaron stared at his grandfather's back, then shrugged. He slid the paper over toward him, spreading it out and snagging a forkful of eggs. He glanced first at the date: July 21, 2004. That was enough to make him lose his hunger with the first bite.

The headline stopped him in mid-swallow.

CALIFORNIA ATTACKS U.S. BORDER
Associated Press Services

RENO, Nevada. Forces of the California Elite Guard yesterday attacked the U.S. Army outpost at Brennen Pass, Nevada. Casualties were rumored to be heavy. Sporadic gunfire was reported throughout the night. General Schwarzkopf's office refused to confirm early casualty figures, but reliable sources have said that as many as twenty of the Guard were killed in the fierce night-long skirmish.

This marks the fifth time in the last month

that the uneasy truce between the Californian Republic and the United States has been broken, and leads to speculation that the peace talks scheduled for the end of the month will be canceled.

That was as far as Aaron read. His eye was caught by a strange photograph and the next headline down.

GREEK TEMPLE APPEARS IN HOTEL
United Press International

CHICAGO, Illinois. A time storm ravaged downtown Chicago last night, leaving portions of what appears to be a Greek temple lodged in the foundations of the Hyatt Regency Hotel on Wacker Street. The storm lasted over a minute and involved manifestions from several different eras, all within a three-block area. Seventeen people are known to be missing, and three buildings, including the Hyatt, have suffered structural damage. Three unknown people were found in the structure, all speaking a dialect of ancient Greek. They have been taken into custody, following the standard emergency regulations.

The time storm is the first to have occurred in a major urban area, and the furthest to have occurred from the apparent center of the disturbances, somewhere in southern Illinois. Scientists are worried that the Chicago storm indicates that these temporal dislocations will occur more frequently and in even more distant localities. Dr.

David Fitzpatrick, Chairman of the History Department at Notre Dame University notes that the apparitions are historically accurate. "The temple columns, the transepts, the facings—all correspond exactly to what we'd expect of the architecture at the time of the Parthenon."

"Gran'pa"—Aaron's finger pinned a photograph of the transformed Hyatt lobby to the table—"What is this? When did California start fighting the rest of the nation? When did these time storms start?"

Carl looked at him as if he'd grown an extra head. "The damn war's been going for fifteen years now," he said. "You registered for the draft on your eighteenth birthday like everyone else, boy. You remember how happy we all were when your student deferment came through?"

Aaron remembered no such celebration, but he wasn't going to say so. His grandfather stared at him strangely. After a moment, Carl began speaking again. "These storms began two summers after you left. I saw the very first one—all kinds of weird landscapes and things flickering across the lawn, right here. The last lightning flash left that big pile of rock sitting next to the house, just before the storm ended. No one believed me, though. They all called me crazy until a time storm hit right in the middle of Green Town a couple of weeks later. There were dinosaurs, walking right out in the middle of the square— for a few minutes, at least."

"Yeah, well, I . . ." Aaron stammered. He didn't know what to say. To cover his confusion, he rustled the paper, flipping through it quickly. The rest of the stories were just as incomprehensible: an article about the Czars (who had *always* ruled in Russia); another article about a new recording from Elvis (who wasn't dead); and one about Queen Elizabeth (who apparently was) of the European Empire. The world was scrambled; worse, it seemed that it had always been that way.

A sudden fear came to Aaron, along with a suspicion.

"Gran'pa, you said they never found Jennifer or Peter."

"Nope. Jenny's mom still holds a birthday party every year for her. Saddest blame thing I've ever seen, Mrs. Mason just sitting there in the middle of the kitchen, the cake blazing with candles, and her just bawling and staring at the door like she thinks Jenny's going to walk back in while the wax runs down, melting all over the icing. Everyone calls her crazy, like they call me. I don't think she's so crazy. I didn't hold no birthday party for you, but I knew you weren't dead. I knew it."

Aaron shivered at the image of Mrs. Mason's birthday party for her missing daughter, and the thought made him think of Jennifer, and *that* caused a hundred questions to rattle like a skeleton's fingerbones in his head.

None of this made sense. None of it added up, no matter how he tried to explain it to himself. "Gran'pa—"

"What now?"

Something in his grandfather's tone made Aaron's jaw snap shut, clipping off the words he might have said. The old man's smile had vanished. One hand was stroking the stubble of his cheek. Grandfather Carl seemed to have the same harsh edges as the world revealed in the paper.

"Nothing, Gran'pa. Nothing. These are great eggs. Thanks."

Carl *harrumphed* and turned back to his own plate. He poked at his eggs viciously.

"Gran'pa," Aaron ventured when he thought it might be safe, "don't you think that we ought to tell someone what happened? I mean, I know why you didn't have a chance to tell anyone yesterday but I'm back now and I can *prove* what happened. I can show them the roadway. Jenny and Peter had to follow me. Let's go into town, tell Sheriff Tate and have him come back here—"

"No," his grandfather said. "*No* one comes out here. You understand that? No one! And no one needs to know about you, either." His voice had risen to a strident bellow. The muscles of his neck stood out like ropes under the skin.

For a moment, the old man just sat there, breathing heavily and staring at Aaron. He dropped his fork onto his plate and stood up, toppling his chair. Without another word, he walked away and dropped his plate into the sink from chest height. The china shattered, eggs and glass spraying out onto the soiled linoleum. Grandpa Carl just kept walking. He pushed the door open to the back porch.

With a squeal of rusted springs and a groan from the old hinges, the screen door slammed behind him.

*   *   *

Aaron cleaned up the mess, then went prowling through the house. All his old clothes seemed to be gone; he rummaged through his grandfather's closet until he found a pair of pants that almost fit and a shirt that hung on him like a drape and went outside.

Grandpa Carl was standing in the middle of the backyard, just standing there staring outward at the line of trees down the slope. Aaron came up behind him. "Gran'pa?"

No answer. Aaron touched the old man's shoulder. "Gran'pa?"

Carl turned. The two of them were very close. Staring into his grandfather's wrinkle-snagged dark eyes was like staring into the eyes of a stranger.

"Who are you, boy?" Carl breathed. "Which one of 'em sent you? The General over at the Compound or them gray suit types? You're trying to set me up, I know it. You want to prove I'm crazy so you can take my land."

"I'm *Aaron*, Gran'pa—" he began. "Please, just tell me what's going on."

"You know. You have to know. I'll shoot 'em," Carl said. "I told 'em I would and I will. If they don't leave me alone I swear I'll do it. The storms ain't my fault. They ain't. The suits did it when they took that thing out of the woods."

"Took *what* out of the woods, Gran'pa?"

"Why, the path, boy. The path. I told you that, didn't I? They came and got it at night, maybe a week after the three of you were lost. A whole crew of 'em, a convoy of trucks tearing up the driveway, bright lights around the trucks harsh and blue and throwing long shadows across the yard, men looking like dark robots in their uniforms. They went in and brought it out covered in plastic, but I knew what it was. They wouldn't tell me anything at all no matter how much I shouted at them that it was my grandson who was lost out there and how this was my land and my property they were stealing. But I knew. The path—they were taking Travis's path. I knew then that I wasn't ever going to see you again. They were taking *you*, same as if they killed you."

"Gran'pa, hey, you're talking kinda scary. Are you saying that someone found the section of roadway? That can't be—I just came through it, after all, me and—" *Mundo*, he was going to say. Explaining about a large white gorilla named Mundo didn't seem like a great idea at the moment. Aaron tried to laugh; it sounded more like a cackle. "Anyway, it's still down there, I know . . ."

"Maybe," his grandfather said, and his expression changed again. "Unless you're someone that they sent to fool me. They want to get rid of me, you know. They think I'm still hiding something. They think I made the storms somehow. That's why they keep bothering me. That's why I still find 'em down in the woods sometimes."

Carl grinned, then, and the smile was more frightening than anything he could have said. It was a dead smile, a mirthless thing made of fury and frustration and madness. It was a ghoul's smile; with it, Carl turned away again.

Aaron stood there for a moment looking at the wrinkled landscape of the back of his grandfather's flannel shirt. That, at least, was the same as he remembered. Grandpa Carl had always worn the same thing, winter and summer: overalls over a plaid flannel shirt. All this was familiar—the mountains and valleys of red plaid hiding his skinny body, the thin gray hair curling around the collar.

The suspicion hit Aaron all at once. If they (whoever "they" might be) had found *another* piece of the roadway, if Eckels's destruction of the floating path had sent *two* pieces spiraling through time to here, then maybe Jennifer and Peter had found that piece. Maybe they were trapped as he had been trapped, lost in some strange past.

Which meant that, maybe, he could find them again. First, though, he needed to know what was going on here, and it was obvious that he wasn't going to get much here.

"Gran'pa, I think I'll—" . . . *run into town*, he was going to say. Somehow the words wouldn't come out. His grandfather hadn't reacted, anyway.

Aaron sighed. He patted his grandfather on the shoulder. "It's okay, Gran'pa. It's all going to be okay. I promise you that."

Aaron turned and headed for the front of the house and the detached garage at the end of the driveway. The big double doors to the garage were the wrong color, but they were open. Aaron peered into the darkness of the garage. No car—a big haywagon liberally decorated with dusty cobwebs took up most of the space. His racing ten-speed, bought the summer before, he'd always placed in the front corner. It wasn't there, either. Hanging up on a wall bracket was a clunky-looking bicycle: big tires, no gears, no handbrakes. An acne of rust pocked the chrome handles and cratered the fenders. When Aaron took the bike down, he found that the tires were flat, but there was a bicycle pump propped alongside the bike. Aaron put air into the tires—they held. The seat springs screeched in protest as he got on the bike.

It was nine or ten miles to Green Town by way of the road. Aaron and his friends biked it often enough or even walked it through the woods.

When Aaron reached the gravel driveway, he looked back to the rear of the house. His grandfather was still standing there, staring into the woods as if they held a secret that only he could know.

Aaron hopped on the bike and began pedaling away down the road.

DUEL PERSONALITIES

"Why don't you ask the lizard when it's going to take *us* out again?"

"SStragh is a 'she,' not an 'it,' Peter. I'd also apppreciate if you'd stop calling them 'lizards.' And if you'd make half an effort to learn their language, you could ask her yourself."

Hands on his hips, Peter watched Jennifer leave the compound with that Struth lizard. As the odd duo went through the gate of their enclosure, she was already spouting those ugly snorts and whistles that the lizards called a language.

Peter could feel his face grow hot, the residue of yet another argument with Jenny. His fingernails dug moon-shaped divots in his palms. It seemed like all he and Jenny did anymore was argue. He loathed this place. He detested the lizards: their cold stares, stupid customs, and haughty ways.

For a moment, Peter thought of just charging the gate, of breaking it down with the sheer blind energy of his anger and frustration. One of the guard-lizards, almost as if the thing sensed his thoughts, moved in front of the vine-lashed frame and snarled at Peter, displaying twin rows of sharp incisors. The lizard pawed once at the ground, plowing quadruple furrows with its long claws. It looked almost eager, staring at him with bright, green-flecked eyes.

"You'd love to tear me apart, wouldn't you, ugly? You'd really get a kick out of that."

The creature hissed, its long tongue flicking out. Peter scuffed dirt toward it and then retreated.

Coming into this world had started out as a grand adventure, exciting and even dangerous. The adventure had turned into a prison. Before the moment when he and Jennifer had first stepped onto Travis's floating path, neither of them could have imagined anything more incredible and exciting than streaking back in time or finding that the dinosaurs were one heck of a lot more intelligent than Aaron-the-dinosaur-nut or any of Peter's teachers had ever suspected. So much for *their* supposed knowledge.

But as the days wore on and on, all Peter ever saw was the inside of these stupid walls. Every time he was taken out he and Eckels were hobbled like animals and treated like unruly pets. They'd been here well over a month now, as nearly as Peter could tell. A month was about all he could stand.

He couldn't comprehend how Jenny could feel differently. Peter was beginning to think that he'd never understood her at all. Ever.

Eckels came up beside him, putting a hand on Peter's shoulder. "Hey, kid, that's one heck of a scowl."

"Aah, it's Jenny, man. Her and this whole place."

Eckels nodded understandingly. "I think—" he began. Then he shrugged. "Forget it."

"Forget what?"

"I don't like saying anything," Eckels answered softly. He smiled apologetically. "She's your friend, after all, and decent-looking, too. But I know she doesn't like me."

"No kidding. You're very observant."

Eckels shrugged at Peter's sarcasm. His voice sounded so reasonable, so calm. Peter didn't understand why Jenny treated the man like he was some kind of maniac. He was friendly enough, friendlier to Peter than Jenny had been recently.

"Well, I didn't exactly make a good impression when you first met me, and after what that liar Travis told you . . ." Eckels said.

"Hey, you were out of your head then, right? You aren't to blame for this—Travis is. And at least you've got some ideas to get us out of here."

Eckels smiled back, patting Peter's shoulder. "We're gonna do that, too. You and me alone, kid, if your girlfriend doesn't want to join us."

"She's not my girlfriend. Not anymore."

Eckels grinned. "She doesn't exactly have much choice at the moment, does she? You ought to think about that, Pete. Until we make our break . . ."

"When's that gonna be, Eckels? I can tell you this, I'm getting real anxious."

"Then we'll do it soon. Soon. Like I told you, they made a mistake with me, those lizards. A big mistake . . ."

They had moved to the center of the compound, near the hut the lizards had just finished rebuilding for them. Eckels reached into his pocket, bringing out a finger-long, cylindrical metal object, which tapered to a point at one end.

"I've a bunch of these," he started to say, then put his hand back in his pocket quickly. Another of the guard-lizards waddled toward them, stopping just far enough away to be out of range of an annoyed foot. The beast made a sound like a wounded teakettle and sat down on its hind legs, glaring at them.

"I know those things are only as smart as a dog, but I still hate them listening to us," Eckels said. "Why don't we go inside while I lay this out for you, eh? Here's what I'm thinking, my friend. . . ."

Still speaking, Eckels led Peter inside the hut.

"The OColihi is part of all of us," SStragh told Jennifer. "The OColihi links us with our ancestors—all the way back to the All-Ancestor Herself. Each of us, both Mutata and Gairk, carry dim memories of the Mute Ones, of what we were before the All-Ancestor defeated the Fiery Ones and gave us the gift of speech. Slowly, we began to learn how to be something more than just animals. We learned how to cooperate, how to deal with our conflicts with honor, to build, to forage, to gather together in these jhaka." SStragh waved her hand to indicate the village around them. "We found that we should live under the rule of the Eldest, that it was best to join with other jhaka when we went on our Nesting Walks. We learned how to Give our dead back to the All-Ancestor in a way that is pleasing to Her. So much we learned. And all of it, all of that combined knowledge of generation upon generation upon generation, is the OColihi. The Old Path rules us."

Jennifer and SStragh strolled slowly toward the center of the village (or *jhaka*, Jennifer reminded herself, repeating the word in her head so she'd remember it.) The day was incredibly hot and humid, the sun relentless. Between the domes, they could see the marshes steaming far out in the valley. Jennifer's blouse, already ragged from months of constant use and washing, was soaked with sweat just from the short walk from the humans' enclosure. SStragh, on the other hand, seemed to enjoy the heat; her chest and back expanded as if basking in delight. Her color was brighter than usual, the scales on her sides gleaming emerald and azure, like a glistening ocean painted in the brightest metallic hues.

"Then why does OTsio Raajek believe that the OColihi must give way to her OChiihi? If the Old Way has brought you this far, what does this New Path offer?" Jennifer asked.

"That's an old argument between the OColi and OTsio Raajek," SStragh answered. "It is why Raajek left our jhaka many seasons ago. Neither Mutata nor Gairk have changed, not since the time of the Eldest of the Eldest of the Eldest. OTsio Raajek says that the OColihi brought us to our current state, then left us with nowhere to go. She says that the OColihi has become like the scales of an Old One, hard and rigid. Because of that, we are trapped, locked in the OColihi's grip. The OChiihi is both Old and New. It will create new behaviors and allow us to move past the OColihi into a better world."

Instinct. Jennifer could almost hear Aaron saying it. *They're driven by instinct.*

Jennifer remembered sitting with Aaron on the

couch at her house. Cara, her Siamese cat, wandered in. Cara jumped up on the couch near them, then turned around three or four times in the corner before finally settling down with her head on her paws.

"I read once that cats do that," Aaron had said. "In the wild, cats will repeat that same movement to make a little hollow for themselves in high grass, a place where they can hide and be safe. Cara's ancestors all did the same, long before they were domesticated. Housecats still have the same behavior because it's their instinct now—a learned pattern that was once a survival trait and now doesn't make any sense unless you know their history."

Instinct.

That was the OColihi, too, Jennifer was certain. Century upon century of instinctive behavior, now codified and ossified into the Mutata's societal patterns, an etiquette, religion, and set of ethics all rolled into one. It was no surprise that the OColi considered Raajek's OChiihi heretical; in fact, it was a wonder that Raajek had found any followers at all.

"When Raajek left, I continued teaching the OChiihi to those who would listen," SStragh continued. "Mostly, that was to others who had chosen Raajek as their OTsio. There aren't many of us, but there were enough followers that the OColi could not silence me entirely. I think that the OColi knew that without the power of Raajek's presence, they would all eventually cease to listen and the cult of the OChiihi would die." SStragh spread clawed fingers wide in self-deprecation.

"I am not Raajek," she continued. "I do not have my OTsio's power of speaking. The OColi was correct. The belief in a OChiihi *would* have died . . . if the All-Ancestor had not sent the Floating Stones."

"The Stones were a signal," Jennifer said.

SStragh snorted in mocking laughter, her long, wide snout lifted. "Maybe. But everyone argues about just *what* the signal means—the end of the OColihi as Raajek says, or a sign that the All-Ancestor is distressed with us, as the OColi and the Gairk claim. Sometimes, Jhenini, I wonder myself."

The Floating Stones didn't come because of any All-Ancestor, Jennifer wanted to tell her. *It was Eckels and his foul-up. No one else.* But she remained silent. Even in Green Town, it was never quite safe to insult someone else's beliefs.

The two were approaching the open area between the linked buildings of the jhaka. The white, pebbly surface of the mound-like structures seemed to reflect the sun back at them. Jennifer found herself shading her eyes to cut some of the glare. Above the buildings, she could see the black bodies of the strange saorods who had attacked the day before. The Mutata had hung them from tall poles. The corpses hung limply, like black leather flags attended by a whining army of flies: a grisly warning.

Jennifer noticed that the Mutata they had passed so far remained far back from the two of them as if proximity might cause them to be infected. A constant astringent odor followed them, as if each of the Mutata was noting their presence. Jennifer knew that the odor must signify something. She could have asked SStragh, but she figured that it was nothing complimentary.

A bellow echoed among the buildings, answered quickly by another. "Ciosie!" someone called loudly. Jennifer knew that word: the best translation SStragh had been able to give her was something like "the All-Ancestor's decision." The word was a challenge, an offer to fight. SStragh had lifted her head, standing as erect as Jennifer had ever seen. Then she hurried forward, her head bobbing up and down as she trotted quickly toward the central clearing with Jennifer following.

SStragh had once explained the delicate intricacies of the ciosie, rules formulated in the OColihi. Jennifer knew that the only allowable weapon in such a fight was the Mutata thrusting spear, the only weapon the Mutata ever seemed to use. She knew that the spear must be grasped with the left hand foremost, and that only one bloodletting blow would be allowed. Jennifer also knew that such a wound was often eventually deadly since the Mutata had very little medical knowledge. There were other rules, strange nuances and forms that were part of the ceremonial display.

It seemed she was going to see some of that now.

Most of the village seemed to have gathered in the clearing. Jennifer saw two dozen or more Mutata there. SStragh was already speaking with a young male whom Jennifer recognized as Waato, another of Raajek's students or otsioiue. SStragh and Waato were speaking so fast that Jennifer could not catch everything that was being said. " . . . shouldn't ask for ciosie, especially with Lhath. That isn't what OTsio Raajek would want, Waato."

Waato stank. Jennifer could think of no other word. The Mutata's aroused emotions had spawned a welter of vigorous odors that permeated the area. Waato glared beyond SStragh impolitely, his gaze fixed on Lhath. Jennifer could see the long ropes of muscles standing out in Waato's left hand and arm as he grasped the shaft of his spear. The glassy stone of the weapon's head glittered in sunlight, mockingly. The tip of the Mutata's thick, rigid tail flicked back and forth, restlessly, in the shadow cast by the saorod bodies.

"I am sorry, SStragh," Waato said. "But Lhath has continually insulted me and our OTsio. He has just done so again here, in front of many others. I will no longer tolerate it."

"Raajek doesn't want this, Waato," SStragh pleaded. "Remember her teachings. You have fallen into the OColihi, not the OChiihi. Please, I'm asking you for Raajek: withdraw your challenge."

The tail lashed again. Waato rocked back on his massive legs. "I hear your words and smell your concern, SStragh, but I have given the challenge. You know as well as I do that once spoken those words can't be taken back."

"Listen to SStragh, Waato," Jennifer pleaded. Her sudden intrusion into the conversation caused Waato to snort in surprise. He ignored Jennifer's presence entirely, refusing to even look at her.

"The challenge can be ignored if Lhath agrees," SStragh said over the awkward silence.

"Lhath does not agree."

The voice was all too familiar to Jennifer—she turned to see Frraghi standing beside Lhath. The OColi's Speaker was drawn up in full display: his coloring deep and vivid, his chest splayed out, and his spinal frill up. "Lhath will accept the judgment of the All-Ancestor," he said. "We will see if he has said anything to Waato which is wrong."

"The All-Ancestor doesn't speak through ciosie, Frraghi," SStragh answered. "The last thing we need right now is foolishness that injures or kills us. Enough Mutata and Gairk have already been Given in the last hands of days. We are already too few."

"Yes," Frraghi purred. "The abominations of the Floating Stones"—his gaze moved first to the saorod corpses far above them, and then slithered over Jennifer like the blade of a cold knife—"and from the Dreaming Storms have taken our kin. All of which show how the All-Ancestor is angry with the way we are abandoning the OColihi."

"The Dreaming Storms and the Floating Stones are signs that the OColihi is already broken, Frraghi," SStragh answered.

Several of the Mutata snorted at that. "That is what you of the OChiihi keep telling us," Lhath stated. "Well, I say enough. I say let the All-Ancestor guide our spears if words don't convince anyone. Waato has offered me ciosie; I insist on it. Maybe when all of those who listen to your OTsio have been given to the All-Ancestor, She will forgive us. If Raajek and SStragh won't submit to ciosie, at least Waato has the courage to do so."

Frraghi trumpeted his agreement, a sound

echoed by most of the gathered Mutata. With the noise, the cloud of feeding insects overhead shifted over the bodies of the saorods. SStragh's own protest went unnoticed in the general clamor. Jennifer moved closer to her protector; SStragh stood rigidly in front of Waato. Jennifer had never seen SStragh's finely-scaled skin so pale; the dinosaur looked sick.

"Move aside, SStragh," Waato said. Now he did glance down at Jennifer, and his gaze was no more kind than Frraghi's.

"Waato, our OTsio Raajek—"

"I *defend* our OTsio," Waato interrupted. Waato dropped his snout as he turned back to SStragh, a gesture of defiance. "Unlike you."

SStragh looked so distraught that Jennifer could not hold back. She stepped forward, so that Waato had no choice but to look down at her again.

"You defend Raajek with the OColihi, Waato? How can you say you're Raajek's otsioiue when you follow the rules she says are outmoded and no longer useful?" Jennifer burst in. "Waato, that doesn't make any sense."

Jennifer knew that her outburst was a mistake from the moment she spoke. She could feel the hostility around them, could see it and smell it. A derisive hooting erupted, a Klaxon call of irritation. What she said next was very human even though she spoke in Mutata, and was yet another mistake. She looked from Waato to the Mutata ringing the confrontation.

"You're *all* so stupid sometimes!"

She had thought the Mutata were loud before. The noise redoubled, a trumpeting clamor that made her want to clap her hands over her ears—

a tumult that might have shattered windows in Green Town. Jennifer could understand little of the explosion of sound around her. She didn't need to; the message was clear enough.

The Mutata attacked her en masse without bothering to use their spears. Bodies shoved against Jennifer roughly, the scales abrading her skin. Clawing fingers snatched at her, tails lashed. Jennifer was shoved backward. Her feet stumbled over a foot or a tail, and suddenly she was sprawling in the dirt. Panicked, Jennifer rolled— a clawed foot stamped hard on the ground where she'd been, another kicked at her and struck a glancing blow that numbed her shoulder. Jennifer was trying to scramble to her feet and couldn't— the Mutata were closing around her, an impenetrable forest of feet and clutching hands and long snouted mouths open with fury. Jennifer struck back ineffectively, kicking and punching, but it was like hitting an armored knight with a bare fist.

Another kick staggered her; something slammed into her in her back and she was on her hands and knees.

Distantly, she heard SStragh's voice. There was daylight above her. She looked up to see SStragh shoving back one Mutata with her spear. Amazingly—Frraghi was there as well. Together the two Mutata herded and shoved the others back, and slowly the hubbub quieted. Jennifer, bewildered and shaken, rose to her feet.

"Bhieye," Jennifer said to SStragh: thank you. She nodded to Frraghi. "Bhieye," she said again. Frraghi exhaled, wrapping her in the scent of grass.

"I helped only because the OColi gave his word to Raajek that you were not to be harmed yet," Frraghi said. "I obey my OColi. Always. Don't mistake my aid for anything else. Most Mutata consider you nothing more than a curiosity and a beast—that's why they attacked. They weren't going to offer you the consideration of ciosie because you aren't intelligent enough to deserve it. You are a right-handed thing." Frraghi opened his wide, long mouth in a strange grin. "But *I* would give you ciosie if you wanted it, Jhenini Human. I would."

Jennifer stepped back in the face of Frraghi's animosity and she nearly fell again, her bruised legs betraying her. SStragh was suddenly alongside Jennifer, supporting her. Frraghi gave SStragh the same half-grin. "Or you, SStragh," he added.

"I won't do that," SStragh said. "You know why, Frraghi."

Frraghi snorted. "It doesn't matter. You would probably try to trick me the way Raajek tricked the OColi." Frraghi tapped the end of his spear on the ground. "Your abomination knows nothing," he said. "It is a stupid animal. If it were my choice, it would hang with the saorods."

There was too much stress on the word *stupid* and his statements came wrapped in the scent of pleasure, as if Frragh very much enjoyed the thought of Jennifer's body mounted on a pole. Jennifer shivered at the image, afraid. She realized what Frraghi was doing. He wanted Jennifer to disagree; he wanted an excuse to call the challenge of ciosie down on her. And she'd given him the opening.

You just insulted every Mutata here, girl, and you

knew that Frraghi and the others don't like it when the abominations talk back.

She lifted her chin, showing Frraghi her neck in the Mutata gesture of submission. "This abomination *is* stupid," she declared loudly, so that all of them could hear. "It was my anger speaking, not me. I take back my words and hope that all Mutata will understand that I did not mean them as they sounded."

Frraghi sniffed and flared his nostrils. SStragh exhaled a long sigh.

"Enough," Waato said. He had pushed forward again, gesturing at Lhath with the point of his spear. Again, Jennifer felt herself impaled on Waato's glare. "I no longer care about SStragh's abominations. I am Mutata, and ciosie is the way of Mutata. Too much of what Frraghi and Lhath have said is true. I welcome the All-Ancestor's judgment." His voice now had the rhythmic sound of ritual phrasing. "I call again for ciosie with Lhath."

"You shall have it," Lhath replied, his voice like a stentorian horn, the words melodic and precise.

"Are there witnesses enough for you?" Waato asked.

Lhath looked from one to another of the Mutata. "Geedo," Lhath answered. *Yes.*

Jennifer expected SStragh to protest again, but she did not. She only nodded, sweeping Jennifer gently back with one hand as she herself stepped away from Waato. The other Mutata moved aside as well. Lhath, with delicate precision, placed his spear on the ground, the point facing toward Waato. Waato did the same, positioning his weapon so that the points touched and the two spears created one unbroken line. Each of the combatants moved to stand directly behind his own spear.

As one, they reached down and picked them up again, each in his left hand, thumping the butt ends harshly against the ground. They stood that way: their spears in front of them, the dark, glassy blades upright, their right hands at their side. Waato and Lhath seemed locked in a trance, each staring at the other.

Jennifer didn't know what she expected to see: a flashing of spears like a fencing match in an old movie, perhaps, a flourish of thrusts, parries, ripostes and counter-ripostes. Another image came to her: two gunfighters in a western, staring at each other down the length of a dusty street, the townsfolk gathered to watch, eager to see quick violence and death.

She almost missed it. There was nothing fancy or graceful about the ciosie. Waato growled and leapt at Lhath as if catapulted, his spear thrusting. Lhath moved at nearly the same moment, stepping slightly to his left and sweeping his spear to the left to send Waato's strike harmlessly aside. In the same motion, Lhath stabbed back. Waato's momentum drove him right into Lhath's spear tip. Waato grunted as if in surprise, his eyes widening in shock. He kept moving forward, tearing the spear from Lhath's grip; but the deadly blade was already lodged deep in his chest. He lurched, careened. Toppled.

Waato was still alive. He screamed in pain, trying to tear out the spear that impaled him as he thrashed on in the ground. Blood splattered the front ranks of the watching Mutata and stained the dirt. Waato's claws gouged at the earth, his tail whipped and flailed. SStragh was holding Jennifer tightly, even though Jennifer struggled to be loose.

"Somebody help him!" she screamed, not even realizing that she was speaking English. "Let me go!"

Lhath sank down beside Waato. He cradled the dying Mutata head like a lover, stroking Waato in sympathy yet doing nothing to stanch the flow of blood or to remove the spear from the wound. Frraghi sat beside Lhath, taking Waato's hand in his own. The two spoke to Waato in comforting tones. The other Mutata watched, crooning sadly and sending forth an odor of spice to comfort Waato.

They all seemed to share Waato's agony, crying with him.

It took Waato a long time to die. Lhath stayed with him the entire time, and when Waato gave a great sigh and went limp in his hands, it was Lhath who gave a keening ululation of mourning.

"The All-Ancestor speaks," Lhath said, but there was no triumph in his words, no satisfaction.

Each of the Mutata came forward to stroke Waato's long neck. Each of them gave the cry of mourning, of loss, of pain. They touched Lhath, too, as if consoling him for having slain Waato.

Frraghi took Waato's spear from the dead Mutata. After a ceremonial proffering of the weapon to the sky, he broke the shaft in two over his leg. He offered the truncated tip to SStragh.

SStragh didn't move to take it. Frraghi nodded as if satisfied and replaced the broken spear in Waato's hand. SStragh stared at Waato's body, and Jennifer could feel the Mutata trembling from raging, hidden emotions. "Come, Jhenini," SStragh said, her voice soft and her odor strangely subdued.

"SStragh—"

"Be quiet and follow me!" Sstragh ordered in a sudden peremptory tone. The trembling increased under Jennifer's hand and she took a step back. "*Aii*!" SStragh added, making the command imperative.

She began to walk away.

Wondering at what she had seen and what it might portend for the humans, Jennifer had no choice but to walk with SStragh. The gaze of Frraghi, Lhath, and the other Mutata followed them from the site back toward the humans' enclosure.

GREEN TOWN
REVISITED

"I finally make it to the year 2004," Aaron muttered. "And what does it look like?—1920."

Biking down Mill Creek Road toward Green Town only made the familiar landscape seem stranger. First, there was no car traffic at all. Judging from the mud washed across the asphalt from the sides of the road and the weeds sprouting ankle-high through the cracks, Aaron would have bet that tires rarely touched it at all. A quarter-mile down the road, where the woods had once ended abruptly and Mill Creek Road had run into Route 42 at the edge of the town, there was no intersection at all. Old houses sat there now. The woods thinned out, the trees shading expansive lawns. The blacktop rolled unbroken under the leaves into a much altered Green Town.

Aaron kicked down the stand and got off the bike. In the shadow of the trees, he stared and wondered whether he'd made a mistake.

This was a different Green Town, far more different than twelve years of lost time should have made it. Even though most of the town was blocked from sight, Aaron could see that 'downtown' Green Town was smaller and more compact. Mill Creek Road and 42 had been the main intersection—the hub, the one place where

Green Town didn't look like some sleepy little burg. There were supposed to be lights and signs and traffic here. In Aaron's memory, storefronts jostled and crowded one another, with cars glittering in the parking lots, their windshields and chrome throwing back bright Illinois sunshine. There had been noise and music and movement.

That was all gone. The trees in the yards around Aaron were thick-trunked and ancient oaks—they couldn't possibly have grown up here in the last dozen years. *This* Green Town was more like the one his Grandpa Carl had talked about, the Green Town of the early part of the century. The houses sat well back from the road, and ahead stood a sedate town center that might have been a movie set. None of the buildings was more than two stories high, all wood-shingled with a boxy, utilitarian look. A few people wandered there, and three cars as strange looking as the one he'd seen this morning were parked at the curb.

One thing jarred more than the rest. In the center of town, looking very much out of place, was a statue of a dinosaur—a hadrosaur of some variety, with brilliant emerald and blue colors on its scales.

Very weird, Aaron thought.

A man mowed the grass just down the street from Aaron. At first that, at least, looked normal enough, then Aaron realized that the sound was wrong: no roar of a gasoline engine, no whirr of an electric motor—just a rhythmic, comforting *whiss-whiss-whiss* from a push mower.

"Aaron? Aaron Cofield?"

Aaron turned. The man had come from the nearest of the houses. "Bill?"

The person confronting Aaron had to be Bill Withers—one of his friends at Green Town High. But Bill had changed. His hair, once a sea of unruly blonde-brown waves, was cut short and had receded like a tide from the beach of his forehead. His skin was blotched and dry-looking, engraved with new lines around the eyes and mouth. His chin sagged tiredly against his neck and his stomach mounded over the belt of his pants.

Bill wasn't eighteen anymore, and adulthood hadn't been kind to him.

Bill was staring at Aaron, also, and the friendliness that had been in his eyes at first had shifted to something darker and more distant. "Aaron," he said. "My God, you've been missing for— what?—more than ten years. Man, everyone figured you guys were dead, you and Jenny Mason and Peter Finnigan . . ."

"No," Aaron answered. He wasn't sure what to say. He was quickly beginning to regret having come into town. *I should have realized that there'd be too many questions to answer. Gran'pa was right . . .* "I . . . I just ran away, that's all."

Bill just peered at him, up and down. "You haven't changed, Aaron." The statement was more accusation than compliment. "You haven't changed at all."

"Yeah, well, thanks. Neither have you."

Bill snorted. "Right. I know better." He patted his stomach under the blue denim shirt. "Too much beer, too many steaks, not enough exercise. And the hair I'm losing on top is going other places. Married life'll do that to you, especially with Vicky."

"Vicky *Sanderson*? You married *her*?"

Bill nodded. "Yeah. Ain't life funny? Bill got to marry the prom queen, even if she's gotten as big as I have." Then his eyes narrowed, his head shook, and Bill took a step back toward the house. "You look so *young*, man . . . Your grandpa know you're back? You seen him?"

"Ummm . . ." Aaron hesitated, not certain what to say. With his grandfather acting so strange and paranoid, Aaron had the feeling that—if he admitted that Carl knew of Aaron's return—his grandfather would be in some kind of trouble.

As Aaron hesitated, wondering whether to lie or not, the world changed.

The shift wasn't radical, but Aaron felt it an instant before anything actually happened: his vision shimmered like the air above sun-baked concrete and he felt a crackling like heat lightning. No noise, no shuddering of the earth beneath his feet, just a brief quiver that was entirely in his head.

He had been looking past Bill at the house. One moment, the front was white with blue trim. In the next, the trim was green and new curtains had appeared at the windows. Bill hadn't reacted. He was still standing there, arms crossed over what was no longer blue denim but a T-shirt that proclaimed *DON'T BLAME ME. I VOTED FOR QUAYLE.*

Aaron, confused, glanced down the street toward Green Town. Bill's neighbor was still mowing the lawn, oblivious to the fact that his driveway had just disappeared. In the town center, the cars were still parked where they had been, but the chassis weren't quite so boxy. One of the buildings had sprouted another floor, yet another had been replaced by a playfield. The dinosaur's statue was still there, but the scales had changed color to stone gray.

Aaron felt sick at his stomach, as if he'd just been punched. He was puzzled. *Why did I notice the change and no one else? Is it because I don't belong here, because I'm not really part of this time?*

"Hey, Aaron, you hear me? I asked if your crazy old grandpa—" Bill's voice had lost any friendliness it had held. It was as if a switch had been turned off.

"Bill, look . . . I . . . I gotta go. Nice talking to you, huh? You say 'hi' to Vicky for me." Aaron tried to smile; it felt more like a grimace.

"What'd'ya mean, you gotta go? What about old man Carl? Where's Jenny and Peter? Hey, there's a lot of people would really like to talk to you, Aaron. These time storms and all the weird—"

Bill started to reach out as if to grab Aaron's shoulder as he turned to leave. Aaron batted the man's hand aside. For a few seconds, there was a standoff. The two of them stared at each other before Bill seemed to make a decision.

He roared and lunged for Aaron. Aaron did what he'd been taught to do in aikido classes: he stepped back and to one side, grabbing Bill's arm and adding his own power to Bill's momentum so that the man was accelerated past him. Bill went sprawling over the curb onto the blacktop, landing hard on his side. He howled, grabbing his elbow.

"You just made a big mistake, Cofield," he shouted.

"Bill—"

"That crazy old coot's in a lot of trouble 'cause he won't cooperate. Everyone knows he's responsible for what's happened around here. Everyone knows the trouble started on your land. He's gonna get his someday soon. And so are you, now. So are you."

The neighbor had stopped mowing and was running toward them. In the house, Aaron saw Vicky looking out of the window—a much older Vicky, a Vicky whose face was fuller and tired, and who stared at Aaron with a mixture of horror and fascination.

Bill shouted at the woman as he pushed himself up from the pavement. "Call Sheriff Tate, Vicky!" he hollered. "Hurry up! Call Tate!"

Aaron, suddenly frightened and not quite sure why he should feel that way, leapt on his bike. Pedaling furiously, he fled.

Aaron heard the car long before it came into view, the roar of a straining engine loud among the trees. The squealing protest of tires sounded as the vehicle started into the turn just a few yards behind him.

Aaron threw the bike one way and himself another, rolling into a patch of tall grass just as one of the ugly cars appeared around the curve. The bike hit a tree and disappeared on its side in the weeds. Peering through the screen of greenery at the side of the road, Aaron could see Sheriff Tate in the driver's seat with a man and woman he didn't recognize in the back. All three were looking intently at the woods.

Aaron huddled down, trying to burrow into the

ground as well as he could. He didn't dare look up. The tires hushed along the blacktop, their sound growing louder and then—thankfully—softer again as the car passed him.

Aaron rose slowly, brushing the dirt and burrs from his pants as the car disappeared around the next bend in the road. The sound of it lingered long after the vehicle was out of sight.

What in the world have I stirred up? Aaron sighed. It seemed obvious enough that he couldn't simply ride up to the house now. He picked up the bike from where it had fallen, brushed away the weeds that had tangled in the spokes, and then sighed. Looking into the woods, he reluctantly let the bike drop again. His house was only a few miles from here if he cut through. The paths were all familiar.

At least, he told himself, *I used to know these woods. God knows if anything's the same now . . .* Still, the forest seemed a better alternative than the road at this point. With a shrug, Aaron turned his back on the road and entered the domain of trees.

At one time, there had been a wide dirt path worn through the undergrowth not far from here, well used by the local kids trekking from Green Town to the Mill Creek pool, where they could catch minnows and tadpoles. Aaron found a path running in the right direction, but the trail was much narrower than the one he remembered, weed-choked and easy to lose among the brambles and blackberry bushes. Aaron followed the trail along the crest of the hills toward the creek and his house, panting as branches reached out brittle fingers to grab him and vines lassoed his

ankles. The topography seemed to be the same—
at least, the hills and valleys all corresponded to
his memory though other features had altered
mysteriously. Once, where Aaron remembered
that a lightning strike had burned a large section of woods several years back, there was no
grassy meadow, just more of the oak, maple, and
sycamore stands.

Another half-mile on, he came across a strange
area of black sand. As far as he could tell, the
sand was laid out in a perfect circle about ten
yards in diameter. "Very weird," he muttered
as he crouched down next to the sand. It must
have been fairly new—there were only a few animal tracks across the expanse. Aaron plunged his
hand into the stuff: the forest earth was sheared
off as if by a cosmic knife, and the packed sand
went down at least as far as his wrist.

Aaron decided to walk around the sand patch
rather than across it.

Several minutes later, sweating and panting,
he had made his way through the trees to where
the woods came closest to his house. Standing
well back in the shadow of the trees, he looked
out. Sheriff Tate's car was there, parked in front.
The couple who had been in the back seat were
standing on the front porch, scanning the fields
around the house with binoculars. Sheriff Tate (a
bit heftier and balder than Aaron remembered)
was talking to Grandpa Carl near the porch steps.
Aaron could hear nothing of the conversation,
though from the chopping gestures his grandfather was making, Aaron guessed that Tate was
saying nothing Carl wished to hear.

"So what do I do now?" Aaron asked himself.

He wished he could get closer to the house to eavesdrop on the conversation, but there was no cover. From where he stood, there were fifty yards of open lawn to the side of the house, without any place to hide. The pile of boulders might have given him a chance, but it was on the other side. Aaron decided to stay where he was—for the moment, anyway. Maybe when the sun went down . . .

Aaron sat down on a fallen log to wait.

It was a lengthy vigil. Tate argued with his grandfather for a long time. Eventually Carl went back inside. The couple sat on the big porch chairs, the man propping his feet up on the railing. Tate sat on the steps, smoking a pipe. Once, the woman got up and paced the long boundary of the yard and fields, peering into the woods. When she approached, Aaron moved well back.

Hours passed. The sun rested at zenith, then eased itself down the long slope toward evening, flinging long, gold-struck beams of light through the branches as it sank below the hills. Night insects began their chorus; fireflies rose from the grass and danced their whirling arabesque around the house. Lights came on in the kitchen, then in the bedroom upstairs. Tate tamped more tobacco into his pipe and lit it, the fragrant wreath of smoke curling through the glare of his lighter. The woman leaned against the porch railing, looking out across the north field. The man snored in his chair.

Aaron's stomach growled and his throat was horribly dry. "Why don't you *leave*?" he whispered toward Tate's entourage, but it was beginning to look more and more as if they were spending the night on watch.

And it looked more and more like Aaron was spending the night in the woods. . . . He was just about to try to find a comfortable spot when he heard a faint noise not far from him: a footstep disturbing dry leaves. Aaron quickly hunkered down, watching, None of the trio in the front of the house had seemed to notice, but Aaron saw a light, furry body moving quickly and silently across the side yard under the starlit sky, avoiding the splash of light from the kitchen window.

Aaron recognized the form immediately. "Mundo," he breathed. The apelike figure scurried into the shadow of the house, then began to move cautiously around to the back.

The creaky old steps betrayed the creature. The loose boards on the second step let out a screech that carried loudly in the still night. The insects, startled, went silent in response. From the front of the house, Aaron heard hushed, urgent whispers.

"Hey! What was that?"

"Around back. You go that way. Hurry!"

Tate came around the near side of the house. Something metallic glittered in his hand. Mundo had frozen at the sound. Now, hearing Tate approaching, he half leapt, half ran from the house toward where Aaron was sitting, nearly bowling Tate over as both turned the corner of the house at the same time.

"Hey, you!" Tate shouted. "Stop!"

Mundo didn't stop. He was already halfway across the yard. The woman had come from the front as well, and Aaron saw the other man coming at a full run from the far side. Curtains moved in the bedroom window as Carl peered out at the scene.

Sheriff Tate raised his hand, and Aaron saw the unmistakable barrel of a gun. There was a harsh *chuff* like an air hose, then grass and dirt exploded noisily next to Mundo's retreating form. Mundo howled like wild dog, leapt to one side, then burst into a run more desperate than before.

"Stop!" Tate yelled again, then there was a double cough of air as both Tate and the woman fired and Mundo hit the tree line. Aaron didn't know if Mundo was struck or not—he had ducked involuntarily as one of the shots tore leaves into confetti over his head.

Flashlights wove yellow circles of light through the trees as Tate and the two others headed for the woods and Aaron's hiding place. Trying to keep low to avoid banging his head against tree branches in the near-blackness, Aaron ran in a crouch. He heard another barking cough of the guns and flung himself to the ground as a shot scattered debris to his right.

Aaron went left, toward the slope at the rear of the house. Somewhere ahead, he could hear Mundo thrashing wildly through the trees; behind, the night was punctuated with shouts as Tate's group pursued them. Aaron found himself wondering why Tate, who had a reputation for being strict but very slow to use force, would have shot so quickly at Mundo. He wondered, but this didn't seem to be the time to stop and ponder the question. Aaron rather doubted that *this* Tate was going to make much distinction between Mundo and himself, especially now.

Aaron ran, away from the house and deeper into the woods.

You can't go back to Grandpa Carl. Not now— not until it's safe and they're gone. The realization pounded in him like the blood drumming in his temples. Tate's people seemed to be between him and house. He couldn't hear Mundo at all.

Great. The cops on one side and a half-crazed maniac from the future on the other. And neither one is going to be much inclined to help you out of this . . .

Aaron found that his flight had taken him near the piece of broken roadway that led to the Mesozoic. He stopped, leaning against a tree and trying to catch his breath. *Fate*, he thought. *Somehow you wanted to come back here.*

Aaron turned his back on the house, moving further into the depths of the woods. In the darkness, it took him some time, but he found the roadway. Since his pursuers seemed to have lost him, Aaron took the time to camouflage the jagged piece of floating material. As he arranged brush around it, he noticed a faint glow from underneath. On his hands and knees, he peered under the thin surface. An irregular chunk of what looked like a glowing, pale green crystal sat there, embedded in the blackened surface near where the explosion of Eckels's time machine had ripped the path apart.

"Great," Aaron grumbled. "The thing's probably radioactive or something." Getting to his feet, he completed the task of hiding the path from the casual observer, then took a deep breath. From the direction of the house, he heard a sudden rattle of gunfire. *That's weird. Their guns don't make that much noise.* A howl shivered through the darkness, a shrill cry that could only be Mundo. Aaron decided that going back to look would be both foolish and dangerous. He needed help, and there was only one place he could think of to find it.

"This had better work," he said aloud.

Aaron stepped onto the path.

AN ULTIMATUM DELIVERED

The night sky held a brilliant crowd of stars. Without the insistent glare of street lamps and mall parking lots, without the haze exhaled by automobiles and factories, the glories of the heavens lay revealed in crystalline purity, like multicolored jewels strewn in careless heaps across the satin cloth of the sky. It was easy to get lost there, to follow the gleaming strands and revel in the glittering, ancient light of distant suns, to let the imagination hurl one deeper and deeper into the vastness of it all.

"Pretty, isn't it?"

Jennifer, leaning back with her arms wrapped around her knees, didn't look at Peter. She could feel his presence at her side, a warmth in the night chill.

"It's an incredible view," she agreed. "It makes me feel awfully small sometimes, to look up there and realize that there are worlds like this one around some of those stars, or to know that the light we're seeing is thousands or millions or billions of years old. Who knows whether those stars are still shining right now or what may have happened on their worlds? Think about it, Peter. On one of those worlds, eons from now, some being might look up and see our sun shining in the night, and that gleam in an alien sky might be the sunlight that we saw today. So by just sitting here and looking up, we're time traveling."

"What happened today, Jenny? You haven't said two words since the lizard brought you back."

Peter's question shattered her mood. Jennifer stretched, bringing her head down. "I watched one of them kill another," she told him, and the catch in her voice surprised even her. Peter sat beside her, a presence in the darkness limned in faint blue starlight. His red hair was black, his green eyes just flecks of light under his brow. A guard-lizard had followed him over, watching them from several feet away. Haltingly, Jennifer told Peter about the ciosie she had witnessed that afternoon.

Afterward, Peter snorted. "I keep telling you, Jenny—they're bloodthirsty animals, even your precious friends. They'll turn on us again, like they did to you today, and maybe next time you won't have anyone there to keep them back."

"You don't understand, Peter," she told him. "It was horrible, yet . . . I don't know. You see, in a weird way the whole thing was also touching and almost gentle. When Lhath held Waato, when the others gathered around singing their mourning . . . Peter, I could feel their sorrow and their loss. The Mutata were so sad, so deeply affected by the death. The whole ritual was such an odd blend of violence and compassion, like nothing I've ever experienced or heard of. The Mutata aren't primitive creatures, not really. They have a society that's as deep and complex as our own. It's just that this mess Eckels made has changed their whole way of doing things. Some of their customs are so beautiful, really. Left alone, their way is very much in harmony with their world. I like them, Peter. I do."

"Yeah, they're beauties, all right. Look how they've treated us."

"Be fair, Peter. How would we have treated *them* if they'd arrived in our world? I doubt that we would have been kinder." Jennifer could feel herself slipping into the old argument once more. She shivered and scooted slightly away from him.

"Uh-huh," Peter said sarcastically. "I think—" He stopped, and when he spoke again, the strident tone had gone from his voice. "There we go again. I don't want to fight with you again, Jenny. I really don't."

Jennifer felt Peter's hand touch her shoulder. She started to pull away, but something held her. *He's your friend. Your only friend here.* "I don't want to fight, either," she told him. Peter's fingers caressed the length of her arm. Jennifer was almost disappointed when the touch moved away again. She pulled her legs into herself and rocked back. Peter moved behind her, sitting with his legs on each side of her and his arms around her shoulders. He pulled her to him; Jennifer resisted at first, then leaned back fully against him. Voices warred in her head: *Aaron . . .* , then *You need the comfort and the closeness of a friend. You need this, Jen; it's nothing more.*

"I've missed you, Jenny," Peter said. His voice was a low murmur in her ear. She could feel the warmth of his breath on her neck.

"Peter—"

"Shhh," he said. "I know what you're thinking. Aaron's my friend, too, remember. I just . . . well, I've been thinking, too. You remember how Eckels said that he'd been here a long time before we came?"

"He was lying," Jennifer said. "He had to be lying." She started to get up, to turn to look at Peter, but his arms tightened against her.

"I know how you feel about Eckels, Jenny," he said. "I understand. But your lizard friends say the same thing, don't they? Wasn't Eckels the Far-Killer already a legend when we showed up? Jenny, look at the timing. If Eckels *was* here for weeks before we arrived, then we have a problem. Travis claimed that Eckels wrecked the path maybe two *hours* before Travis showed up in Green Town and surprised us. I've been doing some thinking about that. At first I figured either Travis or Eckels had to be lying, but what if they're *both* telling the truth. There's one way that everybody's claim makes sense: if time is slower or faster on one end of the path. If I'm right, then everybody's telling the truth as they see it: Travis, Eckels, your lizard friends. If a few weeks here is only a couple hours in Green Town . . ."

Peter's voice trailed off. Jennifer found her hands tightening into fists. The pounding of her pulse seemed louder than the percussive trill of the night insects. "It could take Aaron days to find the path in the woods," Jennifer said. "A week. Longer."

"Right," Peter answered. "And each single hour in Green Town is maybe a week of time here. They may not even be looking for us yet. We're potentially talking *years*, Jenny. Aaron could come blasting in here fifteeen years from now, still looking and still *being* eighteen. That is, unless—"

"Unless what?"

"Unless we get out of here soon. Unless you work with me to find a way to escape from here and get away from these lizards. You know them. You know how to talk with them."

"Peter . . ." Jennifer sighed. *And around we go again . . .* "I've told you. The Gairk patrol the valley; so do the Mutata. We'd have to worry about the samurai and those flying things, not to mention the Dreaming Storms. If we escape and the Gairk or Mutata find us, we *will* be killed. SStragh and Raajek won't be able to protect us. Without knowing where we're going, all we can do is wander around. They'll find us long before we stumble across our path home again. That doesn't sound like much of a plan to me."

"Believe it or not, I agree. Which is why I've come up with another plan."

"Will your plan hurt Raajek and SStragh?"

"Maybe," Peter admitted. "You'd have to lie to them, and I know how you feel about that. But otherwise we sit here and wait until Aaron or someone comes—maybe years from now—or until the lizards make up their minds. From what you're telling me, it doesn't look like our side is going to be the winning side. I have to have your help, Jenny."

His arms came away from her. His fingers lifted her hair and brushed the nape of her neck. "Think about it," Peter said. "Then come and talk to me."

Then he rose suddenly. Jennifer's back was suddenly cold. Peter seemed to hesitate a moment; then she heard his footsteps moving toward the hut. She didn't look at him.

For a long time after Peter left, Jennifer stared at the stars and tried to lose herself in their beauty once more. But the stars were just random points of light, and the vast blackness between was just an emptiness.

After a while, she got up and went into the hut.

The saorod squealed like a tree-swinger snared in a longtooth's whiplike tongue. Its distress echoed in the confined heat of the OColi's chambers, drowning out the words of the Gairk who had brought the captive. The Gairk, who had announced himself as Klaido, casually unhooked one of his warclubs from his armor lashings and struck the saorod on the side of the head. The blow knocked it sprawling on the uneven rocks as its bound wings thrashed futilely. The creature subsided into a continuous low moaning.

Klaido returned to his speech without even glancing at the injured saorod. "As I was saying, most respected Mutata OColi, we of the Gairk have grown tired of waiting for the problem to be solved. My own OColi is most upset. We have consulted with each of the Gairk OColis within a full hand of days' walk from here. Without exception, they all report evil omens and strange sightings. The disruption to the OColihi and all of our Old Ways is spreading."

Klaido's chest was spread wide in display, causing the leather bindings of his armor plating to creak under the strain. The Gairk skin coloring, always multi-colored, bright, and varied, was especially deep. The copper armor was tooled with symbols and polished with gaita weed, showing Klaido's high status as a favorite of the Gairk OColi.

He smelled of rebuke.

The OColi glanced significantly at SStragh and Raajek. The Mutata were standing in a properly respectful attitude to the OColi's right. Frraghi, on the OColi's left, hissed and released his own scent of displeasure. SStragh struggled to keep her own fear from showing to any of them; Raajek seemed calm enough, her blind eyes lowered as if in contemplation as she listened. SStragh wished she could cultivate her OTsio's apparent indifference to the proceedings.

Klaido's arrival had been incredibly bad timing. It was only yesterday that Jhenini had finally given them some of the information they needed. She had finally told them where they were most likely to find the Floating Stone that led to her world. Jhenini had said that the human OColi, Eikels the Far-Killer, had been listening to the voice of his All-Ancestor. This human All-Ancestor had shown Eikels a way to seal up the Floating Stones so no more invaders could come through. SStragh had hoped that this news would allay the OColi's growing fears, but now it seemed that the Gairk were even less patient than the Mutata. SStragh found it a struggle to keep her rising despair from tainting her smell.

"We're all aware of the omens," the OColi said in his trembling, ancient, and broken voice, nearly inaudible in the chamber. They could all feel the pain of the OColi's attempt to speak; the hurt permeated his smell.

That the OColi had decided to meet with Klaido in his chambers rather than sending Frraghi to deal with the envoy was another ill omen, SStragh knew. That SStragh and Raajek had been invited to the meeting was not a good sign either. The OColi wriggled slightly on his comfortable bed of heated rocks, looking at Klaido with his one good eye, his head cocked sideways. His frill was displayed, still brightly colored despite his advanced age, still magnificent, *unlike* (SStragh thought) *the diseased and ragged frill of Raajek.*

But time had taken his once-strong voice. The OColi waved Frraghi near him, whispering at length. It was Frraghi who spoke the OColi's answer.

"I too have consulted with my peers in all jhaka nearby. The tales they speak all tell me the same thing: the Dreaming Storms foretell a great danger to the OColihi. Unless they can be stopped . . ." Frraghi didn't finish the statement; all of them knew what the OColi meant. Even SStragh felt an aching cold settle into her bones.

"Yes," Klaido agreed, looking at the OColi rather than Frraghi, as was proper. The rank odor of long-dead meat wafted out with her breath. "Our zhiotae (the Reader of Omens) told the Gairk OColi that the Dreaming Storms have worsened for one reason: the Mutata have allowed abominations from the Floating Stones to remain alive here. The humans have infected the OColihi with the sickness of the Dreaming Storms."

"The Mutata do not have zhiotae," Raajek said, surprising SStragh. It was very rude to speak without the OColi's permission; doing so in front of the Gairk representative gave the impression that the OColi was less than respected. "Our OColi is wise and has made no rash decisions he would regret later," Raajek continued. "Our *OColi* is the person who makes decisions regarding the OColihi, not a zhiotae. We Mutata feel this is the better way."

There was a doubled snort of irritation at that: from Klaido, annoyed at the underlying criticism of the Gairk, and from the OColi himself. SStragh suddenly understood Raajek's strategy. She had trapped the OColi into either contradicting Raajek's statement and thus further diminishing his own status, or agreeing and implicitly supporting Raajek.

The OColi saw the trap, too. Normally slow to speak, the OColi glared at Raajek and then hurried into the conversational gap. Frraghi bent down his long neck to listen to the whispering, ruined voice, then looked at Klaido before speaking loudly what he had just heard.

"The Gairk zhiotae are undoubtedly wise and give your OColi the advice he needs. I too am concerned that the Dreaming Storms have come more often, and that the hard-shelled humans come from the Floating Stones, and that these huge saorods have entered our valley." As Frraghi finished speaking, the OColi gestured to the bound creature alongside Klaido. "Five Mutata died in their attack," the OColi said himself, his voice rasping and painful to hear.

"The greatest number of these saorods attacked us, yet we Gairk lost only three." Klaido sniffed;

having defended the warlike honor of the Gairk, he went on. "But even one is too many. The Dreaming Storms have killed two more Gairk, both of them of mating age and one my predecessor as Envoy to Mutata. Our hunting grounds are riddled with areas of strangeness left behind by the storms; we lost a portion of our jhaka fence in the Dreaming Storm yesterday and there is nothing there now but a strange black sand."

Again Frraghi bent down to the OColi, listened, and spoke. "It is our hope that Gairk OColi realizes that Mutata are not responsible for these occurrences."

Klaido reared up to full height. In the confined space of the OColi's chamber, he was a fearsome, dark specter. SStragh took an involuntary step backward, as did Frraghi. As the Gairk flexed his hands, long claws rattled like stones.

"I speak now *my* OColi's words," Klaido said, and his smell was that of remembrance while his voice took on the slow resonance of a formal statement. His head lifted to the ceiling, revealing the muscular expanse of neck and the brightly-colored folds of skin there. SStragh stared at the Gairk, fascinated, certain that she knew what Klaido was going to say and yet fearing to hear the words.

" 'Tell the Mutata OColi that Gairk do not say that Mutata alone have caused the All-Ancestor to become angry,' " Klaido quoted. " 'Yet the Mutata have allowed this to go on for too long. They have not made the gift of blood that would cause the All-Ancestor to smile again. They have not followed the OColihi as we do. Tell the Mutata OColi that we have lost our patience. We have asked that the humans be Given, and the Mutata have kept them alive.' "

Klaido halted, and from his smell and the way that his coloring darkened, SStragh knew that the Gairk was not comfortable with what he was about to say. " 'Perhaps it is because you are leaf-eaters and don't have the courage to consume those you kill, OGhielas approaches—a day of portent, always. If the humans have not been Given to the All-Ancestor by then, the Gairk will not wait. We will come and take them from you.' "

Klaido remained with his head lifted so that he could not see any of them. His voice echoed from the pebbled surface of the roof above.

"Those are my OColi's words," Klaido concluded. He moved his hands away from his weapons, his neck still dangerously exposed, waiting. In the silence, the rustling and frantic mewling of the bound saorod was very loud.

SStragh glanced at the OColi. The OColi groaned as he rose to his feet. Frraghi moved quickly to help, but the OColi waved his Speaker away. He was trembling, his hand very near where his spear rested against the wall of the chamber. It was the OColi's right to strike, to slash open the proffered sacrifice of Klaido's neck. SStragh watched as the OColi took the spear in his left hand, as if he were about to stab the Envoy. The OColi drew his arm back, making a rattling guttural sound deep in his throat. All of them could smell the rage. It soured the air.

Then, quickly shifting the spear to his right hand, the OColi thrust.

The saorod next to Klaido squawked once and died.

"Our OColi is indeed wise," Raajek said softly.

Klaido brought his head down. His scent bland, his stance emotionless, he looked at the slain saorod, at the spear standing upright from its body, and at the OColi. Slowly, the Gairk blinked, as if surprised to find himself still alive. The OColi, sinking back down against the heated rocks, was whispering furiously to Frraghi.

"Tell your OColi that the Mutata OColi does not appreciate threats," Frraghi said, and SStragh could sense mingled eagerness and fear in his stance as he gave Klaido the OColi's words. "Tell him that even leaf-eaters can send the All-Ancestor the gift of a soul, even if we do not eat our Givings."

"I will tell him that I witnessed the Mutata OColi striking dead a bound saorod," Klaido said, and there was no mistaking the mocking tone. "Should I also tell him that Mutata OColi refuses to deliver these humans by the dawn of OGhielas?" Klaido asked. His voice was barely civil, as if Mutata defiance was more an amusing concept than an impressive one.

The OColi did not answer immediately. As if sensing his uncertainty, Raajek spoke. "My OColi, remember what Jhenini has said. If Eikels has the ability to seal—"

The OColi cut off Raajek in mid-sentence. "*If*," he rasped, then spoke again to Frraghi. Frraghi nodded and lifted his snout slightly to Klaido.

"The humans were captured by Mutata and my OColi will not deliver the humans. The All-Ancestor gave them to us, not the Gairk," Frraghi said. Klaido stiffened at that, his hands going unbidden to the handles of his war clubs. His smell became spiced with irritation. "But tell your OColi that Mutata OColi had already come to much the same conclusion regarding the humans. The OColihi demands that they be Given, and OGhielas is as good a day as any. If the humans have not proved their worth in other ways, then the OColihi will be satisified. If Klaido or any other Gairk would care to witness that as well, he is welcome to return here on OGhielas and watch the Giving of the humans."

The smell of satisfaction rose from Klaido. "Perhaps I will. That will be the decision of my OColi. But I will tell him all that you have said."

Klaido's large, armored head moved slowly from the OColi to SStragh and Raajek. The eyes, protected under bony, large-scaled ridges, glistened and narrowed as he looked at the blind Otsio and her student. "I will also say this. Any abomination found outside your jhaka will be Given. We will not risk one drop of Gairk blood for the life of any pale fur-bearer."

"I smell your resolve," Raajek answered. "And I would remind Klaido that the three abominations here are under Mutata protection, as my OColi has decreed. I would also remind you that Jhenini Human called the first Dreaming Storm and struck down your predecessor."

Raajek smiled up at Klaido. "There is a magic to humans. I would be careful of them, were I a Gairk."

"Gairk fear nothing." Klaido spoke each word in a separate, precise exhalation. "As for Jhenini Human, she will be dead on OGhielas, one way or the other."

With that, Klaido lifted his head formally to the OColi, released an odor of respect, and left the chamber. Frraghi accompanied him. SStragh and Raajek made their obeisance as well and started to follow, SStragh leading her Otsio, but the OColi's voice stopped them.

"Raajek . . ." Rasping. The OColi had gone to the saorod, standing over the dead beast.

"My OColi?"

"You played that well, as you always do. But there are no more compromises to make. On OGhielas, it is over unless your Jhenini has done what she has said she can do. I *will* Give them to the All-Ancestor on that day."

The OColi pulled his spear from the saorod's body. The bloodied tip dripped its dark wetness on the rocks.

A THOUSAND REALITIES

Aaron had forgotten the feel of the Mesozoic, but the world gave him an instant reminder. The humidity hit him like a hot, damp washcloth slapped across his face. The incredible variety of sounds shrilled among the leaves, and the scent of wet, fertile earth and greenery carried memories of plowing the fields in the spring. For a moment, Aaron simply stood there and filled his lungs. The air was so rich he almost wanted to bite off each breath and chew it. It was enough to make him forget—for an instant—why he'd come back.

He looked carefully at the piece of roadway almost lost among tall ferns. The blackened torn edges were exactly the same as those of the Green Town fragment. Aaron shook his head and went to find Travis, hoping that the man hadn't gone anywhere in the time Aaron had been gone. *Two days . . . Travis could be anywhere, or any time, for that matter . . .*

But as Aaron pushed through the thick brush that hid the clearing, he could see the time machine exactly where it had been. The scavengers were still tearing at the T-rex's carcass, which didn't look significantly more skeletal than it had when he'd left, two days before. Aaron puzzled over that as he stepped into the open. Even more oddly, Travis didn't seem to have moved either. He was still crouching and peering under the vehicle, in nearly the same attitude he'd been in when Aaron and Mundo had last seen him.

... It's been a dozen years, boy ... his grandfather had said.

Aaron suddenly realized why nothing had changed.

"Travis! How long have I been gone?"

Travis turned. His eyes widened at the sight of Aaron, and the man brushed uselessly at his own filthy clothes. "You haven't been gone ten minutes, kid. Where'd you get the outfit? Where's Mundo? I thought you were taking him back to his time through the roadway."

Aaron gave a chuckle that was half-amusement and half-exasperation. "Travis . . ." Aaron wasn't sure where to start. "That's the problem. His world isn't there, but *mine* is. I mean, Green Town is. Mundo's world is gone. Vanished. I don't know what happened with your time machine, but you were wrong—you didn't take me back to my time at all. You couldn't have. *It's still there.*" Aaron laughed helplessly. "Still there," he repeated.

Travis was staring at Aaron as if the older man thought Aaron were mad. He shook his head, glancing back at the frost-rimed canopy of the time machine as if making certain it hadn't disapeared. "That's not possible," Travis said with his guttural, deep accent. "I'm not trying to trick you. You watched me set the controls. The machine worked; we both saw the world change outside . . ."

"And I'm telling you that something was set wrong or your machine's broken. Green Town's still there." Aaron paused. His mouth twisted into a frown. "Sort of," he added.

"Sort of?"

"Well, it's changed, too," Aaron said. "And time seems to be running faster on that side." Haltingly, Aaron told Travis the tale of his last two days, from the struggle that had taken both him and Mundo through the path to the strangely altered Green Town he'd found there, the twisted history. Travis, to his credit, didn't interrupt except to guide Aaron through the story, though Aaron could see questions and uncertainty flitting across the man's drawn, angry-sad face.

"Green Town's getting time storms like the one we saw here, huh?" Travis said musingly after Aaron had finished. "Your world's still on the other side of the path, but we can't find it when we use the time machine. And your world's changed . . ." Travis's fingers scratched the stubble on his cheek.

"What are you thinking, Travis?"

"I'm not sure. Not yet, anyway. There were theories some of our technicians had, conclusions drawn from the mathematics and hypotheses that were never confirmed . . ." Travis groaned and started to rise. Aaron watched the man lurch painfully to his feet and limp slowly into the time machine. Aaron had almost forgotten how badly injured the man was, how dirty and exhausted he appeared.

Travis returned a few minutes later with two of the rifles. He handed one to Aaron. "Here."

Aaron started to take the weapon, then stopped. "Why?"

"We're going to go take a look at this Green Town of yours and it sounds like people are shooting first and asking questions later. I don't want you, or especially *me*, dead." His dark eyes were weary, with great circles underneath them. "And I'm not so sure that I'm going to be a great help. The fact is that I'm tired, I'm hurt, and I'm slow. I may need you more than you need me, kid."

Aaron still refused to take the rifle. "Travis, I want to know what you're thinking. If you've got this weirdness figured out, I deserve to know. You told me that Eckels destroyed my time, and that isn't true. Have you been lying about the rest, too?"

Irritation flashed briefly in the sky of his eyes. His words were clipped and precise. "I didn't lie to you, kid. Not intentionally, anyway. I *saw* my future after Eckels stepped off the path, just the way I described it. We both saw what had happened to it after he blew up the roadway."

"Then why is Green Town still there, Travis? Why didn't Mundo and I find Mundo's world on the other side of the roadway? There has to be a reason."

"Because Eckels's mistake didn't just scatter the roadway pieces through time." Travis took a deep, rattling breath, and the man's temper receded for a moment. He watched the small scavengers tearing at the body of their larger cousin, then turned back to Aaron.

"Look, kid, back when I was about eight years old, there was a monstrous oak tree in my neighbor's backyard. To me it seemed that the top branches could shred the clouds. I used to think that if I could only sit up there, I could see halfway around the world.

"I happened to be the youngest kid in the group I played with back then. Most of them were a year or two older, which meant that sometimes they didn't want me along—I was too young or too slow or too awkward. One day, just to show the others that I was as big and brave as any of them, I bragged about how I could climb to the top of that tree. The other kids all laughed, which made me angry and red-faced and all the more vehement—I had the same temperament then that I have now, eh? They started to tease me, mocking the way I was saying 'I can so!' They dared me to start climbing, then started laughing at me when I hesitated. So I had one of them give me a boost up to the first branch and started on my way up.

"Funny how you can seem to be so much higher when you're up there looking down . . . I moved up two, three branches. I must've been about, oh, ten or fifteen feet up when my shoe slipped on loose bark and I came crashing and tumbling down through the leaves. I broke my right arm and had scratches and cuts on every last piece of skin on my body. I know that for months afterward, I'd imagine what would have happened if I hadn't been so stupid as to take that dare, if I'd just walked away and let them razz me. . . ."

Travis paused, his eyes intent as he stared at Aaron. "Anything like that ever happen to you— where you make a decision that you regret and you spend the next day or week or year second-guessing yourself and wondering what would happen in a universe where you chose the other path?"

"Sure," Aaron said. "Lots of times. I've read books that used just that idea, too—what if Germany won World War II, what if the South won the Civil War, that kind of thing."

"Well, our lab people kicked around the theory that all those universes actually exist, that each and every decision each of us makes creates eddies in reality, and from these spin off untold millions of little pocket universes, worlds in which you don't climb the tree or you make it all the way to the top, where you turn right instead of left, or the girl says 'yes' instead of 'no.'"

"Then there's a thousand, a million Green Towns."

Travis shrugged. "Maybe. What I understood of the theory was that most of those universes don't last for more than a millisecond, and those rare ones that do can't be reached anyway so their existence really doesn't matter, not from our point of view. No matter what we do when we travel down the timestream, we stay confined to our own individual reality, walled off from all the others. We can't touch the other worlds or affect them at all."

"Except that Eckels tore those walls open."

"Yeah, you got the idea. Eckels opened some of them, maybe," Travis said. "It would explain things, wouldn't it? The pieces of roadway are bridges not only through time, but through entirely different histories. We never saw your Green Town because it's not in my history at all."

Aaron had listened to Travis with an initial sense of relief that slowly turned cold and sour. If Travis were right, and if Jennifer and Peter had taken another piece of the path, then they might well be trapped in another reality. His own Green Town now seemed fragile and malleable.

If . . .

Travis held out the rifle once more. Aaron could see the man's fingers trembling around the stock of the weapon. As Aaron reached out to take the proffered gun, the small hairs on the back of his neck rose and the air around them became charged as if with unseen lightning. The scavenger dinosaurs at the T-rex banquet lifted their heads and scattered as a sudden wind began tossing the fronds of the trees.

The time storm was brief but startling. In the dry lightning flashes, visions of odd worlds marched through the jungle clearing.

Flash . . . the wind scoured a barren desert of purple sand. As Aaron watched, the sand began to sift across the border of the vision onto the green carpet of the jungle . . .

Flash . . . and a beast like an ant crossed with a buffalo, standing in a small circle of tall grass with a pack lashed to its back with ropes, stared at them.

Flash . . . the buffalo-ant vanished. Across the clearing a section of shiny dark blue plastic lay on the ground, marked with geometric, fluorescent yellow lines while flashing, multi-colored lights glittered and sparked above it. The pattern was hypnotic and compelling. Both Aaron and Travis found themselves leaning, then beginning to walk toward the display . . .

Flash . . . and the display was gone. For a moment, Aaron was disoriented. He spun around—behind him a beast, like an elephant in a shaggy fur coat, bellowed in alarm at the motion. The mastadon brandished its huge, curved tusks and glared at the two humans as if it were about to charge.

But before Aaron had a chance to retreat or even shout, the lightning came again. Where the mastodon had stood was only jungle glade again.

The storm left its mark. As the wind ceased and the lightning ended in a fury of blue-white sparks, a last vision came. An enigmatic stone pillar suddenly appeared near the T-rex's body, leaning over the corpse like a drunken headstone. The monument stood easily twenty feet high, carved with swirling bas-relief patterns and painted sloppily with garish primary colors. A two-headed stag lay at the foot of the pillar, its twin throats cut as if for some pagan ritual. Warm blood steamed on the ground, and a dusting of snow melted quickly in the tropical heat of the Mesozoic.

The obelisk remained behind as the emerald roof over their heads became still and the first of the scavengers returned to its abandoned feast. They didn't seem to mind the additional entrée at all. Two of the lizards started squabbling over the mammal's carcass almost immediately.

Travis and Aaron stared at the sacrificial scene. Aaron shuddered and snatched the rifle from Travis.

"Different realities," Travis said again. "Thousands and thousands of them, all let loose . . ." He wasn't looking at Aaron at all.

"I'm ready," Aaron said. "Let's get going."

Aaron remembered crisp winter afternoons with the sun glaring from drifts of thigh-deep powdered snow. He and Peter and a few of the other local kids would crouch just within the woods, their breaths puffing in white cloudlets that left ice crystals clinging to the fibers of woolen scarves. The cold seeped through half-unbuttoned parkas, their fingers freezing inside soaked gloves as they clutched toy rifles and peered up at the snow-covered peaks of Aaron's house. In their minds, the house was an enemy bunker, the hillside was littered with mines, and the mounds of wind-blown snow at the top of the rise were machine-gun emplacements where sentries glared down at the woods, waiting for them to show themselves.

"You go around and up the gully," Aaron would whisper to Peter. "Bill, you come with me around to the left; Martin, you wait a few minutes and then draw their fire. OK? Let's go."

And off they'd go, moving quickly and quietly through the trees to their positions and then suddenly bursting from the trees with yells and bursts of mock gunfire, imagining the answering chatter of the sentries' weapons as they zigzagged up the slope, snow flying from underneath booted feet, until at last they would collapse at the top of the hill, laughing and exhausted, peeling off coats and scarves and boots at the back door, stamping and hollering their way to the kitchen where Aaron's mom or Grandpa Carl would fix them mugs of steaming hot chocolate. They'd clasp half-frozen hands around the warm mugs and blow on the frothy liquid, sipping the dark sweetness as the snow dripped from the coats and puddled underneath the boots.

Aaron remembered all that. Somehow it wasn't as much fun in reality, holding Travis's oddly shaped weapon and shivering in his T-shirt and jeans, the snow piled up ankle-high over his sneakers. The cold flakes had gotten down into his shoes already—his socks were soaked and frigid.

"I left here an hour ago, and it was *summer*," Aaron muttered. "Now I'm not even sure it's the same *year*. Travis, this is too bizarre. God, it's cold."

"I have winter coats in the machine," Travis said. The injured man seemed to ignore the cold better than Aaron. He suddenly laughed. "But it'd probably be a month or so here before I got back with them."

They were crouched at the bottom of the hill, sitting just inside the woods as Aaron and his friends had once done. From here, they could see only the upper story of the house. It looked much the same as it had the last time. The strange mountain of rock still loomed next to the building, frosted now with ice and snow. Icicles hung like crystalline stalactites from the corners of the gutters and sparkling arcs of snow tucked themselves in the corners of the windowsills, hiding from the sun. The brilliant light did nothing to warm Aaron; instead it seemed mocking, an empty promise of heat.

There was no smoke coming from the chimney. The house promised no warmth or comfort. "We can't stay here," Travis said to Aaron as he stared at the scene. "We either go check this out or we go back. We're gonna freeze if we just sit here. Which way, kid? It's your call."

That didn't need an answer. Aaron nodded and moved out from under the ice—

They trudged up the icy slope toward the house. The footing was difficult; they both slipped and fell more than once. Near the lip of the rise, Aaron braced himself and then lay down fully in the snow before raising his head to peer at the house over the wind-sculpted drifts.

Snow had piled up against the banister on the back porch, a long curve of scintillating flakes. Two of the back windows were out, and the screen door hung askew, swinging slowly back and forth on one hinge. Aaron couldn't see any tracks in the snow other than those of raccoons and birds, and though the house obstructed part of his view of the drive, there didn't seem to be any cars there, nor had the snow been disturbed. The house looked abandoned. The windows were like the empty eye sockets of a skull.

Aaron rose to his feet, bringing Travis's rifle up in a ready postion, just in case. Nothing happened. He suddenly felt foolish, standing there like an underdressed, shivering sentinel. He was still scared, but no longer for himself. "Grandpa?" he whispered to the snow and wind. He moved cautiously onto the porch.

The screen door fell off its hinge at his touch. The interior door wasn't locked. His breath a mist before him, Aaron entered the kitchen. He stood there in the middle of the floor, turning wildly around.

The place hadn't been touched in weeks. Dust sat thickly on all the surfaces, untouched. Tendrils of snow had entered through the broken windows to snake in white trails across the linoleum. There were dishes in the sink and a glass coffeepot on the stove with dark stains of evaporated coffee ringing the inside. Frosted cobwebs hung in the corners.

Desperately, Aaron went through the rest of the house, half fearing what he might find. It took him several seconds to muster enough courage to turn the cold doorknob to his grandfather's bedroom door. The rumpled blankets were empty; the surge of relief Aaron felt told him just how worried he'd been.

It doesn't tell me where he's gone, but at least he's not here, dead of a heart attack or something.

Aaron went back downstairs to find Travis waiting for him in the kitchen. "He's not here," Aaron said to the man's unasked question. "No one is. Doesn't look like anyone has been for a long time." Now that the adrenaline rush was over, Aaron was beginning to shiver in earnest. The house wasn't much warmer than the outside.

Travis's face was drawn and pale. "Then let's go back to the time machine."

"Travis, I have to know what's happened here. I have to find my grandfather. He was talking so strange . . ." Aaron stopped. For the first time, the pile of dishes in the sink caught his gaze. The plates were moldy and broken—they were also the same ones Aaron had used this morning. *Not this morning*, he reminded himself. *Not in this world, anyway. Months ago. A long, long time.*

"Travis," he said. "*They* must've taken him—Sheriff Tate and the other two, I mean."

Aaron spied a newspaper piled on top of the icebox. He opened it in a cloud of dust and snow. Headlines leapt out at him like scurrying black spiders. "Yes . . . This is the same paper I read," he told Travis. He tapped the paper with his fingers, causing another brief eruption of dust. "They must have taken Grandpa then, that day or soon after. He didn't buy another paper or cook another meal. Travis, are you listening to me?"

Travis was walking slowly around the room, touching the table, the backs of the chairs, parting the curtains to peer out the window. "I thought . . ." he began, then shook his head. He coughed, holding his side and grimacing. The sound was ugly and wet. "I thought I'd never see anything like this again," he said. "I thought I was lost, that there was nothing in the past but jungle and nothing in the future but Mundo's desert. That damn Eckels . . ."

"Travis—"

Travis turned back toward Aaron. "We've both lost too much," he said, and there was a distant fire in his gaze. "It's time we did something about it."

VIEW FROM
THE HILLS

"Hey, darling, it's time to get up for school!"

Jennifer grumbled and turned over in her bed, pulling the covers up tight to her head. She kept her eyes pressed tightly shut. "Ahh, Mom . . ." she grumbled.

"Now don't you fuss with me, young lady. You know how long it takes you to get ready."

Jennifer felt a hand on her shoulder. With the touch, Jennifer knew immediately that something was wrong. Her mom's fingers gripped her shoulder too tightly, and she could feel sharp claws digging through the comforter and into her shoulder. Terror shot through Jennifer's body like a electrical bolt.

"I said *get up*!" the voice insisted, only now it wasn't her mother's voice but a softly sinister growl. The hand was a vise on her shoulder, tightening and forcing her to slowly turn, dragging her unwillingly toward whatever monstrosity was attached to that hand.

Jennifer tried to struggle but her body didn't seem to want to cooperate. It was as if she were detached from herself, trapped inside her head and helpless, the claws piercing deeper into her shoulder as her head was brought around, her eyes wide and frightened, the *thing* a presence looming over her, its breath wet and eager and loud, the dim awful shape of *something* just coming into view. . . .

"Jennifer, wake *up*! One of the lizards is here looking for you."

Jennifer awoke with a start, her body still trembling from the impact of the dream. Eckels's hand was on her shoulder, and Jennifer angrily jerked away from his touch. He grinned at her. "Ahh, our young lady doesn't want the mean old man touching her," he said in mocking, false tones.

"That's right, Eckels. I *don't* want you touching me. Ever."

Jennifer blinked, driving away the remnants of her fear. Memories of her familiar bedroom made the reality all the more depressing. They were in their caged shelter in the Mutata encampment. The rough, thick cloth of her blankets scratched at her arms as she pulled the covers toward her. Eckels was kneeling on the bare ground next to her bedding. Peter, across the room, watched. Jennifer saw very little sympathy in his eyes— it didn't look as if he were about to intercede for her at all. She suddenly felt very isolated.

"Get away, Eckels. I mean it."

"You know, I'm not the horrible person you seem to think I am," Eckels said reasonably, but he leaned in a little closer to Jennifer, cornering her against the wall of the structure. His sour breath was hot against her face and his arm trapped her. "We've been here a long time now, and now we're all cooperating together at last. Isn't it about time we became . . . friends?" He smiled at her. He reached out with his free hand as if to stroke her hair.

"Don't," she said sharply. Something in her tone or her look made him reconsider. Eckels sat back, frowning. Jennifer glared at him. For a moment, it seemed that he was going to say something, then the light from the doorway was blocked by a large figure: SStragh, peering into the dimness of the shelter. "Jhenini?" she trilled. The dinosaur looked curiously at the scene in front of her.

Eckels snorted. "Lizards!" he said angrily, standing. He looked down at Jennifer. "Remember what we talked about, Jenny. This is our chance."

"So you keep telling me. I'm still not entirely convinced, Eckels."

He smiled grimly. Without another word, Eckels shouldered past SStragh and strolled out into the walled compound. He whistled off-tune, his hands in his pockets as if he were out for a casual walk. SStragh sniffed disdainfully at the man's back, her nostrils flaring with the sound, then glanced back at Jenny inquiringly.

"I'll be right out, SStragh," Jennifer said to the dinosaur in the Mutata language. SStragh inclined her head and backed out of the enclosure.

Jennifer wrapped her blankets around herself and went to dress behind the privacy screen they'd erected. Peter's gaze followed her. "Why didn't you say something, Peter?" she said angrily. "Why'd you let him do that?"

"C'mon, Jenny," his voice came from the other side of the screen. "You were the one who jumped all over him when all he was doing was trying to wake you up. You do that and you gotta expect he's going to try to get your goat a little. Eckels wasn't going to hurt you; if he had, I'd've been right there."

"That's really comforting, Peter."

"You don't need to start in with me, either."

Jennifer sighed. She pulled on her jeans. "I'm sorry, Peter. I . . ." Her voice faded. She wasn't sure what she wanted to say and didn't really feel she needed to apologize at all.

"We need to get out of here, Jenny," Peter's voice continued. "Eckels's right in that, no matter what you think of him. I agree with him and I'm getting tired of being cooped up here."

"I don't trust the man."

"I do. And you agreed the other night to go along with his plan."

"Then I can't say much for either of our judgments." Jennifer finished buttoning her blouse and came out from behind the screen. "But it looks like the plan is on, like it or not. I'm going out with SStragh and Raajek today," she said. "SStragh has located a Floating Stone near where we came through, but the Gairk have been hanging around the area and she hasn't been able to get close. We're going to try to check it out."

Peter sat up, rubbing his eyes sleepily. "Really? They found *our* stone?" he asked carefully. "That's great news, Jenny. Your lizards have come through. We're halfway home."

"They're not lizards," Jennifer corrected him tiredly. "You sound just like Eckels. And as to home . . ."

Peter scowled. "All right . . . Remember that you're not going to identify anything as our piece of the path, even if it is."

"I know. I was always the one on the honor roll in school, remember?"

"Just checking. No need to get sore."

"I still don't like this, Peter. I don't like lying and I especially don't like deceiving SStragh and Raajek, who have done nothing but help us."

"Who've done nothing but hold us prisoner, you mean. We're not on the same side as the lizards, Jenny," he said as if he were talking to a child. "The path's our only way home."

"Peter," Jennifer began. Stopped. She shook her head. "I'm sorry, but you're wrong. We should trust Raajek and SStragh. I'll go along with this because I said I would, but they're on our side, whether you believe it or not."

"Then tell them to set us free. Ask them to unlock the gate and send that baby guard-dragon of theirs away. Make that nasty Fergie lizard give us a hand instead of threatening us. Let us walk around without the hobbles when they take us outside. That'd tell *me* they're on our side. Or am I just being unreasonable about this?"

Jennifer ignored the sarcasm. "SStragh's waiting for me," she said.

"Then you better get going." Peter smiled at her. "Good luck, huh?" He came over to her and hugged her. Jennifer tensed against the embrace, her arms at her side. Peter released her, stepping back and just looking at her with an odd half-smile on his lips.

"I gotta go," she said.

"Yeah. I guess you do."

She could feel Peter's gaze on her back as she walked out.

*   *   *

From the top of the hill, Jennifer could see the entire emerald bowl of the valley.

Below them, small flying lizards banked and wheeled in the swirling air currents; sun glinted from the waters of a swamp near the center of the valley, and long-necked diplodocus undulated like living islands through the dark lakes. A glistening river snaked through the lush foliage, rising from streamlets and shimmering waterfalls in the hills and finally spilling out from the valley to join a much larger cousin. The air was alive with strange hoots and shrills and calls. Beyond the valley's steep, greenery-clad walls, folded and crumpled foothills rose blue and tall, each peak rising higher than the one before until at last they were transformed into the foggy, distant spikes of snow-shrouded mountains along the horizon.

Jennifer found herself gazing in awe on the scene. *It's all so beautiful and unspoiled, I've never seen anything like it at home. Everything's the way nature created it.*

SStragh pointed out landmarks for Jennifer. Alongside them, Raajek stood sniffing the fragrant air as if it were an elixir. Maybe it was, Jennifer decided. She felt refreshed and energetic herself.

"Over there, the hills curve around and end at the white cliffs to form an opening into the valley," SStragh was saying. "See the white buildings among the trees? That's the Gairk jhaka. Gairk always build near the mouth of our valley when they return from their own Birthing Walks. Gairk enjoy fighting, as you've already realized, and they're very territorial. The Gairk are perpetually in skirmishes for their holdings with rival tribes, but at least they keep out the Baosiot and the Floaria so they don't prey on us. In return, since the Gairk don't climb too well or forage, we patrol the heights and report to them on any movement we might see, and we give them herbs and spices that they need. We are their eyes and ears and hands; they are our claws."

"You both need each other," Jennifer said.

Raajek answered before SStragh. "We aid each other, yes, little human—which is the way the All-Ancestor wished it to be." Her blind eyes seemed to regard Jennifer kindly. "For the most part, we're allies. At the same time, it's best to remember that the Gairk are always dangerous, as you found with their Envoy. They are fierce, easily offended, and the taste of Mutata meat is as pleasant to them as any other. There have been years when there was no peace between us, when Gairk hunted Mutata and we fled for our lives. Many Nesting Walks ago, our entire tribe was nearly destroyed in such a conflict. Only one breeding mother was left. So our alliance with them is always uneasy."

"Which means that you don't dare offend them."

"Not if it can be avoided," Raajek said gently.

Jennifer could see from Raajek's stance that there were words left unsaid. Jennifer knew that another Gairk envoy had met with the OColi, though neither SStragh nor Raajek would talk to her about what was said. She thought she could guess what Raajek meant.

*The Gairk have asked them something, and they've
had to agree. But what?*

"We've offended the Gairk, haven't we? Us
humans, I mean. Just by being here, we offend
them, and you've made it worse by not handing
us over to them. That's what they think anyway."

"You guess well, Jhenini. The Gairk have
always sacrificed to the All-Ancestor for Her
good graces. . . ." Raajek lifted her snout, scent-
ing some odor on the breeze that Jennifer missed.
"Frraghi is here," she said.

A moment later, Frraghi emerged from the
trees to their right. "Raajek," he said in greeting.
"SStragh." He glanced pointedly at Jennifer, then
deliberately ignored her. "Why are the two of you
outside with the human?" he asked Raajek.

"Jhenini needed exercise," Raajek said blandly.

"Then why do you not have all three?"

"Jhenini can be trusted; the two males must
be hobbled. With the dangers in the valley, we
didn't want to be slowed by them."

"There must be another reason," Frraghi said.

Raajek didn't answer. She took a halting step
forward, almost colliding with the other Mutata.
"You are in our path, Frraghi," she said.

"I came to tell you to take the human back,"
Frraghi ordered. "There are Gairk out in the valley, some of them very near. It would be dangerous if they saw her. Take her back; I will escort
you. She is hardly safe with a blind Elder and her
student."

Raajek simply gave the nasal trill that was
a Mutata chuckle. "Is that the OColi's order,
Frraghi?"

Jennifer knew that what Raajek had said was an implicit challenge to the younger Mutata—pointing out that Raajek was an Elder and thus Frraghi's superior in status. Frraghi reacted as Jennifer expected: the frill along his spine rose and deepened in color from a mottled, pale aquamarine to brilliant emerald; at the same time, a strong scent of musk came from him. He lowered his head and neck, changing from the normal hunched-over Mutata bodily posture to a more erect stance. He also shifted his spear from his right hand to his left—Jennifer was certain that there was probably a reason for that as well, since the Mutata were so habit-driven. Nearly everything the Mutata did seemed to have its reflection in the OColihi, the codes of behavior. Frraghi's reaction was dangerous but normal.

Jennifer also knew that Raajek had deliberately provoked it for some reason of her own.

"I am the OColi's Voice," Frraghi answered haughtily. "I listen to the OColi and speak for him. I know what the OColi would say."

"But the OColi didn't say it," Raajek persisted. "And I remind Frraghi that I once defeated the OColi in ciosie. If I desired it, *I* would be OColi."

"You bested the OColi with trickery, by ignoring the OColihi," Frraghi thundered. The coloring along his flank had gone deep and saturated; his six fingers flexed on the spear's shaft. SStragh had moved in front of Jennifer and just behind Raajek, ready to defend her mentor if Frraghi should attack.

Raajek didn't deny Frraghi's accusation. Instead, she gave a wriggle of the neck that Jennifer realized must be the equivalent of a shrug. "If the

OColi wishes us to return, we will return," she said. "But the OColi has not ordered it. If Frraghi wishes us to return, then we will stay—because after the OColi, *I* am Eldest, not Frraghi."

Frraghi hissed in response. With the sound, Raajek's own frill rose, displaying the ulcerations and tears that were the mark of the creature's great age. Raajek straightened as well, though she moved far more stiffly than Frraghi. Jennifer could hear the dinosaur's joints creaking and popping.

"I am appalled by Raajek," Frraghi said. "I am ashamed at the manner in which she treats the OColi."

Raajek sounded a short, soft note through her nasal horn. "I have not treated the OColi with anything but respect," she declared. "As for Frraghi, I have treated *him* with all the respect he deserves."

Frraghi trumpeted at the bald insult. He drew back the spear. With a shout, he thrust at Raajek. SStragh bellowed in alarm and Jennifer screamed, but Raajek made no move. Frraghi pulled his blow a scant half-inch from Raajek's unprotected chest. The obsidian tip trembled there as if alive. Raajek, with preternatural calm, reached out and felt for the long, deadly blade. Her wandering hand swept against the edge and gashed her finger. Blood welled from the cut.

"You see?" she said, holding out the injured digit. "Even Frraghi wishes to break the OColihi in these days."

Frraghi was looking at his own weapon, aghast. His coloring had gone pale and the frill along his back had flattened, lying limp over his spine.

Suddenly, the Mutata threw his spear aside. The weapon went crashing downhill through the trees.

"You destroy everything," Frraghi said to Raajek. His voice shook with emotion, though Jennifer could not tell whether it was rage or fear or some combination of both. A welter of scents came from the Mutata, too many for Jennifer to sort out. "SStragh's humans should be destroyed now, as the Gairk wish. And you, Raajek—you should have stayed away from the Mutata. You should have died alone years ago. I don't know why the All-Ancestor allowed you to live."

Then Frraghi lowered his stance, his head lifting in submission and humiliation. "Anger has always been my worst enemy," he said. "I nearly struck at you without following the rituals. For that, I am sorry. For that, I apologize to Raajek, but I do not apologize for anything else I have said."

"You've done nothing to apologize for," Raajek answered gently. "You *should* defend your OColi. There's nothing wrong with that, Frraghi Speaker-for-the-OColi."

Frraghi lowered his head slowly. He regarded Raajek appraisingly and almost respectfully, then turned his head to glare at Jennifer. She gazed back at him as calmly as she could, stepping out from behind SStragh.

"I thank you for being concerned for my safety, Frraghi," Jennifer said, knowing that she was doing so mostly because it always disturbed Frraghi when she spoke. She imagined she might feel the same way if confronted with a talking dog. "But right now I feel most safe with a blind Elder and her student, not with Frraghi."

Frraghi snorted, his previous apology to Raajek drowned out by this new irritation. Jennifer thought that he might say something more, but the dinosaur only turned his back on them and half slid, half climbed downhill to recover his weapon. Then, without looking back, he continued down into the valley in the direction of the Mutata town.

Jennifer watched Frraghi's retreat for a short time, then looked back at Raajek curiously. "You provoked Frraghi on purpose," she said to her. "You deliberately upset him."

The blind Mutata seemed to look at her, the featureless white eyes glistening strangely in the sunlight. Blood slowly dripped from her cut finger to the ground; gnatlike insects buzzed around the wound but Raajek didn't seem to notice or care.

"Yes," she said. "I did, Jhenini."

"You did it so Frraghi wouldn't ask again why you were out here, didn't you? If he had asked you directly, you would have had to answer. The OColi doesn't know you found our Floating Stone, does he? You haven't told him yet."

"You are correct, Jhenini—I acted so Frraghi would forget what he should have asked immediately. And no, the OColi does not know. He has also neglected to ask me."

Jennifer looked at the two Mutata, both standing silently and calmly before her, like twin statues. "I thought . . . I thought that you had to obey the OColi in all things."

"We do. Always." It was SStragh who answered her this time. "But if Frraghi did not ask the right questions, is it *our* fault that we did not tell him everything?"

Jennifer laughed at that. "I suppose not. But sometimes . . . sometimes I think you Mutata are a lot more like us than you would think."

Neither of the Mutata responded, though Raajek's scent changed to a sudden citrus sweetness. "Let's go down and find this Floating Stone again," she said. "And we should also be careful. In one thing, at least, Frraghi is right. It would be better not to meet any Gairk."

DINOSAUR PLANET SKETCHBOOK

A Record of My Adventures
by Aaron Cofield

Pages 2 and 3: The saorod's surprise attack was swift and brutal, and almost the end of Jenny.

Page 4: A statue honoring a dinosaur, right in the center of Green Town—but not my Green Town.

Page 5: Their days of playing came to an end. It was the Mutata's rite of passage for their young.

Page 6: The giant white ape who personally wanted to end my adventure through time: Mundo.

Page 7: One more return to Green Town. But it was changed, and bad things happened.

Pages 8 and 9: An involuntary traveler through time. I don't know if this beast was more scared or angry, but it was clearly not happy.

Pages 10 and 11: Of all the strange occurrences that happened to Jenny, this must have been one of the most upsetting.

Pages 12 and 13: The time storms brought strange, exotic things and creatures to the Mesozoic, like this beautiful Buddhist temple.

Pages 14 and 15: A panorama of the place Jenny got to know so well during her stay in the dinosaurs' world.

Page 16: Eckles was crazier than any of us could have imagined. He introduced several different kinds of death to the Mutata and the Gairk.

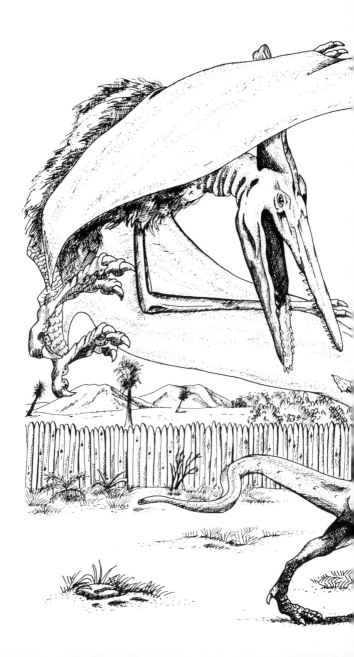

SSTRAGH HELPED FIGHT
OFF THE SAORODS' FIERCE
ATTACK.

IN THE CENTER OF
TOWN WAS THE STATUE
OF A HADROSAUR.

VERY WEIRD!

THE MOST
IMPORTANT TIME IN
THE YOUNGLINS' LIVES—
THE DAY OF NAMING.

MUNDO THOUGHT I
HAD TRIED TO KILL
HIM-- AND WANTED
TO RETURN THE FAVOR.

APPEARING AT
GREENTOWN I
SAW GRAN'PA AGAIN
RIGHT BEFORE I
WAS SHOT.

THE MASTODON WAS
ABOUT TO CHARGE US,
BEFORE IT VANISHED
INTO THE TIME STORM.

JENNY WAS LED TO
A HUMAN BODY
BY TWO OF THE
BIRD-LIZARDS.

OUT OF THE TIME STORM
BEYOND THE BRONTOSAURS,
A BUDDHIST TEMPLE
APPEARED.

FROM THE TOP OF THE HILL,
JENNIFER COULD SEE
THE ENTIRE VALLEY.

ECKELS HAD A
DEADLY SURPRISE
FOR THE GAIRK
ENVOY.

ESCAPE

Outside in the darkness, someone was shouting.

Sudden adrenaline gave Carl an agility that belied his years. He was at the window in an instant, thinking how stupid it was to be poking his head out where it might get shot.

The thought had barely had time to register when—terrifyingly—a weapon *was* fired, almost immediately below his upstairs bedroom window. In the faint light from the house, Carl saw an explosion of grass and dirt out on the lawn. Someone—some*thing*?—in a white, shaggy coat was running hellbent for the cover of the trees; that last shot had struck only a few inches from its feet. Carl could see Tate, his bald head reflecting moonlight like a waxed billiard ball, an air-dart clutched in his hands. One of the two government goons was with him, the one Carl thought of as Cold-And-Icy—Captain Michaels—and Michaels had produced a weapon as well. Both she and Tate fired again as White-Coat plunged into the trees. It was impossible to tell whether they hit the intruder or not.

Tate and Michaels took off in pursuit.

"Aaron?" Carl whispered. The apparition hadn't looked like his grandson, but Carl had a chill, a premonition that Aaron was nearby, very close. Carl wrapped his bathrobe around him and headed downstairs in bare feet at a run. He threw the back door open and went out on the porch.

To his right two more shots sounded from within the midnight confines of the woods. Carl squinted into the darkness. "Damn it, Tate, you said you just wanted to talk to the boy!" he shouted to the night, his hands cupped around his mouth. "You hurt Aaron and I'll have your head!" Carl ran out into the grass, cold dew wet on his ankles, to where the back yard dropped off toward the trees.

"You hear me, Tate?"

Through the black lace of the branches, Carl could see frantically swaying lights as Tate and the two suits pursued the intruder. There were a few more shots, followed by angry shouts. Carl could hear Tate and Michaels thrashing through the woods, cursing the limbs that snagged their clothes and slapped their faces. Their weapons were quiet, and they'd stopped running. The erratic shafts of light seemed to be growing brighter now.

A few minutes later, Tate emerged from down the hill. The beam of his flashlight caught Carl full on the face, and Carl raised his hand to shield his eyes from the glare. "Tate, you're a damn fool!" he shouted. "You hear me?"

"Who—was that—, Cofield?" Tate answered. The sheriff was out of breath. The question came carried on great gasps of air as he trudged up the hill toward Carl.

"I don't have the foggiest idea," Carl said. "And if you don't take that flashlight out of my eyes, I'm going to use it to knock some sense into that ugly hairless skull of yours."

"I'd love—to see—you try," Tate answered, complete but he snapped off the flash. Tate was completely winded by the time he reached the crest of the hill. It took him several seconds to regain his breath. "I'm asking you once more, Cofield," Tate said after he could speak again. "Who was that?"

"You got something stuck in your ears, Tate? I already told you. I haven't any idea."

Tate shook his head. "Cofield . . . Carl . . . We've been friends since we were kids—"

"We *were* friends," Carl interrupted. "Until you became *their* friend." Carl pointed back down the hill, where Tate's two companions were just emerging from the cover of the trees.

"Look, Carl," Tate said, whispering. "I don't like the suits much more than you do, but the law's on their side and I have to uphold the law."

"That law of yours include shooting at people you don't know?"

"If I *hadn't* shot, they'd I've had my hide, Carl. You know that. You also know that what I can see, I can hit, even at my age—if you take my drift." Tate adjusted his pants around the mountain of his belly. "Now answer me straight, Carl. Was that Aaron?"

"No, it wasn't."

"I didn't think so. Then what was it?"

"Someone dressed up in his mother's old fur coat in the middle of summer," Carl answered. "Heck, Tate, I don't *know*. It wasn't anything I ever saw before."

"We've had enough of your lying and evasion, Mr. Cofield." Ms. Cold-And-Icy's voice came from behind Carl. Michaels had arrived in time to hear his last answer. "Don't you think it's time you tried the truth?"

"Captain Michaels—" Tate began.

"No, Sheriff." She cut off his protest with a quick wave of her hand. "I've had my fill of Cofield's incessant disruptions. He's been living here by General McWilliams's leave—"

"This is *my* land!" Carl shouted at her. The darkness under the woods seemed to swallow the protest. "I don't need no damn General's permission."

Michaels ignored him. " . . . by General Mc-Williams's leave," she repeated slowly and deliberately, challenging him with her unblinking gaze, "for the last several years. You had strict orders to inform us of any new developments immediately. Immediately, Mr. Cofield. You failed to do that."

"Aaron's my *grandson*—"

"He says he is. You say he is. The report I have states that the person claiming to be Aaron Cofield looked and acted eighteen. Your grandson should be thirty, Mr. Cofield. Maybe he's Aaron and maybe he's not. Maybe he's really that . . . that *thing* we just chased. And maybe, just maybe, he's responsible for all the destruction and chaos that have afflicted us, the affliction that started *here* on your land, Mr. Cofield, and seems to be rapidly spreading over the entire globe. The affliction, Mr. Cofield, that caused the President to declare martial law throughout our country two years ago."

Captain Michaels turned to Sheriff Tate. "And by the authority given me by that declaration, Sheriff, I am placing Mr. Cofield under arrest."

"Captain—"

"*Do* it, Sheriff," Michaels barked. "We'll be taking him back to the Compound. He can bring a few personal items. That's all. See to it. I'll be waiting by the car. Come on, Sergeant." She wheeled and strode off toward the house, her companion following in her wake.

Tate rubbed a hand over his bald skull, scowling at Michaels's back. Carl stood with his shoulders slumped, not knowing what to say or do. He wanted to scream and rage, but he knew it wouldn't do any good. No good at all.

"Carl . . ."

"Just shut up, Tate. You gonna arrest me like the suit said?"

"I don't have a choice."

"Oh yes, you do." Carl peered angrily at Tate, his face twin-shadowed with moonlight and the glare from the porchlight. "Tate, you're just like the others—too scared to make that decision."

"I got a family, Carl—"

"And I *had* one. Once." Carl sighed. Down the hill, the leaves rustled in the warm night breeze. Clouds brushed the face of the moon and chased their shadows across the fields. "I ain't to blame for this, Tate. I ain't."

"I believe you, Carl. I do. It's just . . ."

"I know." Carl shook his head. "Okay, let's get going."

"You want to get some stuff from the house? The captain said—"

"There's nothing back there I want. Nothing I need. Just let me get some clothes on, okay?"

It was spring again, a spring that had blossomed like an impossibly quick flower in the hour or so it had taken to cross the pathway to the Mesozoic once more, get into the time machine, and set the machine down on the pathway. Vehicle and all had suddenly materialized back in Green Town, and Travis had flown them at treetop level out of the forest to set the machine down on a lush green lawn that had only a few minutes before been covered in snow.

Another of the time storms must have hit in the months between, for the truncated stump of a gigantic tree squatted near the house. The stump was at least ten feet in diameter, and looked as if it had been axed down, thick gashes like half-moons showing white through the bark. As the time machine hissed and sighed to a halt, Aaron decided that he didn't want to meet the person who had wielded that axe.

Aaron was out of the machine first, running to the house with an instinctive hope that he tried to bury but couldn't. The disappointment hit him as soon as he walked in the unlocked front door.

"Gran'pa?" he called quietly, but he knew there'd be no answer. The dust had settled deeper on the floors, the sediment of loneliness. Birds had come through the broken windows and made nests on the sills; a raccoon had left its distinctive, delicate handprints along the kitchen counter.

No one lived here. No one had lived here for—now—a year or so.

Aaron went back outside. Travis was leaning against the time machine as if exhausted. He looked horrible. "Still the same?" Travis asked. Aaron shrugged his answer. "Sorry, kid," Travis said. "I really am."

"Yeah," Aaron said. The word caught, quavering. He cleared his throat harshly. "Now what?"

"Get in," Travis said. "We're taking a short hop."

"Back?" Aaron asked hopefully.

"Forward," Travis answered. "As an experiment."

"Travis . . ."

"Don't worry. I'm going to help you with your grandfather. There's just something I need to check first. If I'm right, we'll know a lot more than we did before. Controls out," he said, and the sexless voice of the machine answered "Activating . . ."

Back inside, Aaron watched the weary Travis set the controls for Travis's own time. Aaron didn't say anything; he could understand Travis's need.

We can always travel back in time, remember. There's no need to be impatient. We have all the time in the world. Aaron watched from his own chair, memorizing the steps Travis took to recalibrate the machine. After a few minutes, Travis sat back, groaning with the motion. "Now," he said.

The time machine howled and shuddered, the engines building up to their familiar whine, but there was a sudden Klaxon alarm and the whine subsided to a mechanical cry. "Calibration error," the computer said. "Calendar settings wrong. We are currently in HomeTime. Reset calendar?"

"No," Travis said. "Controls in, please." As the panel slid back into the wall, Travis swiveled in his chair to face Aaron. "Did you understand that?" he asked.

"I . . . think so," Aaron answered carefully. "You told us that your time machines can only go into the past, not the future. For some reason, the computer thinks the year 2005 or whatever it is here now is your HomeTime. Is it broken?"

Travis grimaced as if some inner pain prevented him from answering, then shook his head. "No, there's no error."

The underlying implication came to Aaron, as if an inner light had revealed a hidden landscape. "We're in another reality entirely . . . You were right, Travis!" he said excitedly. "We never found Green Town when we went UpTime from the Mesozoic because that was *your* Mesozoic, not mine—your whole *universe*, not mine."

Travis nodded wearily. "Eckels destroyed my world, but not yours. Your own present, where the end of the roadway is rooted, became HomeTime as soon as we crossed between the worlds, which is why the machine is confused. Except . . ." He took a long shuddering breath.

"*Is* this your world, kid?" he asked. "You told me it's changed. You *saw* it change." Travis's eyes were closed as he leaned back in his seat. "That can only mean one thing," he said. "It means that someone here is playing around in the past, too. Not enough to have destroyed everything the way Eckels did, but like Eckels with the butterfly—everything's slightly twisted."

The other section of the path, the one Gran'pa said they brought out of the woods . . . Aaron had a sudden hunch that he knew what had happened, but he said nothing to Travis. "We gotta go back," Aaron said. "That night, when Tate shot at Mundo and me—we gotta go back and get Gran'pa. They took him." Aaron stared from the open door of the machine to the empty house. "No," he said. "We go back further, even before I showed up. We'll get him then."

"No, we won't." Travis answered softly.

Aaron whirled around to confront the man. "Why not? If we go back to the night when they must have taken him, Tate'll be there, and the other two. That's stupid."

Travis sighed. His eyes opened slowly. "Time Travel Lecture Number 1: never play with paradox. If we go snatch your grandfather before you show, he couldn't have been there when you arrived. Therefore, it never happened."

"Huh? Travis—"

"*No*," the man said emphatically, and the word brought Travis forward in the seat, his pain-wracked eyes alight with intensity. "Mess with time, and it messes back. Haven't we seen enough of that lesson already? If you change history, you change *everything*. We have no idea what will happen as a result. So far, the changes haven't been pleasant."

"Travis, we're going back. Now."

Travis sunk back in his seat. "Yes, we'll go back. I promise you that. But not now. We both need to rest."

Carl went into the house with Tate following. With the sheriff watching, he dresssed and pulled his old, worn boots on his feet. They didn't talk;

there didn't seem to be anything more to say. Carl moved slowly. Everything seemed to have taken on a strange clarity: the fine cracks in the ancient leather, the feel of the laces running over his fingers, the soft, knobby texture of the bed's coverlet on which he sat. He hadn't really *looked* at the room in years; now there wasn't enough time to see it all.

They went downstairs and out to the front porch. Carl started to lock the door, then tossed the keys to Tate, who caught them and silently stuck them in his pants pocket. Carl held his hands out toward Tate. "You gotta cuff me, right? I know that's the procedure."

Tate snorted. "You never could outrun or outwrestle me, old man." The ghost of a smile touched the sheriff's lips and fled again. His eyes glinted under the ridge of his brow.

Carl let his hands drop back to his side. "Thanks. Thanks for that, Phillip."

"You haven't called me that in years."

"Figured it might be my last chance." Carl gave a last glance at the woods, at the house. "Okay, let's go," he said.

Michaels was standing beside the car, Sergeant Waters next to her with the driver's door open. The engine was idling. Michaels strode toward them, her flat-soled shoes crunching on the gravel driveway. Michaels glanced at Carl, then her chilly gaze went to Tate. She shifted her air-dart from one hand to another. "He's not cuffed," she said.

"Nope, he's not," Tate replied flatly.

"That's not procedure, Sheriff."

"Probably not, Captain."

For several seconds, there was a standoff, Tate standing alongside Carl with his hands folded, Michaels glaring at the two of them. Finally, Michaels sniffed in annoyance. "All right. You're responsible for him, Tate. You understand? If he causes trouble, I'll have someone else doing your job tomorrow."

"Yes, ma'am." Carl noticed that Tate managed to make the agreement sound like an insult. He grinned despite himself as Michaels's eyes narrowed angrily.

"Get him in the car," she said to Tate.

As Carl entered the cramped vehicle, smelling of leather and brass and oil, he saw the flickering out in the field. For a second Carl wasn't sure that he had even seen anything—it was like a glimpse of motion caught with the side of the eye which disappeared when you tried to look at it directly. Then he saw it again—a shimmering in the air as though someone had thrown a rock into a still, vertical pond. He heard something as well, a high keening whine like an engine driven beyond its limits.

The others heard it as well. Tate had straightened alongside the car; Waters was standing openmouthed as he stared out at the field; Michaels had brought up her weapon, sighting down the barrel into the empty landscape.

The not-so-empty landscape. Suddenly, there was *something* there. Without ever having seen it before, Carl knew what it was.

Travis's time machine.

The sleek metallic body hissed and popped, releasing cold white streamers of fog. A filigree of hoarfrost spread wildly over the body of the hovering vehicle, then vanished as quickly as it had come. A door slid upward on the side of the body; silhouetted against the light from inside the time machine stood a familiar figure.

"Aaron!" Carl shouted, involuntarily.

"Gran'pa!" came the faint reply.

Carl heard the sinister *chuff* of Michaels's rifle being fired. Aaron spun, then fell back into the vehicle. Carl shouted, not even knowing what he was saying, and tried to leave the car—the door was locked. Before he could scramble over the seat to the front, Tate had plowed into the seat behind him, covering him. Someone was firing something else, but the sound of the weapon was quite unlike that of the air-darts: percussive and loud. Glass shattered above him, showering both Tate and him with crystalline shards. The weapon kept chattering. Carl tried to look up; Tate shoved his head back down. Carl caught a glimpse of Travis, bright fire sparking from the muzzle of the weapon at his shoulder; at the same moment, Waters's body hit the side of the car hard, and streams of bright blood were running down the sides and over the peaks of broken windshield.

Michaels half dived, half collapsed into the car. Her head low, she slammed the engine into gear and stomped the accelerator to the floor.

Waters's body went spinning away. Gravel kicked and spattered underneath them; Carl was jolted with the movement, Tate's weight nearly knocking the breath from him. There was a sound like someone repeatedly striking the side of the car with a hammer—more glass shattered; low on the door, a round hole appeared, letting in a puff of dust; almost in Carl's ear, Tate grunted in surprise and pain.

Then the car swung around the turn onto Mill Creek Road, and the hammering stopped.

Above Carl, Tate was cursing low and continuously. As the car sped down the blacktop toward Green Town, Carl could only think of Aaron, of seeing the young man tumble backward into the time machine with Michaels's shot . . .

THE FACE OF DEATH

Beaded scarlet and yellow lurked beyond a broken wall of emerald vines.

"Be still!" SStragh commanded in the Mutata language, adding the imperative "Aii" and a scent of cinnamon.

Jennifer froze in mid-step. Frraghi had been right. She could smell something else now—a miasma of rotting meat, mingled with the sound of an asthmatic giant's breath and the rustling of a heavy body as it moved among the leaves. SStragh snapped her spear up to a ready position and sidled closer to Jennifer. Last of the trio, Raajek, her ancient body leaning forward, continued to plod onward, ignoring SStragh's warning.

"OTsio Raajek," SStragh shouted. "Be careful."

"I know," Raajek said. "I smell the Gairk. Let it come out if it wishes, or let it hide back there like a coward pretending that no one can see it."

That brought a hissing like an overheated steam kettle from behind the screening bushes. A Gairk stomped out, crushing the foliage under the pistons of its massive, clawed feet. Tiny shrewlike mammals scampered from its path. Jennifer took an involuntary step away.

She had met only one Gairk in her time here, and that Gairk had been a formidable, dangerous presence until the first Dreaming Storm had killed it. Though younger and smaller than the unfortunate Envoy, this creature was no less impressive. The muscular beast stood seven feet tall, built like a scaled-down version of an allosaurus with its long snout a wicked hedge of snaggled, razored teeth. It had unlashed one of the two spiked bludgeons at its waist and brandished the weapon as it stalked forward, the dull copper armor plating lashed around its body clashing like cracked cymbals.

"I was not *hiding*, Elder," he said in his growling accent. Despite Jennifer's growing proficiency with the warbling hoots and snorts of the dinosaurs, she still had trouble understanding the creature. The sound of it was like a bass drum talking. "I am Khiika, and I am of the Gairk OColi's eggs. Gairk do not hide nor do we fear *anyone*, especially not leaf-eaters."

He said the last with a disdainful look at SStragh and her spear.

Khiika seemed to see Jennifer then for the first time. The Gairk hissed, and his savage head drew back on the thick neck. The club jabbed in her direction, dangerously. "That is one of the abominations," he said. "Move aside so I may dispose of it, Elder."

"This 'abomination' is under my protection, Khiika," Raajek said blandly. Her cataract-white eyes blinked.

"*Your* protection?" Khiika snorted. "Mutata have an odd idea of what constitutes protection. I don't see any such protection."

"Perhaps," Raajek said placidly.

"The Gairk OColi himself gave me my orders," Khiika said ponderously and slowly, as if searching for the right words. "I am to search for new Floating Stones. I am to kill any creature that has escaped from them. That"— Khiika pointed the club at Jennifer —"came from one of the Floating Stones. You cannot deny that."

"So you must kill her," Raajek finished for the creature. Her undertone of sarcasm was apparent even to Jennifer; she wondered how the Gairk could miss it. "I applaud your admirable demonstration of logic, Khiika. Unfortunately, it is misplaced. You can't have this one. She is precious to us and under my protection."

"My OColi's commands are not subject to the whims of a Mutata, no matter how venerable she might be," Khiika answered. "Nor is this my decision to make. I was instructed in what I must do. More strange beings appear every day around our valley. Already this day, I have killed a . . . soft, pale *thing* very much like your abomination, from a Floating Stone that I've not yet found. The Dreaming Storms have come four times in the last hand of days, and the last storm left behind a lake of foul water near the mouth of our valley. The Mutata OColi knows this, yet you have not given us the abominations you keep. Klaido told the Mutata OColi to give them to us."

The club pointed again at Jennifer; this time she noticed the gory remnants snagged between the jagged obsidian blades protruding from the wood. "But now I find an abomination outside the Mutata jhaka," Khiika said. "I will take the body back to show my OColi."

Jennifer was too startled to react. She was trying not to think about what Khiika had said: "... *I have killed a soft, pale thing very much like your abomination* ..." The words thundered and crackled in Jennifer's head.

Aaron would have come after us. If he found the path, he would have followed it once he realized that we were lost. Please, please don't let it be Aaron. It can't be Aaron ...

"This abomination is special," Raajek repeated. "This one is protected."

"Elder, again with no disrespect, but protected by *what*? A blind elder and a young leaf-eater with an unbloodied spear?" Khiika answered disdainfully. To Jennifer, the Gairk attitude sounded all too much like Frraghi's. "That is not protection. Elder, you are keeping me from my duty and I will not tolerate that. You will move aside."

"No," Raajek said softly. "We will not."

"I give you formal warning now, Elder. By the OColihi."

"No."

Then the Gairk took a long, slow breath. Then, without further words, the Gairk charged the group.

SStragh bellowed her own response, her spear thrusting at the Gairk as she shielded Jennifer. Khiika spun with surprising grace, letting the spear's tip graze the armor to leave a long, shiny scar in the copper surface. In the same motion, the Gairk whipped his armored tail around. The metal-wrapped tip caught SStragh on one shoulder, sending the Mutata sprawling with the force of the blow. The Gairk snorted in brief victory, then turned to Jennifer. He raised his club as

Jennifer scrambled for safety. The first blow missed, cratering the soft ground where she'd stood a moment before. The Gairk pursued, bringing the deadly club back yet again.

Raajek was moving also. The ancient dinosaur took three quick and deliberate steps, her head cocked as she listened intently to the sounds of the struggle. With the third step, she was between Jennifer and Khiika as the Gairk shrilled and swung his bludgeon once more. Jennifer screamed, knowing that the blow would strike Raajek rather than her, the blade-studded weapon scything toward the Mutata's head. Raajek made no motion to avoid the blow. She stood—as Khiika brought the weapon down, as the Gairk's war cry echoed in the valley.

Impossibly, Khiika pulled the strike in mid-arc, a scant inch from Raajek's skull. The club trembled with the tremendous effort required to halt the blow; the Gairk's nostrils flared in rage and tendons stood out like massive ropes along his arms.

This is twice now in the last two hours that someone's stopped just short of killing Raajek, Jennifer thought. *That is one lucky dinosaur.*

"Elder, you are very brave and I admire that quality as any Gairk would," Khiika grumbled. "I am also sorry, but now you must move or be killed."

"It's a good thing that Khiika has displayed such impeccable logic and excellent control," Raajek said slowly. She made no effort to get out of the Gairk's path. "Perhaps then he will be able to understand all the ramifications of his actions. You see, Khiika, I am Raajek, Eldest next to the Mutata OColi. I have made twenty-three Nesting Walks and laid eighteen clutches. I tell you this so that you know that I have seen enough to be wise, and so you know that I have done all I need to do. I don't fear meeting my ancestors or telling the tale of my life to the All-Ancestor."

Khiika frowned and stamped his feet. "So instead you will talk me to death."

Raajek gave the wide-mouthed leer that was a Mutata smile. "Perhaps," she said. "But be patient for a few more moments—the human can't outrun you. Khiika, I have been given the responsibility to protect this human. To reach Jhenini, you are going to need to kill me. You can easily do that, as you know—I'm old and blind and no match for a strong youngling like you even if I chose to defend myself. However, if you kill me, then you will also have to kill SStragh, both because she would be honor-bound to avenge the death of her OTsio and because the Mutata OColi has charged her with the responsibility for Jhenini beyond me. SStragh is young and strong too, and she knows the way of the spear very well—her weapon is not unblooded, as you think, and you may find her more of a problem than you believe."

Khiika glanced back at SStragh, who had regained her feet and had moved to a defensive posture just behind Raajek. "I don't worry about dying," Khiika said. "No Gairk worries about death. By the OColihi, an honorable death is always rewarded, as a wise Elder knows. And you *are* trying to talk me to death."

"Perhaps. But listen still, Khiika . . . Even if you give SStragh that honorable death, you must then deal with Jhenini herself. She is not simply an abomination, Khiika. You must know of the Envoy that the Gairk OColi sent to us many hands of days ago, the one who was struck down during the first of the Dreaming Storms. This is the Jhenini who, it is said, pointed and called the first storm. With one gesture, your Envoy was torn in half. I wonder how that would feel, Khiika? I wonder whether your being food for the diejeks will make your OColi feel better when the Mutata OColi declares formal war because of your treatment of me and SStragh? I wonder how the ancestors will treat you when you tell them that you struck down the one human who might help us end the strangeness in our valley. I wonder how many of your people will die because you felt you had to obey your orders so literally?"

The Gairk snorted. "You are trying to confuse me."

"No," Jennifer said softly. She had come up to stand by Raajek. "Raajek is saving you from making a mistake."

Khiika lurched backward, startled, crushing a bush and causing a cloud of large-winged insects to screech away. His fierce visage glared down at her, his head lowering like a crane. "It *speaks*," he trilled in surprise. "And very badly," he added. His nostrils widened as he sniffed in her direction. "It smells confused."

"I apologize to Khiika for that," Jennifer answered, using the formal phrasing SStragh and Raajek had taught her: the OColihi of politeness. One of her schoolteachers had pointed out that the more bound by politeness and etiquette a civilization was, the more violence lurked beneath its surface. That seemed true enough of both the Mutata and the Gairk. "This one is a poor student and hasn't had the advantages of a Gairk OTsio to guide her."

The Gairk snuffled at that, then seemed to accept the excuse. "Is what the Elder Raajek says of you true? Did you call the Dreaming Storm?"

Jennifer glanced at Raajek, at SStragh. She could not decipher Raajek's empty gaze; SStragh seemed to be listening intently; she gave the barest nod of her head. "Yes," Jennifer said.

The Gairk peered intently at Jennifer's hand. "It's an ugly claw, but it doesn't look dangerous. I will wager my broaii against Jhenini's finger." Khiika brandished his club.

Jennifer was certain that he was about to attack again. Feeling very foolish, Jennifer pointed her finger like a gun and sighted down it until her fingertip seemed to point between Khiika's eyes. As a bluff, it seemed very unconvincing.

"Bang!" she said.

Khiika staggered backward again with the sound. The sudden fear in his crocodilian eyes was almost comical. The Gairk hissed and placed his weapon between himself and Jennifer's finger as if to ward off a blow.

"Don't make me do it, Khiika," Jennifer said. Raajek had begun the bluff; Jennifer realized that she had to take it further if they were to stop the Gairk's attack. "I have no desire to rob the Gairk OColi of someone as valuable as you, but if you insist on ciosie, I will have no choice."

"This is not the OColihi," Khiika snarled. "Ciosie is between equals, and the Gairk OColi has declared you an abomination. This magic of the abominations is not OColihi."

"No," Jennifer answered him. "It is the OChiihi, the New Way."

"That is why you must survive, Khiika," Raajek added, her soft, quavering voice insistent. "What has happened in this valley has already crushed the OColihi. It is my belief that those who keep to the Old Path will be destroyed with it."

"We hope that Jhenini—this abomination, as you call her—will help us restore the OColihi, or at least end the Dreaming Storms and the attacks from the Floating Stones," SStragh added. "If you kill her, you end any chance of that. Your Gairk OColi already knows this. Three days ago, your new Envoy came to our OColi and told us this: the Gairk OColi has given our humans their lives until OGhielas. Surely you know that."

"I have been away from the jhaka for a hand of days," Khiika said. "Is this true? If it is not, then, by the OColihi, I will come for you."

"It is true," SStragh said.

Khiika looked from SStragh to Raajek, snorting. His coloring had gone dark and the leather lacings on his armor creaked audibly as he expanded his great chest. He blinked slowly. Jennifer was as startled as Khiika by what SStragh had said, but she decided that if she were going to be killed, she might as well be bold about it. Raajek had taken the chance and gotten away with it—now it was her turn.

"Take me to the abomination you killed," Jennifer ordered, as if she were the Gairk's elder. "Now. It's important that I see it. Or do you *want* the creatures from the Floating Stones to continue to plague you?"

She didn't think it would work. Khiika growled and swung his club once in the air before her, the broaii making a murderous *whuff* as it whirled, the black, sparkling blades slicing air. Then he placed the weapon back in its thong as Jennifer released a breath she hadn't known she'd been holding.

"Follow me," Khiika said. Turning away with a last baleful glance at Jennifer, the creature went crashing back through the underbrush the way it had come, like a great, scaled bulldozer given life. Khiika didn't look back to see that the others were following, but there was no mistaking the crushed path he left.

"You don't believe in violent confrontations, do you?" Jennifer said to Raajek. A sickness lay in her belly like an undigested lump, gnawing at her insides. With each day here, she'd become closer to Raajek and SStragh. Each day she had thought that she had understood their language a little better, thought that she'd understood *them* better. In her mind, she knew that she thought of them as humans trapped in reptilian shape. The Mutata were simply people—strange-looking ones, admittedly, with odd habits—but *people*, not much more different than someone from the plains of China or an African rain forest or the Siberian steppes.

Somehow, Jennifer had mentally clothed the Mutata in the trappings of humankind. She had colored their responses with her own.

The chimera dissolved before her eyes. Raajek was something alien and cold. "That was the second time today I've seen you stand in front of someone with a weapon and get away with it."

"I have been very lucky, Jhenini."

"You lied, Raajek. You told him that I killed the Gairk ambassador, that I brought on the Dreaming Storms. You never told me about this other Gairk Envoy, either, or about any OGhielas deadline."

"I didn't lie, Jhenini. I said that others believe you called the Dreaming Storm, and that is true— I've heard other Mutata say it. Even Khiika must have heard that, I simply let the Gairk believe what he wished to believe. It is not my fault that the Gairk OColi sends out impressionable younglings who do not listen carefully. *You* were the only one who lied."

"What about the new Gairk Envoy? What about OGhielas—whatever that is?"

"As for the envoy and his deadline, Jhenini, you never asked, so there is no lie there at all."

"Raajek, you know what I said earlier about you Mutata being awfully like humans?"

"Yes, Jhenini?"

Jennifer was glad that Raajek could not see her. "You're worse," she said.

Glaring at Raajek with her jaw set, Jennifer wondered what else she'd not known to ask, and just how deadly that lack of knowledge might be.

Jennifer, SStragh, and Raajek stumbled down the slope through the crushed plants and torn vines left in Khiika's wake. They came upon the Gairk again standing in a small clearing next to an outcropping of rock. Jennifer's throat constricted suddenly, the blood pounding in her temples as she walked into the open area. She recognized the wall of gray limestone—the entrance to

Eckels's cave was there, hidden behind a screen of tumbled boulders. That meant that the path back to Green Town wasn't far from here.

And *that* meant that Aaron might well have come this way if he'd followed Jennifer and Peter across time to this place. Which meant . . .

No, she told herself, *you're not going to follow the rest of that thought through.*

Khiika was standing near the rise of stones. The Gairk stepped aside as the trio entered the clearing, revealing a body mostly hidden in the tall, flowering grasses. Two of the scavenger bird-lizards—the jhiehai or Creatures of the Giving, as the Mutata called them—were perched on a boulder nearby. Jennifer's fingernails dug small crescent moons in the palms of her hands. She didn't need to see more to know that the sprawled body was human—she could see leather hiking boots on the feet, and blue jeans just like . . .

No. Don't think it. It isn't Aaron. I won't LET it be Aaron.

"This is the abomination I killed," Khiika said, and Jennifer shuddered at the blatant pride in his voice. It made her want to scream at the Gairk, to shout and rave. *Don't you know that's a PER-SON you killed? Don't you know that I—* Jennifer cut off the unspoken words. Khiika was glaring at her. "You wanted to see it." he said to Jennifer. "Come and look."

"I—" Jennifer began. She didn't want to take the few steps. A breeze swayed the grass around the body; the dark mound of the man lay unnaturally still.

Jennifer had seen death before. Her summer work as an aide at the hospital had made that inevitable, but she had never seen enough to become casual about it, as most of the medical staff seemed to be. Once, Jennifer had gone into a room to give old Mrs. McKnight her dinner tray and found the woman asleep—so she thought. She touched Mrs. McKnight's hand to wake her. The fingers had been so cold, so icy . . . and then Jennifer had noticed the preternatural *quiet* in the room, the stillness. The sound of Jennifer's own breath seemed somehow irreverent. Jennifer had nearly dropped the tray; the clatter had brought in the duty nurse, and Jennifer was ushered out of the room while the Green Cart was rushed in and the resident came flying down the corridor.

They were all too late. Jennifer knew it. She'd seen Death's handiwork there.

She saw it again now.

SStragh's hand touched her shoulder and she nearly jumped. "Jhenini," she said, whispering. "You must look. Whatever has been done can't be undone. You're the only one who can tell us whether this person has come from your world. I will go with you if it will help."

Jennifer took a deep breath. She remembered Mrs. McKnight's sunken cheeks, the way the husk of her body simply lay there as the doctors feverishly tried to return the departed breath. She could not imagine Aaron that way. Right at the moment, it didn't matter that only minutes ago she'd been looking at SStragh and Raajek as if they were monsters. "Thank you," she told SStragh, and patted the dinosaur's clawed hand. "I think I'd like that."

A moment later, Jennifer was staring down into the staring, lifeless eyes. The eyes seemed to gaze past her, heedless of the blinding sun. The mouth was open in a soundless plea.

"Do you know this human, Jhenini?" SStragh asked behind her.

Nothing seemed solid to Jennifer. The world spun around the axis of that dead face.

"Yes," she said, and she could not help the sobs that started then. "Yes, I do."

SHOOTOUT AT
THE COFIELD CORRAL

Three days' rest had indeed improved Travis's condition. He and Aaron moved the time machine into the barn as a precaution, though they saw no one but occasional deer, raccoons, squirrels, and birds during the whole time.

Travis spent most of his time sleeping. Aaron tended to his companion as best he could with the medical kit in the time machine. Travis gave Aaron instructions on the use of some of the more esoteric instruments after Aaron spent ten minutes puzzling over something that looked like a stainless steel hairbrush that had mated with a nutcracker.

More than once (and for many reasons), Aaron wished that Jennifer were there. Aaron suspected that Travis's health was far more fragile than either of them wanted to admit. The man hunched over at odd times with internal spasms, and a hacking cough would leave him helpless. His breath was sour and he wheezed when he moved too quickly. Travis's eyes had a tired, jaundiced look and he moved slowly and carefully, not like the hunter of great beasts he'd once been.

For Aaron's part, the three days were endless. He explored the barn—that took a few hours, pawing over things that looked half-familiar yet somehow strange. He came across a compound bow and some arrows, all well-coated with dust and all looking as if they'd been used quite regularly for a time before being interred here. Had the 'Aaron' his grandfather remembered had archery as a hobby, something Aaron himself couldn't remember because he wasn't exactly the same young man?

Aaron shook his head.

Too many paradoxes. Thinking about the conundrums of time travel made his head hurt.

Impatience gnawed at Aaron—he wanted to *do* something, wanted to be in motion. While Aaron understood that Travis's attempt to recuperate made sense, he couldn't shake the sense of urgency. Each hour that slid by on the console's clock seemed to mock him. He tried to keep himself busy; he spent most of the first night helping Travis reconfigure the software so that the time machine knew the correct date. That involved the sighting of various stars with the instruments aboard the machine.

"May 15, 2006," Travis said at last. "We got it. That sound about right to you, kid?"

Aaron could only shake his head. A few days ago, to him, it had been 1992 . . .

Aaron also explored the woods. He thought he might find some clue as to Mundo's whereabouts, as well as his grandfather's. Aaron wondered if poor, crazed Mundo had survived that night, the wild chase in the darkness, or whether the strange being's corpse might not be lost under a season's leaves. If so, Aaron never found it, nor did he see or hear anything that might have been Mundo's trail.

Once, Aaron went into the house with the intention of rummaging around and seeing what clues he could discover that might tell him about the dozen years he'd missed here. But ghosts seemed to walk the rooms, whispering images of the past. The imagined specters drove him out quickly.

He stayed away from the house after that.

Travis had indicated that he would prefer to stay a week or more, but on that third evening a time storm whipped through the fields around them, giving them more glimpses of bizarre landscapes and creatures: a steaming caldera in an empty volcanic landscape; a diplodocus munching contentedly on a treefern; the interior of a Roman bath, with startled patrons running as water spilled from the broken pools; a writhing creature that looked like something out of *Jabberwocky*; a Japanese pagoda from which Aaron swore a Native American was staring.

The last of the lightning flashes tore away the rear of the barn, leaving in its place the base of a tattered, mud-wattle hut only a few inches from the time machine. The proximity of the ruin scared them both, as they realized that Travis's vehicle could have been wrecked or lost altogether at the whim of the storm. The time machine was their only weapon in this strange war.

They didn't even have to speak. Travis looked at the hut and the missing back wall of the barn, which appeared to have been snipped away with cosmic shears. He gave Aaron a long stare, shook his head, then went to his seat and strapped himself in. After a last glance around his old homestead, Aaron did the same.

"Controls out," Travis said to the machine.

As the panel extended from the wall toward him, Travis glanced at Aaron. "Where're we headed, kid?"

Aaron remembered the paper he'd read, the one whose dateline had so startled him and which was still sitting on the table in the kitchen of his house. *"Picked one up yesterday in town,"* his grandfather had said, "July 23, 2005," he told Travis. "Very, very early that day, just after midnight of the twenty-third, maybe."

Travis keyed in the date, confirmed it with the computer.

The time machine howled like a banshee and fled. And materialized again under a moonwashed sky.

Aaron was out of his seat even as the frost on the windshield started to dissolve, revealing the scene. Travis had shunted them slightly in space as well as time—they were in the field in front of the house. Aaron could see the black, ugly car in the drive, light gray smoke curling from its exhaust pipe. He recognized the face in the back seat.

Aaron slapped at the door contact. "Aaron!" The call came from the car, faint yet clear.

"Gran'pa!" Aaron yelled back as the door hissed fully open. Sheriff Tate was just stepping into the car; the man was standing on the side nearest the time machine, with the woman behind him.

Aaron, his attention on his grandfather, saw the motion just a second too late. The woman had raised her strange weapon to her shoulder. The sound and the impact came almost simultaneously.

Aaron, like all his friends, had seen his share of action-adventure movies and television shows. In the middle of a running gunfight, the hero grimaced and lifted a hand to a suddenly bloody shoulder. He looked down at his fingers in surprise. "Nicked me . . ." The hero was never much hampered by the wound. He immediately flashed back into action as if it had never happened. He could still climb walls, dive through windows, duck and roll, or wrestle his opponent to the ground. No problem.

Wrong. The reality was far, far different.

It was as though Aaron had been hit by an invisible truck. The force of the impact turned him sideways and sent him staggering backward. There was a moment of blackness, and Aaron found himself sitting bewildered on the floor.

For a moment, Aaron thought his shoulder had been torn off entirely. His shirt was ripped open; underneath, there was a hole that seemed to be the size of Illinois. His whole side was wet; the blood looked black in the dim light. When he tried to sit up, he felt bone grating against bone in his arm. The pain exploded in starburst fireworks before his eyes. Through the whirling, Aaron was aware that Travis had come running from his seat, that Travis was firing back at the woman. The shots sounded incredibly loud and percussive in the confined space of the time machine.

"Hey, Travis," Aaron started to say. "Watch where you're shooting. That's my Grandpa out there," but the words seemed somehow comical and he wasn't sure he got them out. Aaron started to laugh.

He was still laughing when the world went away entirely.

Carl knew where they were. Everyone in Green Town knew the Compound. Once the site of a pharmaceutical company, the series of long, low buildings in the town of Ripley, just downriver from Green Town, had been enclosed in a net of security fences when the defense conglomerate Harriel-Jovi had bought the site from DuPont, the original owners. During the sixties and seventies, the Compound (as it was already called) had been used for Harriel-Jovi's research and development in chemical warfare.

When the Pentagon budget cuts had curtailed that particular operation in the early eighties, Harriel-Jovi had shut down most of the Ripley operation, devastating Ripley's economy in the process, and also hurting Green Town, since several of its residents worked there. The majority of the buildings had been sealed; a few others were used for shipping and transport. Much of the output of the chemical research was still stored on-site; Harriel-Jovi retained the shell of the security team for the Compound for that reason.

That was the way the site had remained for nearly a decade—until dinosaurs were seen walking in the midst of Green Town. Until the bizarre time storms started to plague first the Midwest and then the rest of the country. Until a strange, floating piece of plastic had been brought in from the woods not far away. Until martial law had been declared and a military/scientific force had been installed on the Compound grounds.

In the last several years, the Compound had blossomed to life again. The old buildings were opened and a few new ones were built. A few people from Ripley and Green Town were employed as construction workers, as administrative support, as janitorial staff—but not many. Most of the jobs were taken care of from within, by people brought in from outside or by the soldiers stationed there.

The Compound was a ripe source for Green Town gossip. Those who lived nearest the site spoke of strange noises and odd lights coming from the area. There were rumors that the President had even flown in once or twice in secret to view the operation. Some said that a top-secret government project was underway there and that the time storms were actually a product of some experiment that had gone awry.

That last was the opinion of those who weren't already convinced that all the strangeness didn't somehow stem from crazy old man Cofield who had murdered his grandson and two of his friends. After all, didn't the FBI go through the woods? Hadn't there been a day when a big army flatbed truck left the Cofield property with something covered by an olive drab tarp on the back, and didn't that same truck head right for the Compound? Didn't the ones the townspeople called suits—the ones the soldiers addressed as "Major" and "Colonel" but who never wore uniforms— pay a lot of attention to old man Cofield?

Carl knew he would have the opportunity to discover the truth about the Compound now. What he wondered was whether he would ever get the chance to tell anyone about it.

"Get a squad up to the Cofield property *now*! Make sure they're armed. Move it!"

Michaels was shouting. Their car was pinned by the glare of spotlights. Michaels's arms, gesticulating, threw dusty shadows through the blue-white beams. "Waters was hit. I had to leave him behind, and I've got a wounded man in the back seat. Come *on*! Move!"

Carl had a confused impression of people leaning into the car, of the doors being yanked open and hands pulling him out. Tate was half-conscious. Blood had soaked the right side of his uniform shirt; it looked black and wet in the spotlights. Other vehicles pulled up, emergency lights flashing blue and white. White-coated arms helped Tate from the car and onto a gurney.

"Cofield!" Tate called hoarsely. Carl shrugged away from those around him and went to the man.

"Yeah, Phillip?"

"I'm sorry, Carl. I really am."

"So am I. Listen, you're gonna be all right."

"Sure I am. It's going to take a lot more than this to take me out."

Carl would have said more, but suddenly Captain Michaels was there alongside him and the doctors were wheeling Tate away. "They killed Waters," Michaels said, and her voice seemed very quiet and cold in the hubbub. "I saw his face, saw death in his eyes. I'm holding you responsible for that." Her face was dark against the false suns of the lamps; they made a glow of her disheveled hair, like a mad halo.

"*You* were the one who overreacted," Carl answered angrily. "That was Aaron in the—"

He stopped.

"In the what, Cofield?" Michaels asked. "In the time machine? Both you and I know that's what that thing had to be, don't we?"

Carl didn't say anything. He clamped his mouth shut, muscles bunching in his jaws. Michaels gave a harsh laugh. "So you *have* known more than you told us, all along. I'll be—Well, follow me, Cofield. You might as well see the rest, because until we know everything you know, you're not leaving here. I can promise you that."

"I want to talk with my lawyer, Michaels."

"You don't have that right, Cofield. Not here. Martial law, remember? National Emergency. Until you're charged with a civil crime, I can do anything I want. I'll get around to charging you, eventually, but not right now. For the moment, You're under General McWilliams's jurisdiction. He'll decide who you can call, and when. Now, if you'll follow me . . ."

Carl followed. He didn't have any choice. He was behind the gates and walls and electric fences of the Compound. He suspected that the Compound was as effective at keeping people in as out.

With two soldiers keeping careful step just behind him, Carl followed Michaels into the nearest building.

Carl had served in the Army, many years before. The interior of the building reminded him instantly of every base he'd ever been on. It was clean—all bases were spotlessly clean, since there was no shortage of noncoms to keep them that way. But somehow the overall impression was dreary. The decor was Early Cement Block, brushed with a thick, semigloss paint that was supposed to be a cheery off-white but instead only managed to look dingy. The carpeting was an indoor-outdoor variety of some indeterminate color between green and brown. The furniture looked as though it had come from several sources, none of which stocked anything beyond the utilitarian.

The lighting was provided by long fluorescent tubes—that was the only modern touch. Only a few buildings in Green Town could afford electricity. The lights were evidently newly installed, since the gas lamps that had adorned these corridors a decade ago were still in place.

Interiors were supposed to be dim—that was normal. But here the sun never seemed to set. The world economy might be in a shambles everywhere, but it looked as if General McWilliams had a very generous budget.

Michaels led Carl down a series of identical corridors differentiated only by trim colors at the tops of the walls. They finally came to a set of double doors. Michaels nodded to the guards stationed there and pushed the doors open.

It took Carl several seconds to adjust to the light in the large room beyond. He blinked, not certain what he was seeing. Tears blurred his vision for a moment and he wiped his eyes with the back of his hand.

In the center of the room, hovering a few inches above the floor, was a jagged, torn piece of what looked like thick white plastic, roughly six feet long and perhaps four feet wide. It appeared to have been ripped from a much larger piece, the jagged edges of it blackened as if from some violent, fiery eruption. Underneath, Carl could see a basketball-sized chunk of machinery embedded in the cracked material. Carl knew instantly what he was seeing—Travis's roadway from the Mesozoic. He knew the hell that had flung the fragment into this time, when Eckels's time machine had met itself and exploded in a shattering paradox.

"Do you know what that is, Cofield?" Michaels asked at his side. Carl could feel her watching him, staring at his face.

"No," he lied, not daring to glance at her at all.

"I think you do," she answered. "But let me tell you anyway. That, Cofield, is a portal into the distant past." She stopped, waited, then gave a quick, unamused laugh. "You just stand there silent. You don't chuckle, you don't protest, you don't say 'Captain, that's the craziest thing I've ever heard.' You know what?—I didn't think you would."

"Captain, after losing Aaron, Jennifer, and Peter, after seeing what I've seen in the time storms myself and what I've read about what they've done elsewhere, I'm really not that surprised at much anymore."

"Good answer." Michaels applauded ironically. The sound echoed faintly from the hard tile walls of the windowless room. "A very good answer. Exactly what I might have said in your situation. Well, let me tell you about our floating anomaly there, just in case. Step on that thing, and you'll be transported to a marsh, in a forest that's composed of tree species we've never seen except in fossils, under a sky where small flying lizards fly while dinosaurs prowl below. We know that, Cofield, because we've sent mechanical probes through the portal and they've come back with the videos—those of them that made it back at all. Look—"

Michaels swiped at a set of switches with her hands and the lights flickered out. Through the wash of afterimages, Carl began to see a faint green glow underneath the path, a glow which seemed to be coming from the machinery embedded in it.

"When they first saw that, none of our scientists had the foggiest idea what it was or what the compound was composed of. We've examined it, studied it, even managed to manufacture something very close to it ourselves. We also know that if you remove that hunk of half-melted metal from where it's sitting, then you don't go anywhere on that floating path. Nowhere at all. And you know what, Cofield? Knowing something is possible gives you lots of incentive to duplicate the feat. We've even been able to make our own time traveling device—a little one, just a small mobile box with a camera. We can send it back in time, oh, maybe a century or so, as near as we can determine—we have photos of this site as it was before the Compound was built, when Green Town was just a sleepy little nineteenth century burg a mile or two upriver, where adults remember fighting in the Civil War and grandparents were eyewitnesses to Indian raids. In fact, we were performing one of those experiments when I received the news that your grandson had been seen in town."

Michaels flipped the lights back on and the soft

emerald light was gone like the stars at dawn. Carl squinted at the woman. "Why are you bothering to tell me all this?"

"Now, don't play stupid with me, Cofield. I know you better. We both know this was found in your woods. We both know your grandson and his friends must have gone through this thing. You're no bad B-movie mad scientist, working away on a time machine in your basement. I know you didn't *create* the path, but you or Aaron *found* it and since it's been found, some awfully strange and dangerous things have happened. And now Aaron's come back, and from what I saw out there, he came back in a machine that travels through time."

Michaels sighed. The scowl softened and the lines at the corners of her dark eyes relaxed. When she spoke next, the harsh, clipped tones were gone, and her voice was sympathetic and warm. "Mr. Cofield, please. I can understand your position and your grief, I really can. I'm not an ogre. I have nieces and nephews and I know how I'd feel if they suddenly disappeared one summer day. All I'm asking is that you tell me what you know. Tell us how to contact Aaron. Maybe, along with what we've been able to discover here, we can find some way to stop the time storms before they get worse, before chaos is loose everywhere. I'm asking for some help that only you can give."

"Captain . . ." Carl began. Then something stopped the words in his throat. He didn't quite know what it was. Maybe the unsmiling guards beside him, maybe the facile way she'd shifted gears on him when she realized that threats weren't working, maybe just remembering the sight of her only an hour ago, sighting down the barrel at Aaron and pulling the trigger. . . .

"No," he said.

The sympathy in her face shattered like glass struck by a hammer. "Get him out of here," she snapped to the guards.

In that second between Michaels's abrupt order and the guards' movement, Carl made a decision.

You always loved books about dinosaurs . . .

The guards half expected Carl to bolt. He saw them close ranks to cut off his path to the doors. But they hadn't expected him to run the other way. Carl's rush past Michaels caught them flat-flooted. He had a yard's head start on them before they moved.

He needed every inch of it. The guards were young and fast, and Carl's body had absorbed all the abuse it could tolerate already this night. Every joint burned with angry fire as he ran, and he heard Michaels's shout and the sudden stac-cato thunder of the guards' pursuit.

"No!" Michaels cried. "Stay off the path, Cofield! You don't know—"

He half leapt, half stumbled onto the hover-ing wreckage. He turned to grin triumphantly at Michaels. Even as Carl saw the two guards halt their own headlong rush, even as he watched the flush of rage and failure color Michaels's face, he felt himself dissolve into a whirlwind coldness.

Aaron, I hope you're on the other side . . .

Carl fell into another world and another time.

"Take out the mechanism. Now!" Michaels ordered the guards. Cofield was gone, lost, and she wasn't about to risk anyone by sending the guards after him. She wanted the path dead. That was the way she'd wanted it always kept, except that the lab people had overruled her. She watched, angrily, as the soldiers removed the two large pieces of blackened, torn metal and the embedded chunks of odd glowing material from underneath the floating roadway.

The General was going to be furious.

The pathway had been rendered inert once more. She nodded to the guards and was about leave. Michaels turned, then gaped in wonder.

"That's not possible," she said.

But, of course, it was.

A PATH
NOT TAKEN

"Who is it, Jhenini?"

Jennifer didn't answer at first. She choked off the sobs, though they were a violent floodstream gathering behind the frail dam of her control. She could manage nothing in answer to SStragh's question, not daring to speak or move for fear that the effort would break her.

After the first shock of recognition, Jennifer couldn't bring herself to look at the face again. Her eyes refused to cooperate, wanting to drift away to find trees or sky or earth or anything else but that accusing lifelessness. She forced herself to contemplate instead the two horrible wounds the Gairk's weapon had torn in the blood-soaked shirt and the unprotected body beneath. She regarded the horror almost analytically, as she imagined the doctor she wanted to be might, noting how the force of the blow had shredded the fabric, how the blood had already begun to darken and coagulate. Then she wrenched her attention upward again, past the sprawled arms with the hands still spread in useless, mute supplication, to the chest so achingly still, to the mouth gaping awkwardly, to the eyes wide with empty, lost astonishment.

"He's . . ." Jennifer began. She brought her fist

up to her mouth and stopped the scream that threatened to rise from her throat. When she thought she could talk again, she swallowed hard. " . . . Aaron's grandfather," she said. "Carl."

The words were like a barrage of mortar shells, falling explosively into her world, all thunder and flame and destruction. The dam of emotion shattered and broke under the impact, loosing a grief that she could no more hold back than she could stop a tsunami's fierce rampage. "No!" she shouted in denial, knowing that it would change nothing but needing to scream to the universe her refusal to accept this as real.

"It's not right!" she raged, not knowing whom she was accusing. "It's not *fair*!"

The tears blurred her vision and ran salty into her mouth. Her wrath found a burning focus, and Jennifer wheeled toward the Gairk Khiika. With a guttural cry, she launched herself at the creature, not knowing what she intended but wanting to strike out at this *thing* who had murdered Carl so casually.

SStragh's arms were suddenly around her, wrapping Jennifer surprisingly tightly to the dinosaur's body even as she flailed and struggled. Through the shimmering curtain of tears, Jennifer could see the Gairk staring at her blandly, as if watching an amusing but suddenly insane pet.

"Your human is leaking," Jennifer heard Khiika tell SStragh. "Is that normal? And does it always make these horrible noises?"

SStragh's short arms tightened around Jennifer's chest as the girl redoubled her efforts to get to the Gairk. The dinosaur's breath sounded like a bellows. Jennifer could feel SStragh's scales like a fine, warm chain mesh pressing against her, and the smell of the dinosaur was a complex mixture of anise, cinnamon, and mint. "It is a human defect," she heard SStragh reply, grunting, her voice a rumble. "They are subject to these fits."

"No! You let me go, SStragh! That monster killed Carl!" she fumed, not even realizing that she was ranting in English. The Gairk cocked its head quizzically at the sound. "You're liars! You're all liars!"

"Is it ill, then?" Khiika asked SStragh. "It *sounds* ill."

"We will care for the human, Khiika," Raajek told the Gairk. "I would suggest that you return to your OColi and tell him what you have seen here."

Khiika sniffed. The Gairk's tail thrashed ponderously, causing the jhiehai scavengers around the body to flap their wings and rise into the air. "Yes," he agreed. "I have much to tell. Though I'm not sure exactly what it is I *have* seen."

"You can't just let him *leave*—" Jennifer started to protest, then realized that she was still speaking English. The Mutata words were all scrambled in her head; she couldn't find the ones she needed.

"*Yeie*," she shouted, the Mutata denial: *No!* As Khiika turned ponderously to glance back at Jennifer, he pointed to Carl's body. "*Werada*," he said.

The Mutata and Gairk had several words for "killing," a separate term for everything from the accidental death to murder, with subtle distinctions as to who caused the death and what type of creature was the victim. Werada was one of the "left-handed killings," or the deliberate murder of one sentient being by another. Khiika snorted, his great, dangerous head coloring slightly as if in annoyance, and he glanced at the body.

"*Werada yeie*," he answered, and there was an almost human mockery in his voice. He pointed the brutal head of his weapon at the body. "*Whiaso*." Whiaso was a "right-handed" killing, the justified and unlamented death of an animal. Khiika sniffed once, nodded to Raajek respectfully, and turned away again. Jennifer, still locked in SStragh's careful embrace, could only struggle futilely as Khiika trundled slowly away, smashing undergrowth loudly underfoot. Only when the Gairk was safely gone did SStragh release her. She nearly fell to the ground.

"He called Carl an animal," Jennifer spat out. "He thinks we're less than Gairk or Mutata, that we're no better than jhiehai."

"Yes," Raajek answered softly. "He does. So do nearly all the Mutata." She seemed to shrug. "SStragh, where is your Floating Stone?" she asked, casually, as if the incident were over and forgotten.

"Very near, OTsio," SStragh answered. "On the other side of the hill and down in a hollow. It is hidden at one end of a small marsh, as Jhenini told us it would be."

"Let's go on, then. Jhenini, speak the word of your Giving to this Caiarl and we'll go on."

Heat flared on Jennifer's cheeks. "How can you say that? I'm not going anywhere yet. That's *Carl* lying there. I can't just leave him."

"He is dead, yes?" Raajek asked, with a puzzled tone in her ancient, quavering voice.

"Yes. Thanks to that Gairk."

"Then we are wasting time. We came to see your Floating Stone and it is nearly evening already. Unless we hurry, we will need to spend the night out here."

The obvious bewilderment with which Raajek said the words was like a spray of cold water, shocking Jennifer.

In that instant, with Raajek gaping blindly at her and SStragh's smell still clinging to her, the two dinosaurs she thought of as friends and allies were very alien. The strangeness wasn't that Raajek didn't care about the body—Jennifer knew the Mutata rite of Giving all too well. She knew that they considered it proper to let the jhiehai feed on the corpse; she knew that if it were impossible to bring the body of a dead Mutata back to the Giving Hall, they would leave it where it had fallen. She knew that they didn't have the fetishes about death that her society seemed to have.

She knew all that. She expected it. But she hadn't expected *this*: this callousness, this coldness, this disregard for her emotions. Even worse, she could tell that Raajek hadn't a clue that what she had said should be upsetting to Jennifer, nor did she seem to care.

"I have to bury him," Jennifer said. "I'm not leaving here until I do that."

"The jhiehai are already here waiting, Jhenini," SStragh answered, and her voice held the same puzzlement as Raajek's. "Why would you steal their meat? Why would you hide this one from the Giving?"

"Because that's what we do."

One of the jhiehai flapped its hairy wings and

hopped awkwardly toward the body. With a shrill cry, Jennifer charged the bird-lizard. "Shoo! You get away from him!" The creature bent back its long neck as if offended, cawed angrily at Jennifer, snapped once at her with its hooked beak, and then took two wobbling steps back from the arm-waving apparition in front of it. The thing settled down with its kin, watching carefully as Jennifer found a thick stick, sank down on her knees beside Carl's body, and—crying openly—began jabbing furiously at the dirt as if the earth itself were Khiika.

Raajek and SStragh watched patiently enough, but neither of them moved to help her dig the shallow trench, nor did they help her roll the body into its crude, shallow grave. Not until Jennifer had said a brief prayer over Carl and begun to cover him in the dark soil did she feel a presence alongside her.

SStragh silently helped her mound the earth over Aaron's grandfather. "This is the human OColihi?" she asked. "The human Giving?"

Jennifer didn't want to answer. She didn't want SStragh near her at all. *They're just lizards*, Pete had said. At the moment, she was tempted to agree with him. "Yes," she said. "The human OColihi."

SStragh looked at the dark earth of the grave. Whatever she was thinking, she said nothing.

Every time I think I am starting to understand the humans, they do something bizarre . . .

SStragh puzzled over Jhenini as she led the human and Raajek through the forest. Raajek smelled of mingled bewilderment and apology.

but Jhenini continued to thrash through the undergrowth ignoring the unsubtle, scented plea from Raajek.

It was incredibly rude of Jhenini to ignore Raajek's scent that way without remarking on it or sending a sympathetic odor of her own. SStragh knew, of course, that Jhenini could not alter her own scent as the Mutata did, but she *was* able to smell. Jhenini already recognized most of the Mutata scent modifiers to speech, but missing this one was inexcusable. Especially since, as far as SStragh could see, Raajek had done nothing at all to offend the human. Nothing at all.

SStragh added her own scent to Raajek's, thinking that perhaps the intensity of the odor was too slight for Jhenini's poor human nose, but it made no difference. Jhenini followed them silently and angrily, her own scent—as always—faint and unreadable.

. . . *Strange* . . .

There was no time to brood over it now. SStragh pushed through the last screen of horsetails to expose a small clearing in a marsh. Huge dragonflies scattered at their approach while some of the smaller, unintelligent cousins of the Mutata fled for their hiding places.

"Here," SStragh said softly.

And here, like a piece of smooth white slate held on some invisible hand, lay the Floating Stone. From the intake of breath behind her, SStragh knew that this was also Jhenini's Floating Stone, the one that she claimed had brought her and Peitah to their world. In mute confirmation, she could see the prints in the mud near it, human prints made by the odd dead things they wore over their feet, *new* human prints that must have been made by this Caiarl the Gairk had killed.

Raajek knew it too. SStragh could scent OTsio Raajek's own certainty, could see it in the eager forward cant of Raajek's old head as she listened and sniffed the air, in the way she held her crest.

"Do you recognize this?" SStragh asked Jhenini, more because she was curious as to how Jhenini would answer than because she needed confirmation.

Jhenini *did* hesitate, and SStragh was certain that she was going to lie uselessly. SStragh knew that Peitah and Eikels made Jhenini tell lies for them frequently when SStragh asked the humans questions; they didn't seem to realize that SStragh could nearly always tell when they were doing so. Jhenini breathed loudly in that strange mournful way that humans had.

"No," she said. "It's not."

Raajek gave a scent of disappointment, the smell of an OTsio rebuking her student. "That is not the truth," she said.

Jhenini hesitated for a long time before answering again. "No, it's not," she said, but there was no posture to indicate an apology, no odor of shame. All she said were the empty words.

"Would you have answered differently if the Gairk had not killed your Caiarl? Would you have told us that this was your Floating Stone then?" Raajek asked.

Jhenini's odd, flat face twisted as if it were a stream flowing around pebbles. The atrophied peak of skin that passed for a nose on the humans wrinkled.

"I don't know, OTsio," she answered, and this time SStragh heard the truth in her voice. "Peitah . . . he and Eikels asked me to lie. But I made the choice. Part of me believed that Eikels was right. I really don't know. This Floating Stone . . . it's our only way back, OTsio. Do you understand? Without this, we are lost. We can't go back to our own kind any other way."

Raajek's shoulders slumped. Her wrinkled, arthritic fingers flexed as if she wanted to stroke Jhenini's long fur, as one might pet a dhieka brought into the sleeping hall for the younglings to play with. "I understand, Jhenini," the old Mutata answered. "But I'm sad that you no longer trust SStragh and me."

"I . . ." Jhenini began. She stopped, with a sound like she was about to begin giving eye-moisture again. Her gaze went from Raajek to SStragh and back again. She stretched out a hand and touched SStragh.

"I'm sorry," she said, using the form of apology which indicated a failure of obedience but forgetting to raise her chin. "I'm especially sorry toward you, SStragh. You've protected me when I didn't know what was going on; you started teaching me your language; you found OTsio Raajek and brought her back to help us. But I wanted out of your world so badly . . . Everything's so mixed up . . ."

The hand slipped away from SStragh's side. "What will you do now? Will you tell the OColi about this? He'll set guards on it, as you've done with the other Floating Stones that have been found. The Gairk will insist on it. Please, I ask you not to say anything."

"Then it is also a lie that Eikels can seal up the gateway," Raajek said without answering. "You have given us a lie to give to the OColi."

"Yes . . . No. . . . I really don't *know*," Jhenini said. "Raajek, when is OGhielas, and what happens then?"

"OGhielas is a hand of days from now, and that is the day the OColi has said that you humans must be Given unless you have shown that you can help us. If Eikels cannot seal the Stones, then . . ."

Raajek didn't finish the statement. She didn't need to.

"Do you agree with him?"

"It's not a matter of agreement." Raajek sat wearily on a knoll of wet grass. "Jhenini, the OColi has a difficult task. You know that the Gairk OColi is furious because none of the humans has been Given to him as he has demanded. Our OColi isn't able to withstand the Gairk's anger any longer— not when the Dreaming Storms come so often; not when new, fierce animals come from Floating Stones we haven't yet found, not when attacks from the Floating Stones we guard continue as well. I have done all that I can do, and you give me lies. You make me wonder whether the OColi has not been right all along."

"Then we're dead—Peitah, Eikels, and I—one way or the other."

"I am telling you what I know, Jhenini. Only the All-Ancestor has your answer."

With the words, Raajek gave a warm earthy scent and she spread her arms wide and squatted, in the protective gesture of a creche-mother, telling Jhenini without words that Raajek intended to guard the humans from any threat as long as she could.

But Jhenini did not respond as she should have. Instead, SStragh saw the muscles tense in her arms, along the line of her short neck.

"In that case, I'm sorry again," Jhenini said, then shouted something in her own language.

" . . . You're saying that no matter what happens, we'll be handed over to the Gairk, and they'll kill us."

Raajek simply gave her old, tired nod. A scent wafted toward Jennifer in the breeze, but it was hard to distinguish from the muddy odor of this swampy hollow. Raajek had spread her arms apart in what looked like a shrug. "I am telling you what I know," Raajek said, and with the emotionless words, Jennifer felt the decision harden inside her.

Look, just tell them that Eckels knows how to seal up the gateway, but it's a difficult process and he'll need our help—our unencumbered help. We need our arms and legs free. When we get close enough, we make a jump for the path . . .

That had been the plan as Peter had outlined it to her, but like a house of cards, it had collapsed in ruin.

I know you're going to think I've abandoned you, Peter.

"Then I'm sorry again," Jhenini said in Mutata, then switched to English. "I'm out of here."

With the last word, she broke and ran.

"Jhenini!" SStragh bellowed at her back. Jennifer ignored the shout, her focus on the pathway, on the way home. Mud splattered under her headlong rush; she slipped, catching herself and coating her arms to the elbows in umber goo. SStragh had lumbered into motion behind her, and Jennifer knew that the Mutata's long, powerful legs would make up the distance between then in a few steps. The ground shook under the impact of SStragh's pursuit.

The roadway was so close . . .

Jennifer, with a desperate cry, gathered her strength and leapt.

She hit the path, the shock nearly causing her to fall. Jennifer regained her balance, expecting the sudden rapture of the cold, the whirling dizziness of the passage across time, expecting to tumble out into the woods behind Aaron's house.

Home. She had the scheme set in her head: to get Aaron, gather all the help and manpower she could, and come back in a rush to rescue Peter and Eckels, knowing what would be waiting for them on the other side and being prepared for it.

If Peter and Eckels's theory was right about the different rates of time on opposite sides of the path, she could easily return before Raajek and SStragh got back to the village with the news.

But nothing happened. Jennifer was standing on the Floating Stone, yet there was no cold and no dizziness and the world she saw was that of the Mutata. After several long seconds, Jennifer turned, standing on the buoyant pedestal of the broken path, still hoping that it would suddenly jolt into action and knowing that it wouldn't. SStragh had stopped her pursuit, and was standing looking at Jennifer with unfathomable eyes.

"I guess we bought one-way tickets," she said.

And the tears came again.

MUNDO'S RETURN

The world came back slowly.

Aaron opened his eyes to see a blurred face filling his field of vision. "Grandpa?" he said, but the face mumbled something he couldn't quite hear, the words all jumbled together and sounding as if they were coming from the end of a long tunnel. A dragon (who looked somehow familiar) seemed to be sitting on his chest and breathing fire on his shoulder, and Aaron couldn't quite feel the rest of his body.

"Go away, old Smaug," he said.

Smaug didn't move.

It seemed easier to let his eyes close again, so Aaron did.

When he opened them again, the blurry face and Smaug had both gone away. Aaron could see the ceiling of the time machine. His mouth felt full of the driest cotton ever picked. He was in one of the seats to the rear of the craft; the seat's back had been cranked horizontal into a makeshift bed. Aaron tried to sit up, but the craft did an odd little whirling dance step at the same moment and he lay back down abruptly. Aaron vaguely remembered being shot in the army— about a century ago, it seemed like. He thought he should raise his shoulder to see if still worked.

It did, after a fashion. Aaron managed to lift his hand all of four or five inches before the darkness returned, filled with painful skyrockets.

This time, Travis was in the seat beside him. "You know, you're not the smartest kid in the world," the man said. "But you *are* stubborn."

Aaron tried to sit up, but Travis gently pushed him back down. "That's exactly what I mean," Travis said.

"Where's Grandpa Carl?"

"And you have a one-track mind, too," Travis clucked. "You want this sugar-coated, or are you feeling good enough for the straight truth?"

"Travis—"

"All right, all right." The man leaned back, his thin face and dark eyes looking away. "They took your grandfather. I don't know where, and I wasn't in much position to go after them with you bleeding all over the floor, so I came back UpTime to where we'd been before. I managed to get the bleeding stopped—those popguns of theirs use a nasty little barbed dart, and my bet is that the tips are laced with a poison. I thought . . ." Travis paused, and Aaron could read the concern in the man's face. "Anyway, I managed to clean everything out. You look okay now."

"How long?"

Travis shrugged. "Oh, a week or so."

"A *week*—" Aaron began. "Oh," he said after a moment. "I guess the time's kind of irrelevant, isn't it? When you have a machine that can pop you back—"

Travis had looked away again. "Not entirely," he said.

"What does *that* mean?"

Travis shrugged. "We've been doing a lot of jumping. The power supply for the machine isn't unlimited, you know. We're getting low."

"How low?"

"I can keep the lights and heat on for a long time yet. We can move around in space fairly well, though this thing isn't exactly a speed demon. But moving through time . . ." The thin shoulders lifted in another shrug. "One or two more. Maybe three if we're lucky. Everything depends on how far DownTime or UpTime we jump and how much of a cushion they've built into the gauges. Basically, we can't go very far, and not very often."

Aaron got up on one elbow. He licked his lips and cleared his throat. "Travis." he said slowly and deliberately, "we *are* going back."

The man gave Aaron a slow smile. "Stubborn, like I said. I figure I owe you that much, at least. Okay. We'll make a deal. You heal up. When you can touch the top of your head with your left hand, we'll go."

It took three weeks.

The time machine sobbed like a heartsick whale and the windshields roiled with the fog of BetweenTime. When the mists cleared, they looked out on an empty night field in front of Aaron's house.

"We're about fifteen minutes after your grandfather was taken away," Travis said as he unbuckled the harness to his seat and went to the door.

"Not long after I took off with you for our HomeTime here, but enough of a time gap that we didn't meet ourselves and repeat Eckels's mistake. Here—we may need these again."

He handed Aaron one of the hunting rifles with a flashlight mounted on the barrel. This time, Aaron took it without hesitation.

The field wasn't quite as empty as they had thought.

Near the driveway there was a dark mound. As the two approached, they saw that it was the man who'd been with Sheriff Tate and Aaron's grandfather. The man was bleeding badly, lying on his side with his limbs splayed out. His shirt, once white, was soaked with so much blood that the fabric looked red. His eyes were open and he moaned as they stood over him.

" . . . can't move . . ." he said. His voice was a wrecked whisper. They had to strain to hear him. " . . . hurts . . ." His fingers twitched in the open hands. Nothing else moved.

"Travis, we can't just—"

"I know," Travis said. "I'll be right back. Let me get the medical kit." He ran back to the time machine.

Aaron set his rifle down on the grass and knelt beside the man. He could almost see death waiting. The sight of the horrible wounds sickened Aaron. The man's eyes never moved, continuing to stare upward past Aaron at the stars. "Where's my grandfather?" Aaron asked as gently as he could. "Tell me where they took him."

" . . . help me . . ."

"Travis is getting something. A pain-killer and something to stop the bleeding. Don't worry.

You'll . . ." Aaron choked on the word. "You'll be fine. But you have to tell me. Where did they take Grandpa Carl?"

" . . . can't . . ."

"You *have* to," Aaron said urgently. "Please. I'm the one you were trying to capture. I'm Aaron Cofield. You wouldn't have been after me if you weren't worried about all the strange things happening around here or if you didn't think I had some clue to help. Well, I do. Travis and I are starting to figure some things out, but before I help, I have to know where my grandfather is. I have to know he's safe. Please," he said again. "Please tell me."

The man seemed to sigh, a wet gurgle rattled in his throat. He coughed, and pink foam spattered his lips. " . . . the Compound . . ." he gasped. " . . . Compound . . ."

"The old place down by the river? Is that what you mean?"

" . . . there . . . you should . . ." The man shuddered and groaned. His hands clawed at the air. Aaron took one hand in his, holding it, as the man groaned, as his back arched in a spasm of helpless pain.

The man went limp. He exhaled wetly, started to take in his next breath . . .

. . . and Aaron realized that the breath was never going to come. The field was suddenly very, very quiet except for the sound of Aaron's own inhalation. Slowly, he lowered the hand to the man's chest as Travis came back with the medical kit.

"Too late," Aaron told him. He was still kneeling beside the body. He wanted to reach out and close the dead man's unseeing eyes, but was somehow afraid to touch the body now. Travis set the medical kit down, crouched, and brought his hand over the face to bring the eyelids down.

"You okay, kid?"

"Yeah." The word was just a gasp. "Well, no. It's just . . . I mean, I've never seen anyone . . ."

"Die? I have. It's hard to miss in a war. I know saying this doesn't help you at all, but it gets easier after the first one. Maybe that's unfortunate. There might be a lot less killing if it didn't."

Aaron nodded and got to his feet. He looked out over the field, just breathing slowly and deep and not looking down. "The guy told me where they took my grandpa."

"Where?"

"The Compound. It's an old abandoned—" Aaron stopped. They both heard the sound: laboring, noisy engines coming from behind the screening trees, the clamor growing louder as the vehicles approached from the road.

Travis uttered a quick curse. "Come on," he said. Travis grabbed the medical kit and ran for the time machine; Aaron followed. As he reached the door of their vehicle, they could both see the yellow beams of headlamps throwing columns of light through the intervening trunks and hear the crunch of gravel as the first of the cars turned into the drive.

Travis was already busy at the console. "You're taking us back UpTime?" Aaron asked.

"Uh-uh. Not if we're interested in coming back. Close the door and get yourself in a seat, kid—I'm going to move us back into the woods."

The time machine lurched and rose in a steep climb as harsh, blue-white spotlights began to rake the field. None of the beams found the time machine in its flight, nor did anyone seem to notice the whine of the vehicle over the diesel roar of their own engines. Aaron and Travis were quickly behind the first line of trees, moving slowly and carefully at treetop level.

"Rear view," Travis said to the console. "On," replied the computer. A corner of the windshield went opaque and then lit with a camera-view behind and below them. Through the branches, they could see four vehicles in front of the house. Black figures moved through the beams of the headlights toward the body on the ground.

Travis was cursing softly under his breath again. "They may wait until morning to do it, but then they're going to fan out and search the area. That's one of their buddies on the ground there, and they're not going to be in the best of moods."

"But *they* started the shooting," Aaron protested. "Not us."

"That's the second thing about war," Travis replied. "Once bullets start flying, it doesn't really matter who started things. You see your friends die in front of you and suddenly you don't worry about who pulled the trigger first or who's right or wrong. You just shoot back. You shoot because you're angry and because you're scared and because those slugs are still flying past you. Which isn't right and isn't smart, but it *is* what happens. We need to find a place to bring this machine down, kid. We're sitting ducks up here, and we're about as high as she'll go."

"These woods are pretty thick. After all, they've never found the part of the path I came through on."

"True enough. Well, I guess that's where we go right now. We need to figure out what we're going to do next."

Travis nosed the craft south, making a large arc around the house until they were well to the back of the Cofield property, then moved slowly into the deepest section of the stand of trees.

"Here looks good enough," Travis said finally. "We're far enough away from the path that if they find us, they won't also find the path, but we're close enough that we can run for it if we need to." He brought them down in a clearing barely large enough to hold the time machine, branches scraping the sides of the craft as they landed.

Travis just sat there for a long time after they landed, his eyes shut, his mouth locked in a tight grimace. "Travis?" Aaron said at last.

Travis opened his eyes. "Sorry, kid," he said. He sat forward in his seat, and Aaron saw the effort that the movement cost. "A little relapse, that's all."

Travis rose from his seat and then crouched in front of the console. He gestured to Aaron to do the same. As Aaron watched, Travis reached under the panel and pulled out what Aaron recognized as a small circuit board about the size of a credit card. Silver lines glittered in its ebon surface as Travis twirled it in his fingers. "Part of the Chronos software," he told Aaron. "Without this, the machine can't go into time travel mode. You see the slot for the card?"

"Yeah, sure. Travis, why are you showing me this?"

Travis shrugged, coughed. The cough didn't sound very good at all. "I'm not really sure. I got you into this mess without really intending to, and I know I haven't been the most pleasant company either. Despite all that, you still took care of me. Right now, I have to figure that those people up at your house know we have a time machine. They've been fooling around in the past themselves—that's why things aren't the way you remember them. They haven't been able to make wholesale changes yet, the way Eckels did in *my* time line, so they haven't done too much damage. What I don't want to happen is to hand them a working time machine.

"Here—" Travis handed Aaron the card. "I'm giving this to you. You know how to work the machine by now. I'll let you make the decision when and how to use our last few trips in time." His laugh had a bitter edge. "It doesn't look like there's much use for time traveling back in *my* world unless you like big blue snails."

Travis got up and went to the door. He took one of the rifles from its holder there. "You stay here, kid. Leave the door open so you can hear. I want to scout around."

Travis stepped out of the hovering craft onto the leaf-carpeted floor of the forest. As Aaron watched, Travis moved away into the shadowed darkness under the trees. Here, Aaron could see Travis's skill as a safari guide—the man made almost no sound. In a few moments, he was another shadow among shadows, lost to Aaron's eyes.

Aaron sat down in the open doorway of the time machine, letting his legs dangle so that his feet scuffed at the leaves. Night sounds reasserted themselves: the cheery rasp of crickets, the mournful call of a barn owl, the treble sigh of the breeze through the high branches. Once, faintly, he thought he heard a distant shout from the direction of his house, accompanied by a clanging like metal striking metal; even more faintly, a steam whistle shrilled from the direction of the river, making Aaron wonder if steamboats still plied the muddy waters in this version of his world. Maybe they did—it didn't seem that the technology here was as dependent on fossil fuel. Now that Aaron thought about it, since he'd been in this time line, he'd never seen a plane or jet streaking across the sky, as they so often had in his 'real' time. Maybe there was no air travel here, or only on a very limited scale. Primitive.

On the other hand, some of that might actually be good. Aaron mused. He dug at the dirt underneath the leaves with his shoe heel, his head down. *There might he less pollu—*

A white form screamed as it hurled itself at him, and Aaron was suddenly knocked away from the time machine while hands clawed at him and a furry weight bore him down. Two years of aikido training kicked in: Aaron let himself roll easily with the force of the attack, bringing his hands up as the fighters went sprawling on the ground. That shook off the clinging hands and sent his attacker tumbling as well.

Aaron managed to get to his feet, dead leaves cascading from his shirt and jeans. His newly healed shoulder throbbed painfully—Aaron could barely bring the arm up into a ready stance. The white form had also done a neat tuck and come up easily about ten feet away from Aaron. Aaron recognized him immediately: Mundo.

The apelike figure was more gaunt than before, and there was a long dark streak on the right arm where the snowy fur had been torn away to reveal skin. The wound was new; a little blood, too light and thin to be mistaken for human, trickled into the matted fur underneath. Mundo snarled at Aaron, almost hissing in his effort to speak.

"You lef' me to die. You lie' to me. You trie' to kill me with—" Mundo paused and Aaron felt something like a cold hand touching his mind. "—rifles," Mundo continued in the strange accent that blurred all the hard consonants. Mundo brushed his injured arm.

"It wasn't me who shot you, Mundo," Aaron said. "They were aiming at me, too." Aaron gestured at his own shoulder. "The same people."

"You lie again," Mundo spat. "That is an *ol'* woun', alrea'y heal'."

"No, you don't understand. This—" Aaron shook his head. The explanation was too long. "Forget it. I'm not your enemy, Mundo. I really thought I was bringing you home when we stepped through into this world."

Aaron judged the distance to the time machine. He was closer than Mundo. If he could get in and hit the door contact before Mundo . . .

Mundo's flat, dark snout wrinkled. The dark, eerily bloodshot eyes narrowed. They both moved at the same time.

Mundo was a lot faster than Aaron expected.

THE DAY
OF NAMING

"We're stuck here. There isn't any way back." The finality of the words brought the tears brimming in Jennifer's eyes once more.

"That can't be right," Peter insisted. There was a wild anger in his eyes. "You must have done something wrong."

"Like *what*?" Jennifer snapped back. "Peter, all we did was *step* on the roadway, remember? There aren't any knobs to push or buttons to press or incantations that have to be spoken. I stepped on it and *nothing happened*."

That answer hardly seemed to mollify Peter. "You were going to run."

"I was going to get help."

Peter was huddled in a corner of their hut in the Mutata enclosure, near the fire they'd built to take the edge off the night chill. Firelight brushed his form with wavering yellow and plucked Eckels's lanky figure from the shadows near the door. Jennifer sat near her bed with her arms around her knees.

"The roadway didn't work for any of us," she continued. "Both Raajek and SStragh tried it, too."

"*Carl* got through," Peter said. "Unfortunately for the old man."

"Which means the transfer works in the other direction. That doesn't help us."

"What are the lizards going to do?"

"I don't *know*," Jennifer answered. "They . . . they really didn't talk much on the way back, either one of them. I asked them not to tell the OColi about the path, even if it doesn't work, but SStragh wouldn't answer. She just kept saying that OTsio Raajek needed time to think."

No one seemed to want to talk. A vast weight seemed to press down on Jennifer's shoulders, making it hard to breathe. The tears kept threatening to overflow and she didn't want to cry in front of either Peter or Eckels, not wanting to deal with either their sympathy or their scorn. Something inside her seemed to be missing and she realized that the vanished part of her was Aaron, was her parents, was Green Town and the new school year and a sense of normalcy.

Jennifer felt fragile and threatened, and the feelings were terrifying. Somehow during all that had happened, she had never quite felt so lost. The door home had always been open, however distant. Amidst all the strangeness and danger, there had always been the certainty that somehow Aaron would find them, that SStragh would protect them from the whims of the OColi and the Gairk, But now . . .

If Aaron came, he'd be trapped here the same way they were all trapped, and Jennifer was no longer quite sure how she felt about SStragh and Raajek. The door home had been slammed shut right in her face, and cold fear threatened to swallow her.

"I'm going outside," she said, getting to her

feet. "I think I want to be alone for a bit."

"We have to decide what we're going to do," Peter said. His voice sounded almost angry, and the fire blazed ruddily in his eyes. Eckels watched, silent, from his post.

"There's nothing to decide," Jennifer told him. "We don't have any choice. The way back is closed. We're here and we're going to stay here, so we'd better do what I said to do all along—find a way to get along with the Mutata. They're going to be our neighbors from now on."

With that, Jennifer went toward the shack's door. On the way out, she passed close to Eckels. She could hear his breath, could feel his gaze on her. In his pocket, his hand jingled something metallic. For a moment, they made eye contact. His stare was cool and appraising.

Jennifer wrenched her eyes away and left.

In the dark, the tears came easily enough, and it didn't matter that the guard-lizard watched her. Jennifer stood with her back against the rough timber walls of their enclosure, arms crossed against the chill, watching silver-edged clouds skate across the star-speckled sky. Beyond the walls, the Mutata slumbered in their cone-shaped buildings, uncaring.

"You thinking about Aaron?"

Jennifer started; Eckels had come up on her while she was moon-gazing. She blinked hard, half turning from him while she swiped angrily at her face with the back of her hand. She sniffed. "Some, I guess," she said, glad that her voice sounded normal enough.

"This has to be hardest on you." Eckels's voice

was sympathetic, pitched low and soft. "I remember how it is when you're new in love." Blue light poured over his shoulders and swept like a tide across his chest as he shrugged. "I knew a young woman.once . . . Angela. We met in school. When we started talking, there was a spark, a fire, a searing brightness. I could hardly bear it when I didn't see her for a day. There was an aching cavern inside of me when I didn't hear her voice or have her beside me. My God, just to touch her hand and link our fingers together . . . I never felt whole unless I was with her. Angela seemed to make me complete somehow, as if she filled in a part of me I didn't know was missing before. I thought of her almost all the time, at the oddest times. Just about everything I saw or smelled or touched reminded me of her in some way."

Jennifer looked at Eckels with surprise. The man had never struck her as being anything but a boor and a danger before. He'd never opened up with her, never shared anything, never really even said much of anything. Yet what he described, the feelings . . .

No. You don't like the man. This is another ploy on his part.

"I never thought you were the romantic type, Eckels."

Eckels's face twisted with one of his half-smiles. "I'm not, I guess. But I know how it feels when you first meet someone."

Neither of them said anything for a time. The insects called to each other, some animal yowled in the far distance. At last curiosity prodded Jennifer. "So what happened between you and Angela, Eckels?"

Another shrug and another waterfall of moonlight. "After a while, the magic just wore off. The sun stopped shining brighter when she smiled, and odd little affectations like the way she laughed at nothing or always brushed her hair back from her eyes went from charming to irritating in a strange rush. I got *used* to her. Like a cheap, gaudy bracelet, the shine on our relationship got all tarnished and dull."

"That's very poetic, Eckels, but if you're saying that Aaron and I—"

"Sure, you don't want to admit it, but that's what happened with you and Peter, didn't it?" Jennifer felt the heat of a blush and was glad for the darkness that cloaked her. Eckels seemed to sense her unspoken answer, for he laughed shortly.

"I thought so," he said. "You see, Jenny, we're not so different, are we? We're a heck of a lot closer than you are to your lizard friends. You think your Struth ever fell in love? You think she ever felt the thrill of a first kiss? From what you've told me, they don't have *any* kind of relationships, not the kind we're talking about. They don't have families, don't fall in love or marry. They lay their eggs once every couple years, and most of the time they don't know who the fathers are, and don't care."

After what had happened that afternoon, Eckels's words were a barrage, each word a blow that made her want to turn away and begin crying again. Her friendship with SStragh and Raajek, already cracked and dented by Carl's death and the Mutatas' strange indifference, threatened to shatter entirely.

"What are you trying to say, Eckels?"

"Just that I think you should remember who *really* understands you and cares about you. You've been on the lizards' side from the start, and maybe you were right and maybe you weren't about what was the best way to go about surviving here. You've made it very clear that you don't like me— that's fine. I can understand that even though I think you've got me pegged wrong. But you also hurt Peter, and that I *don't* understand. He's your *friend*, Jenny. He's someone you've known for years and years and yet you're keeping him at arm's length. I know you and Peter were together for awhile, and how when you split up, you started going with Aaron. I realize why you think you should act that way. Jennifer, after what you've told us tonight, the likelihood is that you're never going to see Aaron again. There are exactly two other humans in this whole world besides you. Two and no more. So unless you're entirely happy with the lizards, you might want to rethink your attitude."

It was easily the longest speech she'd ever heard Eckels make. He was usually short and sarcastic, lurking on the edges of whatever Peter and she said like a critical parent. His criticism stung, but she had to admit the truth in it. She turned away from him, because she didn't want him looking at her, not with that odd sympathy in his face.

I don't want to like you, Eckels. I don't trust you.

But she found that right at the moment, she wasn't sure she trusted SStragh any better.

Feet shushed across the ground and Jennifer felt a heat at her back. Eckels's hand touched her shoulder. Before, Jennifer would have thrown it off angrily. This time, she didn't move at all. The hand stayed, was joined by another on the oppsite shoulder. Eckels squeezed her shoulders gently, then stroked her neck under her hair before withdrawing. The warmth left her back and he sighed, a sound that might have been satisfaction or only empathy. Jennifer couldn't tell, and she wasn't going to turn to him. She lifted her head to the night sky again, trying to find an answer in the slow dance of the stars and the soft symphony of the night creatures.

After a time, she heard Eckels walking away. He was whistling softly, hands in pockets, and that odd metallic jingling accompanied his off-key tune.

"Eckels," she said without moving.

He stopped. Silence.

"I . . . I'll think about what you said."

She could almost hear his nod. Then the sound of his footsteps drove away the chorus of the insects.

OJaielas: the most important day in a youngling's life . . .

A breeze warmed by thermal hot springs wafted hot and wet across SStragh's face. She closed her eyes, luxuriating for a few moments in the glorious bath of air, then moved further into the room to let OTsio Raajek enter.

Only a few of the other Mutata were there, though most were filing in quickly behind SStragh and Raajek. They found spaces on the tiered levels around the circular hall, the eldest taking their preferred seats nearest the top, where the heat and

umidity were the highest and curling tendrils
of steam swayed brightly in sunlight streaming
through the mica panels set at the dome's summit.
SStragh escorted Raajek to a seat on the topmost
level and then came back down to find her own
place. Each OJaielas, which came once every two
years, she was allowed to sit a tier higher; this year
she was Eighth Tier, only two below the Tenth,
when SStragh could become an OTsio herself.

The central pit hissed and bubbled, belching
out a scent of sulfur and coating the damp landing
and the lowest seats with a yellowed crust. The
younglings who were to be new otsioiue—students of an OTsio—splashed in the pool, sending
wavelets crashing against the first row of seats and
reminding SStragh of the Shallow Sea near the
Nesting Grounds. There the mothers dug their
nests and placed their clutches in that careful hollow while rolling, glassy waves climbed the sand
toward the grassy dunes in cascades of foam. The
sound—rhythmic and comforting—pervaded all
of SStragh's memories of her own two Nestings.
Whenever she looked at younglings, the slow,
gentle thunder of the Shallow Sea returned to her
mind and filled her nostrils with the scent of salt.

As the elders filled the hall, the younglings'
play subsided and they lay quietly in the pool,
lifting their long necks in silent acknowledgment
of the adults' presence. The younglings looked
so foolishly fearless with their bright eyes and
their skin, not yet marked by the folds and wrinkles of a full-grown Mutata and still white-striped
with childhood's coloring, though the pigmenta-
tion was already beginning to change into the
brighter adult colors.

Those in the pool were the Mutata who were approaching their second OGhielas: LongDay when the sun reached its highest point and the sky and the ColdLady of the night was at Her weakest. Many nestlings died before their first OGhielas, which came as the Mutata began the long trek from the Shallow Sea and their Nesting back to their home valleys. Many more died afterward, of sickness or accident or stupidity.

That was normal. That was expected. No one grieved over those deaths except perhaps the CrecheWatchers, who were charged with caring for the younglings until this day: OJaielas—the Day of Choosing, the Day of Naming—when the younglings picked the elders who would be their OTsios and received their adult names.

There were twelve UnNamed younglings left from the latest Nesting Walk, twelve out of ninety or more eggs; twelve out of the sixty or so egglings who had hatched that spring in the nest and who had managed to survive the predators who raided the Nesting Grounds; twelve out of the thirty-three who had walked back into the valley during the delicious lingering heat of the late summer.

Twelve would normally have been enough, enough to replace the adults who died between the bi-annual Nesting Walks with perhaps two or three to spare. Enough in normal times, but these were not normal times. Since the coming of the Floating Stones, since Eikels the Far-Killer had come and had begun his distant killing, since Jhenini and Peitah had arrived and the Dreaming Storms had begun to ravage the valley, there had been too many deaths.

Already twelve was three short of the count, and more would yet die.

SStragh knew that, somehow. She knew it as if the All-Ancestor sang the words in her very bones. The Mutata had never been very fruitful, and life was always hard. The ancient songs told of Mutata jhaka where killings or disease sent the population below the level at which the tribe could sustain itself. Raajek herself had told SStragh how another jhaka had nested near them once, and the young Raajek had come to know some of these Mutata from a distant place. For five Nesting Walks they had been there, just over the first hill where the land curved out into the shimmering waters of the Shallow Sea. Raajek had noticed that each time there were fewer of them, until on the sixth Nesting after their meeting, none of that jhaka had come at all.

SStragh shivered, imagining the empty Nesting Grounds, glistening crystals of wind-driven sand covering the pits where mothers had once nursed the egglings.

This may happen to us. This may be the potent Jhenini brings—not sudden, violent death, but a lingering slow failing, more terrible because we see it approach and yet won't let ourselves do anything to stop it.

"The younglings look especially puny this year." A smell of affectionate disdain accompanied the statement.

Frraghi's voice dragged SStragh from her reverie. The Speaker crouched beside SStragh, his tail wrapped comfortably around his feet. SStragh involuntarily glanced up at the top tier where Raajek reclined. Yes, the OColi was there—evidently he'd entered while she'd been musing.

"I was thinking that myself," SStragh answered. "But then each OJaielas they look younger and smaller to me."

Frraghi gave a soft chuckle and nod. "Of course. It's certainly not because we're getting older, is it?" Then, with a shifting of odor and a glance. "It is nearly OGhielas, SStragh," he whispered, leaning close to SStragh. "Two more days."

"You needn't remind me of that, Frraghi."

"I don't believe that your Jhenini truly sealed the Floating Stone, do you know that? I think it was already broken."

"She sealed it," SStragh insisted. "She has shown that the humans should live. Not even the Gairk can argue with that."

"The OColi is not sure. He wants another test."

SStragh moved away. Frraghi's maleness bothered her suddenly. Maybe it was because the younglings reminded her of the Nesting Walk and choosing a mate for the Nesting. SStragh's last mate had been Caasrt, but it was best for Mutata to choose a new mate each time: that was the OColihi. In any case, Caasrt was dead, a victim of the Far-Killer Eikels. Frraghi was strong and healthy; he would be good choice if a Mutata wanted her younglings to grow strong and be among those in the pool on the Day of Naming.

Frraghi's thoughts were the same, for SStragh could smell the faint tang of the courting scent in the male—just a hint, enough to tell her that a tentative offer was being made. The implicit invitation drove away thoughts of the humans.

"The Nesting Walk is still hands and hands

and hands of days away, Frraghi," SStragh said. "There's no choice to be made now." Others were crowding around them. SStragh pitched her voice low so that none could overhear their conversation.

The embarrassing scent disappeared and he was simply Frraghi again. "I see that Raajek offers herself as OTsio again," he said, looking up. "Who would be fool enough to choose her now, I wonder?"

"*Fool* enough?" That nearly caused SStragh to shout in fury, but suddenly there was no time for further conversation, for the OColi had risen. He did not speak, only gestured down to Frraghi. Frraghi rose, and his voice filled the chamber.

"The Mutata are gathered for OJaielas," he said in tones stiff with ritual. "Have the Un-Named made their choices?"

The younglings, who had gone still, answered in a ragged chorus, lifted their snouts high in respect and faced not Frraghi, but the OColi. "We have, OColi."

Again Frraghi spoke for the OColi. "Then we begin," he said. The OColi now lifted his hand. One long finger pointed down through the steam and mist, picking out one of the younglings. "You will choose first," Frraghi said to the youngling.

The others had sunk lower in the pool. The youngling looked up past Frraghi and SStragh. "I choose Deasst to be my OTsio," he said. With the words, there was a sigh of satisfaction and the sweet odor of acceptance. Deasst, of the Eleventh Tier, made his way down to the pool, where he stood before the youngling who had chosen him. For several seconds, Deasst regarded the youngling, who kept his head lifted high in respect, not looking at Deasst.

"I name you Poasai, because you remind me of the trees that grow near the Shallow Sea," Deasst said. Slowly, the youngling's head lowered, and he looked at his OTsio. Their scents mingled and Deasst reached out to help Poasai from the pool. Dark, fragrant water cascaded from Poasai like the egg's fluid from a hatchling, and together the two left the dome of the naming pool as the gathered Mutata crooned the low melody of OJaielas.

Memories of SStragh's own Naming came unbidden through the residual anger at Frraghi's insult.

It was the year in which the rains came nearly every day, when the creeks and river ran full to overflowing, loud and furious as they ran from the hills down into the valley. Even on the day of OJaielas, the rain pattered insistently at the crystalline windows of the dome. The OColi, his voice not yet ruined so that he needed a Speaker, intoned the rites of OJaielas.

SStragh (who was not yet SStragh but only another UnNamed youngling) had made up her mind long before the Day of Naming to choose Raajek as her OTsio. She knew that Raajek was already considered strange, already speaking to the other Mutata of her OChiihi, her New Path. Yet something in Raajek's endless debates stirred a sympathetic chord in SStragh. When the OColi looked down on her and said "And who is to be your OTsio, youngling?" SStragh gathered her courage and said, "I choose Raajek."

The scent of disapproval had wafted down from the tiers then, but she didn't care. She watched Raajek descend, wondering what name Raajek would bestow on her. SStragh looked at her, then glanced up to where the storm outside flung sheets of water at the central windows. "I name you SStragh," Raajek said, "because in you I hear the strength of the wind."

It had seemed a good name, SStragh. She rolled the name around in her mind, trying to judge its feel.

The second youngling had been called to choose her OTsio; she chose Klaaxa, one of the younger males. That was unusual, since the preferred OTsio were usually among the eldest. Raajek was usually one of the new OTsio for that very reason, despite her views. Yet as the younglings chose, one by one, SStragh never heard Raajek's name called.

"Who would be fool enough?" Frraghi's comment kept returning to SStragh. A faint odor of satisfaction was coming from Frraghi as he called the last few younglings. Finally, there was only one last youngling in the pool. Frraghi looked at the UnNamed one.

"You will choose now."

The youngling looked up to the high tiers, where only the OColi—who could not be chosen—and Raajek sat. Then his head lowered. "I choose . . . Tssafi," the youngling said.

Tssafi, three tiers down from Raajek, rose and went down to the pool.

After the Naming, after the last OTsio and otsiouie had left, after the OColi (stinking of pride) had made his ceremonial spiral descent of the tiers and departed with Frraghi, after all the rest of the Mutata had exited the dome, SStragh looked up to the topmost tier where Raajek sat alone, silent and staring blindly down at the steaming waters of the pool.

"OTsio?"

That brought a faint, ironic smile to Raajek. "It doesn't seem that anyone else cares to think of me in that way, does it? No one wants to be contaminated by someone who teaches that the OColihi is dead. No one wants to hear the truth."

"OTsio . . ."

"It doesn't matter, SStragh," Raajek said wearily. "Come here and help me down. I don't think I want to stay here any more."

CAPTURED

Mundo hit Aaron high, like a linebacker trying to tear off the head of a wide receiver. Aaron spun under the impact, adding the motion of his own hips and shoulders to Mundo's rush as he stepped sideways.

This was another aikido move: using the energy of your opponent and adding to it so that the attacker throws himself. Aaron had seen his sensei do the technique a hundred times, and each time the student who was playing the role of attacker would go flying away like a human missile to land with a high fall, *crack* on the mat. The attacker couldn't hold on; the momentum tore his grasp away.

If your attacker were human. If you did the technique correctly.

Mundo wasn't. Aaron didn't.

Instead of flying away into the nearest patch of brush, Mundo dug apish fingers into Aaron's shoulders. Aaron's sensei would have stayed erect as he turned, his center firm and his stance steady; the strength of Mundo's grasp wouldn't have mattered. Aaron was leaning over and bending forward. Mundo's desperate hands snatched at Aaron's shirt. Cloth tore, but the seams held. Mundo tumbled past Aaron, still

hanging on, then his weight and inertia took
Aaron with him.

They went down together in a heap. Aaron
howled in pain as he landed on his injured shoulder. They rolled, Mundo on top.

Mundo's hands were around Aaron's throat
now, a deadly vise. Aaron tried to push Mundo
away, but Mundo's arms were longer than his
and he could get no leverage. "You lie'!" Mundo
was screeching. The fanged snout was all Aaron
could see, the blood-red eyes staring down at him
in hatred. "You los' my worl' for me. You too' i'
all away!"

"Mundo—" Aaron started to say, but then the
fingers locked around his gullet and choked off
the protest. In Aaron's mind, his sensei was
shouting something about remaining calm, about
moving and bending, but Aaron couldn't hear
him. Everything he'd been taught had vanished.
Aaron's desperate hands scrabbled at Mundo uselessly, trying to get under that deathlock hold and
ease the pressure.

Aaron's face felt huge and swollen. His temples
hammered with the insistent rhythm of his own
pulse, and each slegdehammer beat caused the
world to dim a little. His world was shrinking
and turning black; his universe consisted only
of Mundo's enraged glare and the only thing he
could feel was the agony constricting his throat.
Your hands are free, aren't they? His sensei's voice
was amused and soft. *He only has your throat; you
have the rest of your body.*

Desperate, Aaron tried to bring a fisted hand
up. His arms felt like dead oaken limbs, heavy
and uncooperative. Somehow, he managed to get

the fist back and slam it up into Mundo's snout.

Mundo screeched and the pressure eased. Mundo's odd, light-colored blood splattered Aaron from the creature's flattened nostrils, but Aaron didn't care as he tried to drag air into lungs that were on fire, gasping at the relief as he breathed again. On his hands and knees, still gulping air, Aaron tried to crawl away. Mundo, relentless, came after him. Aaron could hear the footsteps, the dead leaves thrashing. He turned in time to put an elbow into Mundo's solar plexus. Mundo *oofed* and staggered back. Aaron looked around for the time machine, disoriented. In their struggles, he and Mundo had moved several yards from the vehicle.

Crack!

Both Aaron and Mundo flung themselves involuntarily to the ground at the sound of the gunshot. When nothing happened immediately, Aaron looked up cautiously, only to find himself staring into Mundo's frightened eyes, gleaming like blood-laced marbles only a few feet away through the dead branches and leaves of the forest floor. In that moment, some silent communication passed between the two, a truce declared in the face of a possible common enemy.

There was the noise of movement on the other side of the little clearing, near the time machine. It sounded like a struggle, a fight, but it was over quickly. There were no more shots, but the sudden silence was worse.

"C'mon," Aaron whispered.

"No!" Mundo grunted. "I don' trus' you."

"Mundo, please. We've gotta *move*! It's not a trick. I promise."

"I don' believe you."

"Believe me or not. If you stay here, the ones with the rifles are going to get you. Make your choice: me or them."

Mundo didn't look convinced, but he finally nodded. Staying down, Aaron crawled as quickly as he could to the cover of the nearest tree; Mundo, quicker and more silent, followed.

"Oh, my *God*, look at this——" someone grunted in the darkness. A form in a military uniform stepped out from the night-shadowed trees near the time machine, followed by two others who had between them a familiar figure, his arms handcuffed behind his back.

"Travis . . ." Aaron whispered it, almost a plea. The man almost seemed to hear him, for in the moonlight Travis glanced over to where Aaron and Mundo lay hidden. He shook his head, slowly and deliberately. None of his captors noticed; their attention was all on the time machine. The first soldier moved toward the open door, his weapon out and ready.

"The kid's not in there," Travis's deep, oddly accented voice was startlingly loud in the night.

"Shut him up!" the soldier hissed to his two companions.

"I mean it," Travis said. "Your woman friend killed him. I dumped the body."

"Just do like the sergeant said and be quiet!" The man on his right hit Travis in the side with the butt of his rifle. Travis's knees buckled in a loud intake of breath, then he caught himself. "That's for Waters," the soldier told Travis. "There's more of the same coming, too."

The sergeant had gone to the open door of the time machine. He pressed his back against the side of the vehicle, then crouched and took a step inside, weapon first. After a few seconds, he straightened. In the light of the interior, Aaron could see the man looking around and shaking his head. "No one here," he said to the others. "I guess our foreign friend here told the truth." He came back out.

"Hensley," he said to the soldier who'd hit Travis, "give a call to the others up at the house and get them down here. We'll need a flatbed too, and a lot of people to get this metal monster out of here."

As Hensley began speaking into a walkie-talkie, Travis again glanced back to where Aaron and Mundo were crouched, and he inclined his head in a sharp gesture. *Get going!* As he did so, Travis gave them a diversion, suddenly breaking away from the soldier holding his arms and running directly away from Aaron and Mundo. The soldiers yelled in alarm as they went in pursuit.

Aaron touched Mundo, pointed away from the clearing, and began moving as quietly as he could away from the commotion. Mundo followed quickly after him. Aaron's memory of these woods saved him several knocks in the head as they moved through the dim, dappled moonlight under the trees. He headed north again, taking the long way back toward the house and angling away from where he thought the rest of the soldiers would come. The noise of Travis's clumsy thrashing through the trees ended abruptly with a sound of angry shouts and blows. Aaron grimaced, knowing that Travis was handcuffed and helpless, but he kept going.

He knew that would happen; it was a sacrifice he was willing to make.

Aaron brought them out of the woods near the barn, using the old wooden structure for cover. Peering from behind a stack of old lumber, Aaron could see that the squad had already responded to Hensley's call. Only two sentries stood beside the trucks in front of the house, smoking cigarettes in the spotlights' glare. They'd covered the body of the man Travis had killed with a blanket; it lay like a strange lump in the middle of the driveway.

"Looks safe enough here for the moment," Aaron said to Mundo. He eased open the side door to the barn, grimacing at the scrape of rusty hinges, then entered the straw-scented atmosphere.

"Wha' are you goin' to do?" Mundo growled alongside Aaron. "I don' trus' you."

"You don't have much choice, do you?" Aaron replied. "Hang on a minute . . ." The soldiers had turned on the headlights of the trucks to illuminate the area around the house. Sharp wedges of dusty light from the lamps stabbed through the cracks of the rough wooden walls. A knife of illumination gleamed on Mundo's white fur, ran jaggedly over the haywagon, and touched the steel and leather gear hanging from nails on the walls, sparking on the dusty glass of an old kerosene lantern.

Aaron went rummaging through the back of the barn where a time storm—many months from now—would leave a void. The compound bow and arrows were there. Somehow it felt better to have some kind of weapon. Aaron pulled on the string, sighted down his arm. "Weird," he said. "If I take it now, it shouldn't have been there for me to find in the future . . ."

He shrugged. *Time travel*, he thought, *a paradox for every occasion*.

He could feel Mundo's gaze on him the whole time. The creature was watching him, judging, and there was still a sense of malevolence in the glittering orbs under that ridged brow. "Mundo, I know you don't believe that I've been trying to help you. Why is it that someone who can pick my mind for the right words doesn't know when I'm telling the truth?"

"I can ge'—get—wor's only," Mundo said, his mouth desperately trying to shape the sounds, though Aaron could already hear the improvement in Mundo's speech. Mundo, whatever he was, adapted incredibly quickly to the language. "I only hear the the top of your min', the language. I don'—don't—hear the emotions, and I don't hear your thoughts." Mundo paused. His muscular hands gripped air. "You di'n't—didn't—lie? You didn't bring me here to kill me?"

"No. We . . . well, we were wrong. Eckels has done more damage than we imagined. I really thought that when you and I came across the piece of roadway we'd be back in your time, not mine. I was wrong. I'm sorry, Mundo. Believe me, I understand what you're feeling."

Mundo shuddered. Bars of lights shivered with the motion. "I'm so *lonely*," he said. "I want to go back to *my* worl' where I am everyone. Where I *can* hear the thoughts—the thoughts of all."

There was a sound in the darkness. Twin glittering lines ran in the canyons of Mundo's face. Aaron realized that the creature was sobbing like a lost child. "Mundo—" he breathed.

Aaron put the bow down and went to him. He placed his arms around Mundo and held the creature. Under the albino fur, muscular shoulders heaved with emotion. Mundo allowed the gesture for only a few moments, then he gently pushed Aaron away.

"You cannot understan'," Mundo said. "I know you're trying to help, but it makes it hurt more. You and I—we can't ever be close, no'—not—the way I am used to being."

"You're right, I don't think I understand," Aaron told Mundo. "A World-Mind, a part of each and every creature . . . I can imagine some of what it must have felt like to be ripped away from all that. I've lost my parents, lost Jenny and Peter, and ended up in a place that's not as familiar as it should be, but still . . ."

Aaron picked up the bow again and went to the double doors in the front of the barn. He put an eye to the crack between them. The soldiers were still smoking. The faint sound of laughter came from them. In the middle of everything Aaron had gone through in the past few days, their amusement seemed entirely out of place, jarring. "I'm not going to lose Grandpa Carl, too," he said to Mundo. "I'm not going to let Travis get trapped here, either. And I'll get you home if I can."

"Wha'—what—are you going to do?"

Aaron slumped to the ground. He laid the bow across his knees. "Y'know, I'm not really sure."

*   *   *

They brought Travis up a few hours later, taking him away in one of the trucks. Three more trucks arrived just before dawn: one flatbed and two troop transports. The day began with the raucous clamor of chain saws, axes and curses. The sun promptly hid itself behind the nearest cloud, peering out reluctantly from time to time.

Before the last tendrils of morning mist had disappeared from the fields, a car arrived and a woman Aaron remembered all too well stepped out. She stood alongside the car for a moment, her gaze taking in the house and barn and fields. Aaron automatically stepped well back into the shadowed interior of the barn.

The woman went into the woods.

Mid-afternoon, she returned, bringing the time machine and the work crew with her. The men looked exhausted: dirt-streaked, with great circles of sweat under their arms and down the backs of their uniform shirts, breathing heavily with open mouths. The vehicle was loaded onto the flatbed and covered with tarpaulins; after a short rest, the soldiers were sent out to search the grounds once more. The house and barn were given special attention.

But Aaron and Mundo were no longer there. They'd gone long ago. They didn't see the woman's strange, reflective stare as, waiting for the searchers to report back, she gazed at the flatbed's burden. They didn't see her unlash a corner of the tarp, lift the canvas and reach out with a hand to—wonderingly—touch the slick painted surface.

* * *

The Compound. That's where they'd taken Grandpa Carl; that's where Travis and the time machine would be going, too, Aaron figured.

The Compound.

The site was about eight miles from the Cofield property, but Aaron couldn't risk being seen. Going around Green Town itself, avoiding the roads except to cross and dart quickly into cover on the side, and approaching the Compound from upriver meant many more miles. Aaron was certain that soldiers would be stationed at his old house for the next several days, at least. Considering that his prime assets were a bow and arrow and an albino gorilla, it seemed best to leave. As soon as Aaron saw the woman and her squad of soldiers head into the woods, he nodded to Mundo and they moved away in the opposite direction, leaving the barn and the house.

Aaron knew that Mill Creek, which ran along the edge of their property, emptied into the river well above the Compound. He and Peter and the other kids had spent a lot of time along Mill Creek's banks, playing at being Lewis and Clark venturing further and further into the unknown west, or Robin Hood lurking in the green depths of Sherwood, or Shawnee sadly watching the inexorable advance of the settlers. They'd even explored the creek mouth where it gave its burden of water to the river—despite their parents' dire warnings that if they *ever* went that far down the creek, they'd all be grounded for life.

Aaron smiled at the memory. They'd been right, his folks; Aaron and Pete and the rest of the gang had done some rather stupid things.

There were open sewers down there, gushing their brackish effluvium into the water. The yawning mouths had been an irresistible invitation. Lewis and Clark and Robin Hood and Shawnee had quickly been transformed into cave explorers, venturing into the unknown depths.

The gratings that were supposed to have kept them out were rusted and old; they yielded to the eager assault of their hands. The first day they went in only to where the sunlight failed. The next they made sure they had flashlights; they entered a maze, a labyrinth of rusting steel and stained concrete, of echoes and silence, of water and moss and furtive eyes. They played there for days, until the morning when a summer thunderstorm hit and suddenly the sewers were a swirl of rapids and angry water. Somehow, they all managed to get out, soaked and filthy, but alive.

They never went back in.

But they had learned where one of the sewer lines led. One of the snarl of pipes had come up inside the abandoned Compound.

The sewers were Aaron's target now.

It was evening before Aaron and Mundo reached their destination. The sun was setting, turning the river into flowing molten gold and burnishing the treetops. From under the deep bank of Mill Creek, the cracked and crumbling ends of the sewage system protruded like broken teeth. Aaron stopped. "Uh-oh," he said.

"Wha'?"

"There used to be a lot more outlets than this. The system's changed: the pipes are bigger and thicker, and this looks like an old main line, not what used to be here." Aaron sighed. "Well, I guess we don't have a choice . . ."

Aaron had brought with them the old, half-filled kerosene lamp from the barn; he lit it now, sending warm yellow light into the concrete cavern. The beam revealed a black, sluggish trickle and, further in, a mesh grating that blocked their way.

"Why are you goin' in there?" Mundo asked. His snout wrinkled in distaste. "It *stinks*. Yeech!"

"I'm not leaving here without my grandfather and I'm not leaving Travis either. This is the best way, unless you think we can just walk up to the gate and ask to be let in."

Mundo glared at Aaron. "This is another one of your tri . . ." Mundo stopped and made sure he pronounced the word correctly. " . . . tricks. You'll leave me in there."

"No, I won't. I promise. Mundo, look . . . I need you. All I want is for things to be *normal* again. If you want to get back to your world, you'll need the time machine. They'll have brought it here. I'm sure of it." Aaron touched the pocket of his shirt, feeling the hard outline of the circuit card Travis had given him. He wondered if Travis had had some premonition of this. "Mundo, I won't force you." He laughed deprecatingly. "I can't—you're a heck of a lot stronger. I'm going in; follow if you want."

As if in response to his words, there was a sudden growl of thunder. They both looked up. A black storm front was hurtling toward them, furious lightning sparking under the thunderheads. "No way that's a natural storm," Aaron said. "There were clouds, sure, but it didn't look like anything was brewing five minutes ago. This came up way too fast."

Thunder grumbled in answer. The sun had disappeared under the assault of clouds. A wind began to lash the trees. The air had a sharpness, an edge.

Time storm. Aaron knew. For a moment, he hesitated. They'd be helpless in the tunnels. If it rained hard, it would all drain into the sewers, all the water gathering to come crashing down . . .

There isn't any other way in. Not that won't be guarded. All you have is you and Mundo.

"Come on!" he said to Mundo. "We gotta hurry."

Aaron ducked his head and entered the dank underworld, lamp in one hand, the compound bow and quiver across his back. Mundo was right—it *did* stink, far worse than he remembered. He went in, set the lamp down, and pulled at the grating. Chain link rattled, but the barrier didn't move. He pulled again with the same result. Kicked it. Kicked it again. Then leaned back against the rounded wall of the outlet pipe.

"When I was a kid, most of these were just *hanging* there," he said.

Mundo was looking in at him. The onrushing storm lent a wild background to his figure, the wind tossing his long white fur from side to side. The ape stepped fully inside the pipe, carefully straddling the central stream of filth. He went up to the grate and laced powerful fingers around the links. Thick muscles rounded under the furred back as Mundo braced himself, then yanked. Metal bolts groaned, shrieked, and gave way with a sound like gunfire. The echoes took long seconds to die out.

"There," Mundo said. He threw the grating down. Sewage splashed back onto his fur, a long black streak of mud that ran from shoulder to hip. "Yeech!" Mundo howled. He brushed at the goo, but that only made the stain worse.

Aaron stared at Mundo. Then he began laughing. The sound of his amusement was strange against the growing clamor of the storm and the howl of wind.

"It isn't funny," Mundo said solemnly, and the look of deep disgust in the creature's face made Aaron laugh even harder. "Why are you laughing at me?"

"I don't . . . I'm sorry . . . I shouldn't . . ." A lightning stroke flared outside the pipe, nearly blinding Aaron, and the reverberating *boom!* of the thunder caused Aaron to jump to his feet and bang his head on the roof of the inlet.

"Ow!" He rubbed at his head, the laughter gone. "I guess I deserved that, didn't I? You just looked so pitiful and strange, and I'm tired, and everything's so weird right at the moment that if I don't laugh, I'm going to go crazy. That make any sense to you?"

"No," Mundo said morosely. He was looking at his hopelessly soiled hands.

"I didn't think it would." Aaron sighed. "Come on," he said. "We've got a long way to go yet."

RITES OF PASSAGE

Jennifer was hobbled this time, as were Peter and Eckels.

SStragh had come early in the morning to take them out. "Where are you taking us, SStragh?" Jennifer had asked. "Why do I have to be tied up like this?" The dinosaur would not answer her.

"SStragh, please. What's going on?"

"Nothing that I like, Jhenini."

A premonition came to Jennifer at that moment, sparked by SStragh's attitude, the way her coloring was pale and her spinal crest drooped as if wilted in the heat. "Today's OGhielas, isn't it? LongDay."

"Yes, it is." She said nothing more.

"What's going to happen?"

"I can't say."

"SStragh, I thought we were—" Jennifer stopped. *Friends*, she wanted to say, but realized that there was no equivalent word in the Mutata vocabulary. No word for friend, no word for companion—only words for indicating status.

"You thought we were what, Jhenini?"

"Equals."

SStragh smiled, and she used the backward-leaning stance that indicated self-deprecation. "In

215

the eyes of the OColi, no doubt we are exactly that," she said. As unsatisfactory as that answer was, it was all SStragh would say.

SStragh escorted the humans from their shelter and out of the Mutata village. The domed buildings were still in sight through the trees when they reached a small clearing. Four other Mutata stood around the grassy swath, spears in hand. There, waiting for them in the center, were the OColi, Frraghi, and Raajek.

A Gairk.

And two pieces of broken, floating roadway.

They had entered in the middle of a demonstration, it seemed. Frraghi held one of the guard-lizards in his hands. Ungently, he tossed the squalling animal onto one of the pieces of roadway, stepping back quickly as if afraid to come too near it. The lizard landed in the center, the road softly dipping as it took the weight, then rising up again. The lizard looked at Frraghi and snorted its protest at the Speaker's treatment, but nothing else happened.

"You see, OColi, it is as I told you," Raajek was saying. With the words, Jennifer knew exactly what that fragment of path was.

The path home.

Frraghi, still inclining his body well away from the path, plucked the guard-lizard from its resting place and took it over to the other Floating Stone. Again he tossed the guard lizard onto it and again the path dipped as the lizard hissed and spat.

And it disappeared, without pyrotechnics or special effects. The lizard just *wasn't*. A quiet, high-pitched thunderclap sounded from the road, as if air were rushing back into a sudden vacuum.

"Whoa!" Peter muttered behind Jennifer. Eckels gave a short, barking laugh.

"Geiree," Frraghi said to Jennifer. *Come here.*

Jennifer approached. As Mutata etiquette demanded, she raised her chin, exposing her neck to the OColi. She stood with both legs carefully even, the stance also indicating her submission. After a moment, Jennifer lowered her head again and looked directly at Frraghi. The Mutata pointed at the patch of white plastic through which the lizard had gone.

"Today is OGhielas," Frraghi said loudly. "And this is the Floating Stone from which the hard-shelled humans come. The other is the one that Raajek says you have closed—we brought it from the marsh where it lay. Is what SStragh tells us true; you have kept Eikels's promise and sealed this opening?"

Jennifer looked at Raajek and SStragh, but neither one of them would look directly at her or speak. Sudden tension burned in Jennifer's stomach, as she wondered how to respond. *Help me here*, she thought at them desperately. *Tell me what I should say.* But neither one spoke for her.

"Jenny, what's the lizard saying?" Peter asked.

"Not now, Peter," she told him, then switched to Mutata. "Who is this Gairk?" she asked Frraghi, stalling.

"It does not matter to you, nor do you have the right to ask," the Speaker answered. "But I will tell you that he is Klaido, Envoy to the Mutata, and he is here to witness for the Gairk OColi. Again, Jhenini, did you close the other Floating Stone?"

When in doubt, try the truth. Her father had once preached that platitude, but Jennifer doubted that he'd ever been in this kind of situation. "If I did," she said, "it wasn't intentional. And I don't know how to do it again."

Frraghi sniffed and a smell of anticipation came from him as his stance widened. Klaido opened his mouth in satisfaction. Raajek and SStragh seemed to sigh and dropped almost into a crouch. "The OColi is done with you, then," Frraghi said. "He will speak now to your Eldest, as is proper. You will be the Speaker for your OColi, and you will tell OColi Eikels that we want the hard-shells' Floating Stone sealed. Now."

"What are they saying, Jenny?" Peter asked again. This time she turned and told them. She looked from Peter to Eckels. "You insisted that I had to tell them you can make the paths stop working," she said. "You had to suspect that they'd want proof."

Eckels only nodded, smiling. "Great. Tell them this. Tell them that I'll seal it for them. But I can't do it alone, and I can't do it without all of us being unhobbled. Remember, this is what we had always planned."

"Eckels, this isn't a joke."

"Just tell them."

Jennifer started to protest, then sighed. Raising her chin so that she could not see the OColi, she translated. Frraghi snorted in protest, but Jennifer heard the OColi's ragged voice whispering. There was another whispered consultation with Raajek, too soft for Jennifer to understand the words. After a time, Frraghi spoke again. "My OColi says that it will be done, but that the humans should know this: if you try to escape, Raajek and SStragh will stand forfeit for the Giving we have promised the Gairk OColi. Do you understand?"

"Geedo," Jennifer answered. *Yes.*

"Then tell Eikels what the OColi has said."

"That's just fine," Eckels said after Jennifer had relayed Frraghi's words. "Just fine."

"Did you understand, Eckels?" Jennifer said vehemently. "SStragh and Raajek have pledged their lives for ours."

"Great," Eckels said blandly. He grinned at Peter, who smiled back.

"You two have something else planned, something you haven't told me about. What?"

Eckels shook his head. "Just play along, Jennygirl. Do what I say and don't worry. We're done with doing things the way the lizards want them done. Now, tell 'em to cut the hobbles."

"Jhenini, what has Eikels OColi said?" Frraghi insisted, pulling Jennifer's attention back to the Mutata and the Gairk. Feeling a sense of inexpressible dread, she told the OColi. The OColi grunted assent, and the Mutata guards were ordered to remove the vine lashings from the humans' feet. "That's better," Eckels grinned as the thick ropes were taken from him. "Much better."

"Seal the Floating Stone. Now," Frraghi said, and Jennifer relayed the order to Eckels, who nodded and then slowly walked around the pathway.

"I really chewed it up, didn't I?" he said. "Look at that—the section's nearly cracked through from where the shrapnel from the time machine hit it. I'm lucky to have come out of that explosion at all."

"Eckels . . ." Jennifer said warningly. The man just raised a casual hand to her.

"Easy," he said. He swept his hands over the surface without touching it. "Tell them that I'm just saying the magic words if you want to help. Abracadabra! Tell them that these things take a few moments, after all. This path goes to the samurai, you say?"

"Yes," Jennifer answered.

"Then we don't want to go through here just to get cut to pieces, do we? Too bad. That'd be easy. Peter, come on over. Why don't you stand over on this side away from the lizards and look like you're doing something important—wave your hands, chant some nonsense. Slowly now, we don't want old Snaggletooth over there to get irritated. That's it. Now how about you, Jenny? Come on, over next to Peter."

Peter and Eckels had positioned themselves so that the roadway was between them and the Gairk, as well as most of the Mutata. Under Eckels's continued urging, Jennifer moved alongside them.

"Eckels, what about SStragh and Raajek?"

"They're *lizards*, girl. Look at 'em—they wouldn't say a word if Snaggletooth there decides to have us for lunch."

"Eckels, I don't like this."

"You don't have a choice," he answered. "Peter, you ready?" The redhead nodded. "Jenny, why don't you ask Snaggletooth to come over here and help?" Eckels said with a twisted grin toward the Gairk, who was watching them intently. When Jennifer hesitated, Eckels repeated the order with more vehemence. "*Do* it!"

"Envoy Klaido," she said with a backward glance at Eckels and Peter before lifting her chin once more and facing the Gairk. "OColi Eikels requests your assistance. Would you come here?"

With a snort, the Gairk lumbered forward, his armor ringing metallically. Eckels stood in front of the beast, looking up at the huge, fierce head. "You are really ugly, you know that?" he said. "And you stink besides." With that, Eckels dug into his pocket and placed something in the Gairk's clawed hands. Jennifer caught a glimpse of a small ball wrapped in paper, a string protruding from it. Eckels took a device from his other pocket. Jennifer immediately recognized the long rectangle of red plastic tipped with metal. She'd seen a thousand of them back home; she might have known that Eckels had one with him.

"When you take someone's gun," Eckels said, looking at SStragh, "you really should make sure you get the bullets too."

With that, Eckels thumbed the wheel of the disposable lighter and touched the flame to the string. As the fuse crackled fiercely, as the Gairk looked suspiciously at the sputtering device, Eckels broke into a run.

"Let's *go*!" he cried.

Jennifer never quite understood why she did what she did then.

Jennifer could have fled with Eckels and Peter, could have rushed past the startled Mutata who stood between them and the rest of the forest, could have been under the cover of the jungle when the packed gunpowder in the homemade bomb exploded.

She didn't.

Jennifer went the other way. As the Gairk turned his evil head and began to bellow alarm, as Frraghi flung his spear uselessly across the clearing at the retreating back of Eckels, as SStragh and Raajek hooted in surprise and the OColi glared, Jennifer hit the Gairk's cupped hands with all her strength, striking from underneath. Eckels's deadly surprise went flying.

It exploded in mid-air.

Jennifer felt the heat on her back from the percussive blast. The concussion sent Jennifer flying; she landed with a grunt facedown on the ground. Shredded foliage and earth showered her; then there was silence except for the ringing in her ears. She levered herself from the ground carefully, wondering how she had managed to miss breaking any bones. She blinked dirt from her eyes.

Peter and Eckels were gone. The two Floating Stones had been flung into the jungle—Jennifer could see one of them wedged between two saplings. Around the clearing, the Mutata were getting to their feet. The Gairk alone was standing, but he reeled, hunched over, holding his head down so that his hands touched the disklike membranes of his ears. With a visible effort, Klaido forced himself erect once more, taking the double war clubs from his armor belt. He shouted rage and challenge and tried to pursue. The creature's equilibrium seemed to be gone; he nearly fell instead. The Gairk Envoy howled in pain and frustration.

And then Klaido's glittering, furious snake's eyes found Jennifer.

CURIOUS ALLIES

The sewer had been a lot more exciting when he was a kid, Aaron decided. Then, the concrete maze had been a fabulous, winding cavern with glittering flowstone walls, intricate fluted columns, and mysterious pits where dragonfire gleamed far, far down.

All Aaron saw now was a sewer system, something to carry away what most people would rather not see. There was nothing even slightly attractive about the place, unless one liked filth and stench and darkness. He was thankful that the sewer seemed to be carrying mostly runoff water, not raw, untreated sewage.

Aaron had to admit that his imagination wasn't entirely dead. The place might not be a site for grand adventures any longer, but it was spooky enough. In the lantern's dim glow, Aaron and Mundo followed the system back. The tunnel of concrete piping went straight in for a time, then turned abruptly to the left. They could no longer see either the wan light of outside dwindling at their backs or the lightning of the coming storm. They moved in the kerosene lamp's glow, but inky blackness pressed all around. Their footsteps echoed strangely, reverberating, and there were other sounds as well: watery splashes and odd percussions like hammers striking metal or sudden whines of machinery.

As they moved quickly through the tunnel, they could hear the crackling of the thunder from the storm outside, muted but still approaching. The two passed side openings into the main tunnel, black mouths from which issued cold foul air and dark streams. Mundo especially disliked those moments. He would press closely against Aaron, staying in the middle of their patch of illumination.

"Yeech!" he would say each time, but the exclamation now grew softer, as if he were afraid that too much noise might wake something horrible that slept in the lost, impenetrable dark.

Aaron found that he agreed entirely with his unwilling companion. Anything that chose to sleep *here*, he'd rather not meet.

Farther along, they came to an open area. Their own tunnel ended in a room from which three smaller pipes led out in various directions. "I don't remember this," Aaron said. He went to each of the openings in turn, but the lantern's light was consumed by the night lurking in the sewers. There were no discernible sounds, no light, no clues to tell him which way might lead into the Compound. He didn't trust his sense of direction, not since the original tunnel had twisted once or twice. Aaron *thought* that they were facing northwest—if that were true, then the left-hand pipe trailed off in something close to the direction in which they wanted to go.

Aaron remembered that in Latin and in chivalry, "left" was the "sinister" side. That was an omen he didn't care for.

Thunder from the storm outside crashed. Mundo started. The storm sounded closer now, too close. Aaron's experience told him that the trickle of water could become a flood far too quickly, and he knew that he couldn't waste any more time. The time storms he'd seen might not have produced rain, but he couldn't take the chance that he was wrong. As Aaron ducked his head and—crouching—entered the leftmost pipe, he suddenly had the odd certainty that Mundo was no longer behind him.

Aaron glanced back, turning awkwardly in the small space. The ape was standing with his head cocked, his red eyes narrowed and his leathery snout wrinkled as if he were sniffing an odor that only he could sense. To Aaron, this tunnel didn't smell any better or worse than the others.

"What's the matter, Mundo? Now's not the time to get claustrophobic. Let's get moving."

"Something's up there, Aaron. Something that doesn't belong here."

"You can smell that with this stench? You gotta be kidding."

Mundo came closer to the opening, peering in. Aaron's lamp struck scarlet highlights from the ape's eyes. "I don't like that smell. I don't . . ."

"So what is it?"

Mundo shook his head. "I don't know. I—it—wasn't there before, though. It's new."

"Well, whatever you're smelling, it's not likely to go away, and we're not going to get where we need to go standing here. So I guess we'll go find out exactly what it is, huh?"

Wishing he were as confident as he sounded, Aaron faced into the darkness again. Moving slowly and carefully through the cramped pipe, he continued on, Mundo at his heels.

After a thorough body search, Travis was dumped into a cramped holding cell in the basement of the main Compound building and left to cool his heels for several hours. He managed to sleep a little, sitting on the cot in the corner of the room and waking when a shaft of sun touched his cheek through the cell window. The rest of the day was mostly boring: he was fed a scanty breakfast, then lunch—metal trays shoved through a slot in the bars. Occasionally, a face would peer in through the peephole in the solid metal door at the end of the corridor.

It was nearly sunset when two guards came through the corridor door, unlocked his cell, and gestured for Travis to come out. He was smoothly handcuffed by one while the other watched, then escorted down a series of corridors to a set of large double doors. There, the handcuffs were removed and the guards motioned Travis to go on through.

Rubbing his chafed wrists, he did so.

"Welcome, time traveler," a woman's voice said.

She was standing in front of his time machine, wearing a baggy gray suit splashed with dirt and mud, her dark hair disheveled as if by wind and sweat. Travis's time machine hovered just behind her, a few inches above the concrete floor. The door to the vehicle was still open, as it had been the night before when he'd been captured.

Even more compelling than the time machine

was the section of the floating path set to one side of the room, the white plastic stained and shattered. This piece appeared larger than the one through which Travis and Aaron had traveled. Travis wondered how many of these fragments might be scattered through the woods behind Aaron's house.

Behind the hovering remnant, the wall of the laboratory looked as though it had been hit with an explosive wrecking ball.

"You really shouldn't be practicing with hand grenades indoors," Travis remarked.

She ignored that, gesturing instead at the roadway. "Interesting, isn't it? I'll even bet you know exactly what it is. But then, I'm forgetting my manners. I'm Captain Michaels, attached here with General McWilliams—but you already knew that, didn't you?"

"No, I didn't," Travis answered, puzzled; but the woman ignored his answer.

"And *your* name . . . ?" She smiled at him, but it was a weary smile and a cautious one.

He didn't answer.

"We'll find out eventually, you know," she told him. "You weren't carrying identification, but there are other ways: fingerprints, dental work, hypnosis, drugs." Michaels sighed. "Mister, I don't care whether you give me a pseudonym or your real name right now. I just want something to call you other than 'hey, you.' It's been a very long couple of days for me, and right now I'd rather be sleeping than standing here, but that isn't in the cards at the moment. So—do you have a name?"

"Travis."

"Travis. Is that your real name? No, you needn't answer that," she said, waving a hand. Dirt stained the cuff of her uniform. "You *are* a time traveler, aren't you, Travis? And this"—she patted the side of the time machine—"is the device you use to go hurtling through the centuries. It's a lovely machine, a beauty. Far more elegant and useful than the little toy we've built. Tell me, Travis, have you seen this room before?" The woman's eyes had narrowed and she leaned forward slightly to watch his face as he answered.

"This room? No."

She didn't say anything for several seconds, staring at him as if listening to some inner debate. Finally she shook her head dolefully and went to the path. To Travis's amazement, Michaels jumped up and stood on it.

He waited for her to disappear.

His disbelief must have shown. She cocked her head toward him. "You didn't know you could deactivate the portal? I'm surprised. It's easy enough. You see?" She stamped her foot on the pathway; it bobbed slightly, but nothing else happened. "I'll bet this was elegant, too, before it was broken. I can see it in my mind, beautiful white paths floating above green fields. What happened, Travis? This looks as if it might've been through a war. This piece showing up in our time was all an accident, wasn't it? *Everything* that's happened has been a terrible accident: this piece, the dinosaurs, the time storms . . ."

Michaels hopped down and came close to Travis. She looked up into his eyes. "Travis, tell me—everything predetermined? Is history made of steel and rock, a structure we can't alter? Are we forced to walk lockstep in the path Fate has designed for us? You must know; after all, you've come from our future."

"History is crystal," Travis answered. "Delicate hand-blown glass. Once you shatter it, you can't ever fix it again."

"Has anyone ever tried?"

"I have. Aaron has. You can see how well we've done."

Michaels sighed at that. "I was hoping . . ." She paused. "It's funny. Even though I can't point to anything and say 'Aha!' I have this, this *feeling* that things have gotten worse here, like there's a misty, fantasy past in my head that I can't quite remember. Every once in a while, the fog lifts and I'm granted a glimpse, and what I see makes me cry. We've made the worst mistake we ever could have made, haven't we?"

There didn't seem to be any point in lying. Not about that. "Yes." Then, after a long breath, "And Aaron and I made a worse one."

"You killed Waters, you know. I . . . I had to tell his wife. I had to see his kids watching me with wide, terrified eyes, wondering why their mom was crying so desperately. The littlest one kept hugging her and saying 'It's okay, Mommy, Daddy'll be back soon. It'll be okay . . . ' Over and over . . ." Michaels's voice broke, and she stopped for a moment before continuing. "I've been in the army for fifteen years, but I've always been in the administrative end. I've never had to fight; I've never had anyone under my command die because of something I ordered him to do. Telling Waters's family was the hardest thing I've ever had to do. I don't ever want to have to repeat

it. If I could do things over, I'd change it all."
She stopped. "Travis, tell me I can go back and
change that. Tell me I can undo death."

Travis moved his head from side to side, slowly. "That would be a more dangerous mistake
than anything you've done yet."

"It wasn't meant to happen that way."

"Someone shot at us first, remember?"

"Yes. I remember." Michaels turned away, but
not before Travis saw the sudden vulnerability in
her face, the unmasked emotions. The woman
went to one of the barred windows of the room
and pulled aside the heavy, opaque curtain. She
stared outward. "I was told that I killed Aaron
Cofield."

Travis didn't say anything for a moment.
"Yeah," he said at last. "You did."

"I don't believe you, Travis," Michaels said
without turning around. "Maybe it's just because
I don't *want* to believe it, maybe it's because I'm
finding that I have a guilty conscience when it
comes to this whole Cofield mess and I don't
want to be responsible for another death. Or maybe it's because for once in my life I've been
granted a glimpse of the future."

Travis didn't know what the woman was talking about. She seemed to be half raving, wandering lost through her own thoughts. "Where's
the boy's grandfather?" Travis asked. He didn't
really expect an answer. He was surprised when
she replied.

"He stepped through your broken path. Late
last night after we brought him here. Another one of my many 'mistakes.'" Michaels was
still gazing through the window. Past her, Travis

caught a glimpse of failing light on the horizon. He was wondering what Michaels was going to ask next, wondering why he had been brought to this room and when she was going to get to the point when Michaels suddenly stiffened and gave a hissing exhalation. With a soft curse, she went to a telephone on the wall.

"Time storm!" she barked at someone on the other end, then slammed the phone back on the hook.

Just then, the first wave of thunder hit.

The pipe narrowed even further only a hundred yards ahead, so Aaron had to begin crawling on his belly. Mundo moaned and complained, but he lay down in the muck as well. They continued in that manner for several yards, until Aaron saw an opening above him. Maneuvering the lamp into position, he noticed black iron rungs leading upward. Tiny circles of light from a floor grating shone above. "Stay there," Aaron whispered to Mundo, then climbed up until he could put an eye to one of the holes.

He was looking at a gray sky. Carefully, Aaron pushed against the lid; it yielded, and he slid it aside until there was enough room for him to get out. Aaron cautiously poked his head up. They were inside the Compound, close to the wall of a building. A door was nearby, and their luck had held: no one seemed to be looking their way. The guards stationed along the wall were all looking outward at the approaching storm. Aaron pulled himself out, then leaned down to grab Mundo's extended hand and pull him up.

A thunderclap rattled the grating. An alarm began ululating.

Someone was yelling nearby; the voice echoed against concrete walls. "Let's go!" Aaron said to Mundo as he ran for the door, praying that it would be unlocked.

It was. Inside, a single row of fluorescent lights gave a wan, greenish light to the interior. Another lightning bolt threw their black shadows down the hall; then the ceiling lights flickered and went out, leaving the building in near darkness. Running footsteps and more shouts could be heard.

It was as good a diversion as Aaron could have wished for. "I must live right," he muttered, calling down to Mundo. "Come on!" he said. "Hurry!"

Curiosity drove Travis forward to the window. He was surprised that Michaels made no move to stop him. "I've been through three of these things," she said. Travis could feel her shiver. "All you can do is pray that it leaves you alone."

The storm strode toward the Compound on jagged legs of lightning, heaving its black spider-bulk of cloud forward. Its herald was the relentless shrill of wind and under the thunderheads, entire worlds were born and smashed and reborn. Alarms began to hurl their own strident voices at the storm. Travis felt a cold wind slicing through the space between the windows, a touch as cold as the grave. A strobe-flash arced near the Compound's outer fence, a quarter-mile away; in that instant fifty yards of concrete, barbed wire, and guardposts were replaced by a peaceful street scene that might have been from Victorian times.

A startled-looking old couple gaped from their truncated front porch swing.

They were as quickly gone again.

Michaels was shaking her head as other histories danced across the wide yard of the Compound. "There's no use hiding," she said to the accompaniment of thunder. "God knows where you go if the storm takes you, but you go. The first time, the squad I was leading was caught outside in the woods not far from the Cofield place. Suddenly the tree next to me was gone, and I was staring at a herd of spiders as big as horses. We looked at them and they looked at us, and I hoped that they didn't start running before the storm took its offering back again. We were lucky."

"I know. I've seen the storms too."

"Then tell me what's causing them. Tell us how to stop them."

Before Travis could answer, a bolt lashed fiery tongues fifty yards in front of the window. Thunder deafened them as the lights went off in the building. Travis found that he'd brought his hands up to his eyes instinctively; when he lowered them, he saw the gift of the storm.

Travis had no name for it, but he had no doubts about its nature. Looking at the beast's glowing white eyes, Travis could *feel* the thing's malevolence. Wrapped in a dark cloud which left only the eyes easily visible, it stood on two massive cyclone legs twice as tall as a man. There were glimpses of its body through the streaming cloud which swaddled it: a chest like a granite mountainside, arms through which bright energy rather than blood coursed, fingernails tipped with curved talons glinting like steel and radiant with heat. Smaller lightning bolts flickered about and through the cloud-beast, sizzling and crackling.

It moved. The thing seemed to rise even taller, the storm wind roaring past it. The beast-head swiveled slowly, looking down on the Compound like a demon.

"Whatever you are, please stay put," Michaels breathed.

It did not. The apparition took a step, a long stride that took it out of the circle of red sand in which it stood even as the lightning flashed once more and the field of red sand became only raw, normal earth. The time storm rushed onward and past, but the cloud-beast remained.

A squad of soldiers rushed forward from an unseen doorway to the right, firing as they came. The cloud-beast snarled at them, and a lightning-armored hand came down and swept them away. Through the window, Travis and Michaels could hear the screams. Michaels ran to the telephone again, shouting something into the mouthpiece. Travis, transfixed, could only stare at the evil figure of the storm-being.

As it regarded the Compound.

As it began again to move.

Someone was using the building for a bass drum.

Whatever it was, it was louder than the thunder. With each mallet stroke, the walls trembled and more dust fell. The mad percussionist wasn't keeping very good time. His drumming had stirred up the Compound like a stick jabbed into an ants' nest.

That was just fine for Aaron and Mundo. As they scrambled from the sewer, they merited hardly a glance in the unlit corridor.

Boom! The gigantic mallet hit the building again; this time the stroke was followed by the sound of an avalanche.

The wall and roof fifty feet to their left exploded into rubble, concrete blocks and plaster spilling out everywhere as nearby soldiers scattered. A being of wind and cloud and storm walked through the opening. Its form was lined in incandescent sparks, its body black as a moonless night. It snarled; whirling tornadoes issued from the emptiness that was its mouth. It reached out with an ebon hand and touched the dangling power lines in the wreckage. Wild surges ran white and blue through its veins. Demon-thing, it stamped its feet and walls fell.

Aaron's response was pure instinct and fright. In one movement, he brought the bow from his back and strung an arrow, loosing the bolt in the same motion. The shaft sped upward toward the unseen chest of the being. A few feet from it, the metal tip suddenly flared blue and dissolved in a shower of molten steel, the shaft burned to ash in a moment. The thing laughed thunder, peering down at Aaron and Mundo through its own storming and the broken roof.

A lightning stroke crackled down from the upraised hand of the demon-thing. Like a god's thunderbolt, it struck the bow, which cracked and burst into blue flame as Aaron cried out and cast the useless weapon away.

The storm-beast started to reach down as if to pluck up Aaron and squash him like an insect.

Then it hesitated, strangely, and Aaron saw the apparition's glowing eyes regarding Mundo.

Mundo, his snowy fur eerily bright in the reflected magnificence of the storm-creature, was hissing and snarling as though he had gone mad, and yet . . . there was a yearning quality to the sound. Mundo spread his arms wide, as if inviting the storm-beast to strike and take him up into its boiling mass as an offering.

Aaron thought the storm-beast was about to take Mundo's proffered sacrifice. The wind howled far above them, the lightning erupting. Aaron readied himself to knock Mundo out of the way of the storm-creature's attack. He crouched, tensed.

But the thing had drawn back, the searing gaze high and distant. Thunder rumbled, but distantly, like a receding stormfront, and the lightning gleamed softly.

"Alone," Mundo uttered as if to himself, looking up at the storm-beast. "You're alone. I know."

As if in answer, the storming of the creature redoubled. It sprayed fireworks from its hands like a Fourth of July finale. Its funnel-legs swayed and the storm-beast began to move again, a juggernaut of destruction. A moment more, and it was past them, tearing through the Compound buildings like a hurricane. Aaron realized that they were now alone in the corridor. Everyone else had fled.

Mundo was staring after the storm-creature longingly. Aaron touched Mundo on the shoulder and the ape started, as if shaking himself from a dream. "That's from your world?" Aaron asked. "You've seen something like that before. You sent it away?"

"Yes," Mundo answered, still looking at the ruinous wake of the storm-creature. "From my world. I was *part* of that before. I *was* that. And now it's alone like me. Alone. It shares my pain. It knew it could not make me hurt worse than I am already hurting."

Aaron heard Mundo sigh; then the ape shook off the mood. He lifted his head.

"This way, Aaron," he said, pointing down the pile of debris that had once been a corridor. Above the roofless, broken walls, the racing clouds of the time storm hurtled to the east, following the storm-beast.

"Mundo—"

"No more talking," Mundo interrupted. "Quickly. This way."

THE ALL-ANCESTOR'S DECISION

"Go after them!"

The OColi's wrecked voice jolted the Mutata guards into action. Obedient, they crashed into the forest in pursuit of Peter and Eckels. Around the clearing, SStragh was helping Raajek to her feet as Frraghi fussed over the OColi.

In the middle of the glade, Klaido regarded Jennifer, his jaws clashing as if he were in pain. Dirt speckled the copper sheen of his armor. Grass hung from his chestplate like seaweed on a dock piling. The Gairk was still stunned, breathing rapidly and blinking. His fingers twitched around the shaft of the Gairk war club.

Jennifer shook her head and groaned. Now that the initial shock was over, the great-grandfather of all headaches was threatening to split her head apart and she realized that she wasn't hearing very well at all. Still, her initial assessment held—she was standing and, beyond a few bruises, she wasn't seriously hurt. *A minor miracle. That's what I get for being a bleeding-heart idiot.*

And then she realized that Peter and Eckels were gone. *Gone.* She was alone.

"Envoy Klaido, are you hurt?" she asked, more

because the Gairk was still staring at her than because she was actually concerned.

"*Yeie*," he grunted: No—though from the way the creature stumbled as he found his footing again, Jennifer knew Klaido was lying.

Jennifer had no chance to ask again. Frraghi gave a roar of raw, animal anger that brought all their heads around. The Mutata turned to the OColi and pointed in turn to Raajek, SStragh, and Jennifer.

"OColi," Frraghi said. "Let me Give them. Here. Immediately. Let me do as you and the Gairk OColi have always wished."

"What?" Jennifer cried at that, though both Raajek and SStragh remained silent and unprotesting. "I just saved Klaido's life, and maybe yours and the OColi's, too."

"The Envoy's life was the All-Ancestor's to take or leave," Frraghi snorted. He stamped the ground for emphasis, and his tail lashed. The mottled blue-green of his scales was the deep hue of a stormy sea. "We thank the All-Ancestor for sparing him, but it was Her doing, not yours. Be happy that She chose you as Her vehicle. Your Eikels has shown me the truth. Humans are *iaso*," he declared, using the term for unintelligent forms of life.

"*Iaso yeie*," Jennifer snapped back.

"*Iaso*." It was the OColi himself who spoke this time. He spat out the word into a sudden silence. "The humans are clever, yes, but too stupid to understand the OColihi. Too dangerous to allow to live, and too dishonorable. Far-Killers. Users of horrible magics." The OColi looked now at Raajek, and the sour stench of rebuke came to them. "So this is your OChiihi, is it, Raajek? This is more of your New Path? Well, I will no longer tread it."

The OColi looked at Frraghi. He nodded permission. Frraghi gave a cry of triumph and raised his spear to Raajek. The old Mutata didn't move, didn't protest. She only lifted her snout in mute acceptance of the OColi's decision.

"No!" Jennifer shouted. "Frraghi! I . . ." She stopped. All of them were looking at her, waiting. Jennifer could think of only one way to stop Frraghi. "I want ciosie, Frraghi," she said. "You're wrong in this. Killing us won't change anything at all."

Frraghi hissed disdain, but let his arm drop. "You call for ciosie? You?"

"Yes," Jennifer answered. "You said that the All-Ancestor moved through me. Fine. Then let your All-Ancestor speak again. Isn't that what ciosie's for?"

"Jhenini," Raajek said quietly. Her ancient voice sounded resigned. "Submit now. The OColi has spoken, and after what the Far-Killer Eikels has done, I wonder if he has not always been right."

"The OColi is *wrong*. I'm sorry to be blunt, but that's the truth." Jennifer looked at Raajek and SStragh. She shook her head at them. "I made a choice when I stayed," she told them. "But I can't just stand here and let Frraghi do this."

"This struggle is useless," SStragh told her. "Jhenini, I've failed you, and I'm sorry. But now is the time to stand aside and give yourself to the All-Ancestor's mercy."

"SStragh, if you feel that way, then humans *are* different from Mutata. We don't submit so easily. I'm asking for one last chance. I'm asking for ciosie. I won't just stand here and be run through with Frraghi's spear, and if I run, you'll just kill me like an animal. I don't believe that the All-Ancestor speaks through any kind of duel, but you do. If that's the only way you'll believe me, then as idiotic as it might be, I want the opportunity. Frraghi, will you give me ciosie?"

"Yes," Frraghi answered, and he smelled of satisfaction. "I accept."

"Ciosie, indeed," came a deep voice: Klaido. He took a step forward, and his club made a low growl as it swung through empty air. "But the humans' lives were first declared forfeit by the Gairk, not Mutata. There will be ciosie, yes, but not with Frraghi. With *me*."

At the time Jennifer had said the words, the decision had seemed right—in any case, in the midst of the crisis no other tactic had come to her. Facing the ferocious Gairk, she was no longer so sure. Maybe she should have run. Maybe she should have cast her lot with Peter and Eckels.

Jennifer could understand her companions' desire to escape, certainly. She would have followed Eckels herself if she hadn't been holding on to the hope that SStragh and Raajek would somehow protect them. She would have followed if Eckels hadn't so blithely demonstrated his callousness.

Eckels didn't care whether any of the dinosaurs died or not. He didn't care that SStragh and Raajek's lives were also in jeopardy. He didn't care how many his grisly surprise might have killed—'*They're just lizards* . . . ' Eckels's prejudices were no better than the OColi's. As for

Peter . . . well, he'd cast his lot with Eckels.

Jennifer cared. She empathized. It seemed that she'd pay for that mistake.

The spear given her by SStragh seemed ludicrous. How was she supposed to use this matchstick against the armored, scaled bulk of Klaido? It was folly, it was insanity. She might as well try to empty the ocean with a bucket.

Klaido breathed the scent of corruption. His shadow was cold. "We will have your ciosie, Jhenini Human," he said. "Are these witnesses sufficient for you?" he asked.

"Yes," she answered. Her voice sounded thin and timid against the bass rumble of the Gairk.

"Then we begin."

Klaido took his broaii in his left hand and laid it on the ground, the blade-studded, blunt head facing Jennifer. Remembering the ciosie she'd witnessed between Waato and Lhath, Jennifer laid the spear's ebon blade next to the Gairk's weapon, the butt end facing her. The opponents moved so that they stood at the ends of the line made by the broaii and the spear; both Jennifer and Klaido then reached down to take their weapons in their left hands.

Jennifer was trembling. She couldn't stop. Jennifer could see the blade shivering as she held it at her side the way she had once seen Waato do, ready to thrust. Her stance felt foreign and awkward. She felt light-headed, almost dizzy, and faced Klaido with no hope in her heart at all. A brooding resignation gripped her, holding her in its grim, soft arms.

As if sensing her emotions, Klaido swept his club noisily through the air a few times. "Lis-

ten to the song of my broaii, all of you," he
chanted. "Three times I have used it in ciosie,
and three times the All-Ancestor has smiled on
me. Three times the one who spoke against me
died. We Gairk aren't weakling plant-eaters like
the Mutata, and our broaii are not spears, which
sometimes do not kill. One bloodletting blow is
all the OColihi gives us in ciosie, and one blow is
all that I have ever needed. But before we start, I
will grant you one chance, Jhenini Human, since
you say you don't believe in the OColihi we follow. Drop your spear and run. Run now, and I will
call you iaso and hunt you down, but for the life
you have given me, I will give you until the sun
rises tomorrow before I find you and kill you."

Jennifer's fingers loosened on the slick wood
of the spear's shaft. She almost cast the weapon
aside and fled. But SStragh was watching her, and
the Mutata's gaze held her. "What about SStragh
and Raajek?" Jennifer asked.

"The OColi Mutata has already spoken their
fate." Klaido shrugged.

"Then you don't really give me a choice,
Klaido. I've said that the OColi and Frraghi are
wrong about me, but they're wrong about
Raajek's OChiihi, too. The Mutata and the Gairk
will need a New Path or they'll fail." Jennifer
closed her eyes, sighed, opened her eyes again.
"It's still ciosie, Klaido."

Klaido's scent grew stronger. His spinal crest
spread in display. "Are you at peace with your
All-Ancestor, Jhenini Human?"

Are you, Klaido? she wanted to respond, but
Jennifer knew that any such bravado would be
utterly false. She simply nodded. "That is good,"

Klaido responded. "Because you are about to meet Her."

With that, Klaido bellowed. The sound broke Jennifer from the paralysis that held her. In desperation, she lunged forward, thrusting at Klaido with a sobbing cry and praying that her weapon would somehow find a gap between the lacings of his armor. If she could cause blood to flow, the ciosie was over. Only a scratch; that was all she needed.

Klaido parried the blow easily with his broaii, knocking the thrust aside and nearly sending Jennifer sprawling. Klaido didn't follow his advantage. He watched Jennifer stumble and regain her balance. The he raised the broaii high and brought it down—almost contemptuously, not using his full strength. Even so, Jennifer was nearly struck. One of the blades notched the shaft of her spear, slicing a deep gouge from the hardwood. Jennifer knew that even such a half-hearted strike would have been a death blow. Klaido seemed amused that she had evaded him. He lowered the broaii nearly to the ground, mocking her with the opening.

She thrust; he parried again. Thrust and parry.

Jennifer knew that the Gairk was toying with her, like a cat teasing a mouse stranded in the middle of the kitchen floor. Soon, she knew, he would tire of the game. Already she was panting, and the adrenaline rush was gone.

Think! She stared at Klaido, focusing on that muscular body, the carnivore's head, the broaii swaying loose in his left hand. Just to gain time, Jennifer jabbed at the Gairk again; once more, the club swept in and knocked her spear aside.

Always the same. She realized it with a start. Each time, Klaido brought the club in from left to right. If Jennifer began her thrust and then pulled back, the broaii might go past, leaving her a brief opening.

If she could hit it. If Klaido did as expected. Jennifer tightened her grip on the spear and took a breath, calming herself.

Now!

Jennifer stepped in, thrusting with the spear. Klaido tried to swat it aside, but at the same time Jennifer brought the spear up as she stepped back again. The club struck nothing, continuing on its arc. For an instant, Klaido's side was open, with the gap between the armor's chest and back plates exposed.

Jennifer, with a cry, drove the spear forward.

The blade never got far. Klaido turned abruptly sidewise. His armored tail whipped around, striking the spear and Jennifer, shattering the wood in Jennifer's hand and sending the tip pinwheeling away. The unexpected blow knocked all the breath from her and sent her tumbling. For several seconds, she lay gasping and helpless. When Jennifer's vision cleared, Klaido was standing over her with his broaii upraised.

"Our ciosie is over, Jhenini Human," he said.

Klaido brought the club down hard. Jennifer screamed.

The impact shook the ground beside her head. Jennifer realized that she was still hearing the echo of her scream. The broaii was standing upright, half-buried in soft loam, the sharp, jagged edges of the obsidian blades sticking out only a few inches from her face.

Jennifer scrambled to her feet, eyes wide with mingled panic and relief.

Klaido picked up the tip of Jennifer's spear. Deliberately, he jabbed his finger with the tip until blood welled up. He let a drop fall to the ground so that everyone could see it, then tossed the speartip away contemptuously. Klaido looked at the OColi.

"The All-Ancestor has spoken," Klaido said to the old Mutata. "I find that I do not wish to kill Jhenini Human. She has won this ciosie. As the All-Ancestor called Jhenini to spare my life, I was called to spare Jhenini. I ask that the OColi Mutata do the same." Klaido spoke it gently enough, but his stance was wide and martial, and his scent was that of a superior speaking to a subordinate. Jennifer, panting and still wondering at finding herself alive, watched as the OColi struggled with that. The old Mutata had risen up, his crest full and magnificent, and he waved off Frraghi, who had come over to speak for him.

"Gairk do not give orders to Mutata," the OColi said.

"I only ask the favor of you," Klaido said, but nothing changed in his stance or odor. "I do not order, and I will certainly abide by whatever decision the OColi Mutata makes and report such back to the Gairk OColi."

The OColi snorted. "As a favor to Klaido," he said, though his tone did not sound kindly, nor was his scent sweet, "I will grant his wish, even though I do not agree."

"What about SStragh and Raajek?" Jennifer asked.

The OColi glared at Jennifer with his one

good eye. He refused to speak directly to her; instead, he whispered to Frraghi, who answered for him. "The OColi abides by the OColihi, always. Klaido has bent the ciosie as he wished, and the OColi says that he no longer holds Raajek and SStragh's lives forfeit for that of the other humans. He will ponder what has happened here and what it means. That is the best answer he can give you."

"Bhieye," Jennifer said to the OColi. *Thank you*. Then, to Klaido: "Bhieye."

The Gairk merely rumbled deep in his wide chest. "We have balanced our deeds, Jhenini Human," he said, and she could find no friendliness at all in his slitted, golden gaze. "Should there be a next time, I will not do the same."

"What would Klaido have us do with the other humans?" Frraghi asked. "Does Jhenini's ciosie free them also?"

Klaido made a sound of disgust. "Let whoever finds them, Gairk or Mutata, do as they wish. They may be iaso, they may be more, but I do not care."

Klaido stooped and pulled his broaii from the ground. Dark, wet earth clung to the blades and head; uncaring, Klaido lashed the weapon to his hip. "I will go tell my OColi what I've seen," he said. He showed his neck respectfully to the OColi, then lowered his head to look at the others.

"And then I will go hunt humans."

THE PATH BACK

Aaron and Mundo crawled over the rubble that had once been a wall into the shell of a laboratory. The time machine was there, the body of the craft chipped and scarred as if a crowd of angry protesters had been throwing rocks at it. Beyond it, the tumbled wall of the lab revealed the grounds of the Compound. The time storm had passed—stars were appearing on the horizon. Alarms were still wailing their mournful dirge, and Aaron could hear police sirens approaching from the direction of Green Town. A spotlight blinked on in a corner of the guard tower, the beam crawling slowly over the wreckage. Aaron motioned to Mundo and the two crouched low as the column of light slithered near them.

"You two really, really stink, did you know that?"

Travis had appeared from behind the detritus. Something had left a long, bloody scratch along his temple; a fan of blood was smeared across his cheek. He limped, but no worse than he had before. Aaron grinned despite himself, happy to see the man alive and free. "Travis! Sorry, but we took the slimy route. I guess Mundo and I could both stand a long, hot shower."

A movement near the back of the lab caught

Aaron's attention, and he turned to see Michaels. The barrel of a handgun leered at them from her fist. Aaron reached for his bow, then remembered that the storm-creature had destroyed it. "I knew you lied," Michaels said to Travis. "I knew Cofield was still alive."

"Where's my grandpa?" Aaron demanded. "Where is he?"

"In the past," she answered. "He went back in time—through that." She gestured behind her, then stopped in mid-wave. Where she was pointing, there was nothing.

"It's gone," Travis told her. "When that thing came through, I saw the path go flying off like a feather in a gale. For all we know, it may not even be in this time line anymore."

"Gone," Michaels echoed. She sighed and the gun drooped. At the same instant, Aaron gathered himself to leap at the woman, but she brought the weapon up abruptly, stopping him in mid-crouch.

The beam from the spotlight found them, blinding Aaron for a moment so that he put his hand up to shield his eyes. The actinic false sun lingered and then moved on.

"What are you going to do now?" Aaron asked her.

Michaels laughed bitterly, glancing around the ruined shell of the lab. "What am I going to do? Oh, yes, I have the gun, don't I? And I suppose help will be arriving shortly, now that they've seen us. Maybe we'll even find the piece of roadway. And as for the three of you . . ." Michaels stopped. "My duty is to arrest you, Cofield." She looked at Mundo and Travis. "And any creatures which come from other times are to be captured for study. Those are my orders from General McWilliams. That's what I gave my word I would do."

"I want to go home!" Mundo wailed. "That's all. I won't bother you, jus' let me go *home*!"

"You're the creature I saw on Cofield's lawn last night," she said. "The one I shot at. I thought you were some kind of animal. I didn't know you could talk." She looked at Mundo's arm, at the bloodied fur and the scabbed skin underneath. "I wounded you too, didn't I? I almost killed you, along with Aaron."

"Yes," Mundo hissed. "You hurt me when all I wanted was to find Aaron and . . ." Mundo stopped, the black nose wrinkled. Aaron knew what Mundo had wanted to do—he'd wanted to kill Aaron. But Mundo looked at Aaron and his eyes narrowed. " . . . make him take me home," he finished.

There were shouts from nearby. Flashlight beams bounced and swayed beyond the heaps of rubble. Aaron judged the distance between himself and Michaels. There was no time left— he could allow himself to be captured or he could make a desperate attempt to escape, but he knew he must make the choice now. If he intended to find his grandfather, there was only one choice to make—somehow, he didn't think there'd be much chance once General McWilliams had them.

A voice shouted from behind screening walls, "Captain! Captain Michaels?"

Michaels was looking at Aaron, and he knew that she had guessed his intentions. She moved back a step, so that it would take more than one step for Aaron to get to her. "Travis told me that history can be altered," she told them softly, not answering the man's call. "I can change it right now. All I have to do is pull this trigger, and I know that everything that's happened will be different. I can roll fate's dice once more. Maybe Waters would be alive in that world. Maybe . . ." Michaels's stare never left Aaron, never gave him even a moment's opening.

"Captain Michaels!"

"I'm here," Michaels called back this time. Then more softly, Michaels spoke to Aaron. "Promise me something," she said.

Aaron frowned, puzzled. "What?"

"Promise that you'll tell your grandfather that I'm sorry." With those words, Michaels relaxed her grip on the weapon. She handed the gun to Aaron.

"I . . ." Relief drove Aaron's voice away. He looked from the weapon he held to Michaels. "I promise you that," he said.

Michaels sank down wearily on an upturned table. Her eyes, ringed with gray exhaustion, looked from one to the other. "It was about two-thirty in the morning, yesterday," she said softly to them. "I saw you then. Do you understand me? You're all twisted around these last few days. If you want to rescue your grandfather, go back to that moment."

Aaron looked at her. He smiled. "Thanks," he said.

She nodded, but there was nothing but pain in her expression. Now she laughed with hollow mirth. "You'll just have to give me one piece of advice," she said.

*   *   *

The time machine shrilled; white mist covered the windshield and hid the blackness of NoTime from Travis, Aaron, and Mundo. The ape howled in concert with the machine, a discordant harmony.

And they arrived. As the frost melted and ran in bright streams from the machine's body, Mundo's howl subsided to a whimper.

They saw before them the laboratory as it had been before the storm-beast had destroyed it. Michaels was gaping openmouthed at them as they materialized; two soldiers were transfixed near the path.

Aaron had already jumped out of his seat, one of the machine's rifles in hand as he opened the hatch. "Uh-uh-uh," he said to the men, one of whom had reached for a gun at his side. "Be nice, now." The soldier relaxed his hand. "Okay, now unbuckle your holster belts and drop them on the floor . . . *easy* . . . both of you. That's good," Aaron said as they laid their weapons down on the tiled floor. "Now, get out of here."

They stared at Aaron, puzzled. "You heard me," he shouted at them. "*Leave!*"

With backward glances at Michaels, the two obeyed. As they left and the door shut behind their retreating forms, one of them hit a klaxon alarm in the corridor outside. "Travis!" Aaron yelled back into the machine. "The doors!" Travis nudged the craft backward until its rear came up against the entrance to the lab, blocking access.

Safe for the moment, Aaron swiveled the barrel to point at the woman. "Captain Michaels," he said. "I'd like you to reactivate the path. Now. We don't have much time."

Aaron saw Michaels quickly recover her composure. Her eyes flashed, the mouth snapped shut. "Not a chance, Cofield," she said.

"I was told you'd say that," Aaron told her. "I was also told to tell you something else."

"*Who* told you all this?"

Aaron grinned at her. "Why, *you* did. Your future self, anyway."

That hit the woman. Aaron could see it. She sucked her breath in through clenched teeth. Anger fought pain in her jade eyes.

"And what were you told to say?" she asked, her voice trembling.

"I was told to remind you that you're angry right now because of what you know: that because of your incompetence, Waters died. Waters—someone you knew, someone you respected. You've worked with him, looked at the pictures of his family, sat down with his wife and kids, eaten dinner and laughed. You know you lost him— because you panicked."

Michaels let out the breath she had been holding in a gasping sob. She held her hand over her mouth for a moment, her eyes closed. "That was very cruel, Cofield," she husked out.

"Was it a lie?"

A beat, a hesitation. "No."

"Then don't compound your mistake. If you don't help us now, then your friend's death was entirely wasted. If you don't help us, I may never find my grandfather again, or Jennifer and Peter."

"How can I be *certain*? You could be lying to me . . ."

"You can't be certain. None of us can be because nothing *is* certain. Time—history—doesn't work that way. But I can tell you this, and you'll just have to take it for the truth. Our world was better once. If we can, we'll find a way to make it that way again."

Michaels closed her eyes again, swaying slightly as she stood in front of the path. The time machine moved slightly as someone pounded at the doors to the laboratory. Mundo spat, like a cat startled from sleep.

"Aaron . . ." Travis said. "We need to hurry, kid. Company's coming."

"Captain?" Aaron asked.

She shook her head at first, then her lips tightened. "All right," Michaels sighed. Her eyes opened. "I'll need help."

"Mundo!" Aaron called, and stepped down from the hatchway. Michaels said nothing about the ape, though she looked at him curiously. With the woman directing them, the three wrestled the heavy pieces of metal and glowing crystal into the blackened crevices in the roadway. It took several minutes, as the commotion out in the hallway increased. The sound of heavy battering came through the walls, a persistent hammering.

When they had finished, Aaron took from his pocket a small vial that Travis had given him from the medical kit on the time machine. Holding the tiny cylinder between the thumbs and forefingers of both hands, he flexed it. Glass cracked.

"Sniff this, Captain," Aaron said. He gave her what he hoped was a reassuring smile. "You're going to need the excuse."

Michaels took the vial from his hand and held it under her nose. She took a deep breath. Her eyes rolled upward and as she slumped slowly to the floor, Mundo lowered her softly.

"Let's go!" Aaron said to Mundo. The two of them swung back into the time machine. As the hatch closed and Travis moved them forward again, the laboratory doors burst open, a squad of armed men flowing in. The hull of the time machine reverberated with metallic *pings* as the craft moved at an agonizingly slow pace toward the path.

"This had better work," Travis grunted. "This thing's not exactly a tank." To one side, they could see a soldier kneeling, a long tube on his shoulder, sighting down the barrel at them. Another man behind him slammed a shell home and slapped the other's back.

"*Go*, Travis!" Aaron yelled. "That's a bazooka, not a rifle!"

The time machine touched down on the roadway as the weapon gushed flame and the shell exploded.

But Aaron, Travis, Mundo, and the time machine were no longer there. They were in another world and another time altogether.

GLOSSARY OF MUTATA TERMS

The sounds of the Mutata

The sounds made by the Mutata (a race of sentient dinosaurs most similar to the duckbills of our prehistory) are produced through their long nasal horns. In the novels, they are omitted for the most part. However, the most common sounds are a nasal bleet, a snort, a full roar, and a trill.

Pronunciation Key

The Mutata language has been transcribed into an approximation of phonetic English. Most consonants are pronounced as they would be pronounced in that language. In most cases, "a" is pronounced as the 'a' in cat; "e" as the 'e' in met; "i" as the 'i' in dim (though an ending "i" is pronounced as the 'ee' in meet); "o" as the 'o' in solo; "u" as the 'oo' in moot; "ai" as 'i' in ride; "ei" as the 'ea' in heaven; "ah" as the 'a' in tall. Some of the Mutata sounds cannot be adequately reproduced by the human larynx. In those cases, the closest English sound has been used, as in "jh," which for the Mutata is a glottal stop much like a very rapid "jeh-eh," the last syllable being a quick aspirant. In some cases, a literal translation of the Mutata word has been substituted, as in "Speaker" or "Giving." There are also subtle posture and scent aspects to the Mutata language which, unfortunately, must be lost in the written form and which humans can never imitate. Any human must always be partially mute and deaf to the Mutata language as spoken by the dinosaurs.

aii
An imperative: to be performed immediately.

Baosiot
Unintelligent predatory dinosaurs—the allosaurus, possibly.

bhieye
"Thank you."

broaii
The Gairk war club, a massive wooden mallet tipped with several protruding blades of obsidian. The Gairk will usually carry two,

one for the right hand, one for the left. Like the Mutata, the left hand is used when striking another sentient creature; the left is for 'non-intelligent' lifeforms.

chodoe "Follow me." An imperative, used only by a superior Mutata to his or her social inferiors.

ciosie A demand for satisfaction. Ciosie means literally "The decision of the All-Ancestor"—in other words, letting the right or wrong of an issue be decided by combat, with the All-Ancestor's influence supposedly determining the outcome.

daii soo Literally, "Pause (or wait) several breaths."

ehei To go outside a dwelling. Also, to wander.

Eikels Eckels

Floraria Unintelligent predatory dinosaurs, possibly the Tyrannosaurus family.

gaedo An affirmative given by a younger to an elder. "Yes."

Gairk   The racial name for a species of sentient, small allosaurs.

geedo   "Yes." As spoken by peers.

geiree   "Come here," or "Approach me." An imperative form.

gheodo   Literally, "I cannot do that," with the added emphasis that the refusal is based on a superior's orders.

Giving   Translation of the Mutata phrase meaning "The time when the spirit is given to the All-Ancestor." The funeral rite for Mutata.

iaso   "Animal"—more specifically, a nonsentient creature, without language or anything more than animal intelligence. The type of being killed with the right hand rather than the left.

jhaka   The village in which Mutata live, each under the rule of its own OColi.

Jhenini   Jenny.

jhiehai   Scavenger proto-birds—these are deliberately enticed to feed on the bodies of dead Mutata.

khiisoo   A demand for obedience: "You must obey!"

LongDay   Or OGhielas. The summer solstice. As with almost all human cultures, the Mutata and Gairk also mark the solstices for religious celebration and ceremony.

Mutata   The racial name for SStragh's species of sentient dinosaurs.

niijeks   Mouse-like rodents which feed on the stored grains within the Mutata encampments

OColi   Literally, the Eldest. The ruler of a particular Mutata tribe is nearly always the oldest among them. Can be either male or female, though the males generally live the longest.

OColihi   The Ancient Path. The code of ethics and behavior which govern the Mutata. This code is handed down via a verbal tradition through the OTsio. The beginnings of the ritualized OColihi are lost in the long centuries of the Mutata past.

oei   A modifier. When used in conjunction with other words, it indicates "many" or "a large amount."

OTsio   Teacher. Each youngling Mutata when the tribe has returned from the first Nesting Walk after their hatching, is assigned an OTsio to guide their development. The OTsio becomes a parentanalogue, though a Mutata of that age is age is considered independent.

otsioiue   The OTsio's student.

Raajek   SStragh's OTsio, and a proponent of the OChiihi, or New Path—a mindset at variance with the old ways of Mutata behavior.

saorod   A species of pterosaur in Dinosaur World, with about a 3-inch wingspan.

Speaker   Translation of the Mutata title-phrase meaning "One who speaks the words of the Eldest."

SStragh   The Mutata who finds and captures Jennifer, Peter, and Eckels, and who befriends Jennifer.

tiafer   The original name of the current OColi

werada   A death caused by a Mutata—specifically, the left-handed type of killing, not the right-handed killing that would be done to an animal.

werata   Pain

whiaso   A "right-handed" killing, or the killing of a simple, unintelligent creature.

yeie   A modifer, indicating a negative: "I will not" or "This is not so." Also used as a quick denial: "No!"

zhiotae   The Gairk "Reader of Omens" or shaman. Functions as an adviser to the Gairk OColi in spiritual matters. The Mutata have no analogue occupation.

APPENDIX–
A SOUND OF THUNDER

by Ray Bradbury

The sign on the wall seemed to quaver under a film of sliding warm water. Eckels felt his eyelids blink over his stare, and the sign burned in this momentary darkness:

> TIME SAFARI, INC.
> SAFARIS TO ANY YEAR
> IN THE PAST.
> YOU NAME THE ANIMAL.
> WE TAKE YOU THERE.
> YOU SHOOT IT.

A warm phlegm gathered in Eckels' throat; he swallowed and pushed it down. The muscles around his mouth formed a smile as he put his hand slowly out upon the air, and in that hand waved a check for ten thousand dollars at the man behind the desk.

"Does this safari guarantee I come back alive?"

"We guarantee nothing," said the official, "except the dinosaurs." He turned. "This is Mr. Travis, your Safari Guide in the Past. He'll tell you what and where to shoot. If he says no shooting, no shooting. If you disobey instructions, there's a stiff penalty of another ten thousand dollars, plus possible government action, on your return."

Eckels glanced across the vast office at a mass and tangle, a snaking and humming of wires and steel boxes, at an aurora that flickered now orange, now silver, now blue. There was a sound like a gigantic bonfire burning all of Time, all the years and all the parchment calendars, all the hours piled high and set aflame.

A touch of the hand and this burning world, on the instant, beautifully reverses itself. Eckels remembered the wording in the advertisements to the letter. Out of chars and ashes, out of dust and coals, like golden salamanders, the old years, the green years, might leap; roses sweeten the air, white hair turn Irish-black, wrinkles vanish; all, everything fly back to seed, flee death, rush down to their beginnings, suns rise in western skies and set in glorious easts, moons eat themselves opposite to the custom, all and everything cupping one in another like Chinese boxes, rabbits into hats, all and everything returning to the fresh death, the seed death, the green death, to the time before the beginning. A touch of a hand might do it, the merest touch of a hand.

"Hell and damn," Eckels breathed, the light of the Machine on his thin face. "A real Time Machine." He shook his head. "Makes you think. If the election had gone badly yesterday, I might be here now running away from the results. Thank God, Keith won. He'll make a fine President of the United States."

"Yes," said the man behind the desk. "We're lucky. If Deutscher had gotten in, we'd have the worst kind of dictatorship. There's an anti-everything man for you, a militarist, anti-Christ, antihuman, anti-intellectual. People called us up, you know, joking but not joking. Said if Deutscher became President they wanted to go live in 1492. Of course it's not our business to conduct Escapes, but to form Safaris. Anyway, Keith's President now. All you got to worry about is—"

"Shooting my dinosaur." Eckels finished it for him.

"A Tyrannosaurus Rex. The damndest monster in history. Sign this release. Anything happens to you, we're not responsible. Those dinosaurs are hungry."

Eckels flushed angrily. "Trying to scare me!"

"Frankly, yes. We don't want anyone going who'll panic at the first shot. Six Safari leaders were killed last year and a dozen hunters. We're here to give you the damndest thrill a *real* hunter ever asked for. Traveling you back sixty million years to bag the biggest damned game in all Time. Your personal check's still there. Tear it up."

Mr. Eckels looked at the check for a long time. His fingers twitched.

"Good luck," said the man behind the desk. "Mr. Travis, he's all yours."

They moved silently across the room, taking their guns with them, toward the Machine, toward the silver metal and the roaring light.

First a day and then a night and then a day and then a night, then it was day-night-day-night-day. A week, a month, a year, a decade. A.D. 2055. A.D. 2019. 1999! 1957! Gone! The Machine roared.

They put on their oxygen helmets and tested the intercoms.

Eckels swayed on the padded seat, his face

pale, his jaw stiff. He felt the trembling in his arms and he looked down and found his hands tight on the new rifle. There were four other men in the Machine. Travis, the Safari leader; his assistant, Lesperance; and two other hunters, Billings and Kramer. They sat looking at each other, and the years blazed between them.

"Can these guns get a dinosaur cold?" Eckels felt his mouth saying.

"If you hit them right," said Travis on the helmet radio. "Some dinosaurs have two brains, one in the head, another far down the spinal column. We stay away from those. That's stretching luck. Put your first two shots into the eyes, if you can, blind them, and go back into the brain."

The Machine howled. Time was a film run backwards. Suns fled and ten million moons fled after them. "Good God," said Eckels. "Every hunter that ever lived would envy us today. This makes Africa seem like Illinois."

The Machine slowed; its scream fell to a murmur. The Machine stopped.

The sun stopped in the sky.

The fog that had enveloped the Machine blew away and they were in an old time, a very old time indeed, three hunters and two Safari Heads with their blue metal guns across their knees.

"Christ isn't born yet," said Travis. "Moses has not gone to the mountain to talk with God. The Pyramids are still in the earth, waiting to be cut out and put up. *Remember* that. Alexander, Caesar, Napoleon, Hitler—none of them exists."

The men nodded.

"That"—Mr. Travis pointed—"is the jungle

of sixty million two thousand and fifty-five years before President Keith."

He indicated a metal path that struck off into green wilderness, over steaming swamp, among giant ferns and palms.

"And that," he said, "is the Path, laid by Time Safari for your use. It floats six inches above the earth. Doesn't touch so much as one grass blade, flower, or tree. It's an antigravity metal. Its purpose is to keep you from touching this world of the Past in any way. Stay on the Path. Don't go off it. I repeat. *Don't go off*. For *any* reason! If you fall off, there's a penalty. And don't shoot any animal we don't okay."

"Why?" asked Eckels.

They sat in the ancient wilderness. Far birds' cries blew on a wind, and the smell of tar and an old salt sea, moist grasses, and flowers the color of blood.

"We don't want to change the Future. We don't belong here in the Past. The government doesn't *like* us here. We have to pay big graft to keep our franchise. A Time Machine is damn finicky business. Not knowing it, we might kill an important animal, a small bird, a roach, a flower even, thus destroying an important link in a growing species."

"That's not clear," said Eckels.

"All right," Travis continued, "say we accidentally kill one mouse here. That means all the future families of this one particular mouse are destroyed, right?"

"Right."

"And all the families of the families of the families of that one mouse! With a stamp of your foot, you annihilate first one, then a dozen, then a thousand, a million, a *billion* possible mice!"

"So they're dead," said Eckels. "So what?"

"So what?" Travis snorted quietly. "Well, what about the foxes that'll need those mice to survive? For want of ten mice, a fox dies. For want of ten foxes, a lion starves. For want of a lion, all manner of insects, vultures, infinite billions of life forms are thrown into chaos and destruction. Eventually it all boils down to this: fifty-nine million years later, a cave man, one of a dozen on the *entire world*, goes hunting wild boar or saber-toothed tiger for food. But you, friend, have *stepped* on all the tigers in that region. By stepping on *one* single mouse. So the cave man starves. And the cave man, please note, is not just *any* expendable man, no! He is an *entire future nation*. From his loins would have sprung ten sons. From *their* loins one hundred sons, and thus onward to a civilization. Destroy this one man, and you destroy a race, a people, an entire history of life. It is comparable to slaying some of Adam's grandchildren. The stamp of your foot, on one mouse, could start an earthquake, the effects of which could shake our Earth and destinies down through Time, to their very foundations. With the death of that one cave man, a billion others yet unborn are throttled in the womb. Perhaps Rome never rises on its seven hills. Perhaps Europe is forever a dark forest, and only Asia waxes healthy and teeming. Step on a mouse and you crush the Pyramids. Step on a mouse and you leave your print, like a Grand Canyon, across Eternity. Queen Elizabeth might never be born; Washington might not cross the Delaware; there might never be a United States at all. So be careful. Stay on the Path. *Never* step off!"

"I see," said Eckels. "Then it wouldn't pay for us even to touch the *grass*?"

"Correct. Crushing certain plants could add up infinitesimally. A little error here would multiply in sixty million years, all out of proportion. Of course maybe our theory is wrong. Maybe Time *can't* be changed by us. Or maybe it can be changed only in little subtle ways. A dead mouse here makes an insect imbalance there, a population disproportion later, a bad harvest further on, a depression, mass starvation, and, finally, a change in *social* temperament in far-flung countries. Something much more subtle, like that. Perhaps only a soft breath, a whisper, a hair, pollen on the air, such a slight, slight change that unless you looked close you wouldn't see it. Who knows? Who really can say he knows? We don't know. We're guessing. But until we do know for certain whether our messing around in Time *can* make a big roar or a little rustle in History, we're being damned careful. This Machine, this Path, your clothing and bodies, were sterilized, as you know, before the journey. We wear these oxygen helmets so we can't introduce our bacteria into an ancient atmosphere."

"How do we know which animals to shoot?"

"They're marked with red paint," said Travis. "Today, before our journey, we sent Lesperance here back with the Machine. He came to this particular era and followed certain animals."

"Studying them?"

"Right," said Lesperance. "I track them through their entire existence, noting which of them lives longest. Not long. How many times they mate. Not often. Life's short. When I find one that's going to die when a tree falls on him, or one that drowns in a tar pit, I note the exact hour, minute, and second. I shoot a paint bomb. It leaves a red patch on his hide. We can't miss it. Then I correlate our arrival in the Past so that we meet the Monster not more than two minutes before he would have died anyway. You see how *careful* we are?"

"But if you came back this morning in Time," said Eckels eagerly, "you must have bumped into *us*, our Safari! How did it turn out? Was it successful? Did all of us get through—alive?"

Travis and Lesperance gave each other a look.

"That'd be a paradox," said the latter. "Time doesn't permit that sort of mess—a man meeting himself. When such occasions threaten, Time steps aside. Like an airplane hitting an air pocket. You felt the Machine jump just before we stopped? That was us passing ourselves on the way back to the Future. We saw nothing. There's no way of telling *if* this expedition was a success, *if* we got our Monster, or whether all of us—meaning *you*, Mr. Eckels—got out alive."

Eckels smiled palely.

"Cut that," said Travis sharply. "Everyone on his feet!"

They were ready to leave the Machine.

The jungle was high and the jungle was broad and the jungle was the entire world forever and forever. Sounds like music and sounds like flying tents filled the sky, and those were pterodactyls soaring with cavernous gray wings, gigantic bats out of a delirium and a night fever. Eckels, balanced on the narrow Path, aimed his rifle playfully.

"Stop that!" said Travis. "Don't even aim for fun, damn it! If your gun should go off—"

Eckels flushed. "Where's our Tyrannosaurus?"

Lesperance checked his wristwatch. "Up a-head. We'll bisect his trail in sixty seconds. Look for the red paint, for Christ's sake. Don't shoot till we give the word. Stay on the Path. *Stay on the Path!*"

They moved forward in the wind of morning.

"Strange," murmured Eckels. "Up ahead, six-ty million years, Election Day over. Keith made President. Everyone celebrating. And here we are, a million years lost, and they don't exist. The things we worried about for months, a life-time, not even born or thought about yet."

"Safety catches off, everyone!" ordered Travis. "You, first shot, Eckels. Second, Billings. Third, Kramer."

"I've hunted tiger, wild boar, buffalo, elephant, but Jesus, this is *it*," said Eckels. "I'm shaking like a kid."

"Ah," said Travis.

Everyone stopped.

Travis raised his hand. "Ahead," he whispered. "In the mist. There he is. There's His Royal Maj-esty now."

The jungle was wide and full of twitterings, rustlings, murmurs, and sighs.

Suddenly it all ceased, as if someone had shut a door.

Silence.

A sound of thunder.

Out of the mist, one hundred yards away, came Tyrannosaurus Rex.

"Jesus God," whispered Eckels.

"Shh!"

It came on great oiled, resilient, striding legs. It towered thirty feet above half of the trees, a great evil god, folding its delicate watchmaker's claws close to its oily reptilian chest. Each lower leg was a piston, a thousand pounds of white bone, sunk in thick ropes of muscle, sheathed over in a gleam of pebbled skin like the mail of a terrible warrior. Each thigh was a ton of meat, ivory, and steel mesh. And from the great breathing cage of the upper body, those two delicate arms dangled out front, arms with hands which might pick up and examine men like toys, while the snake neck coiled. And the head itself, a ton of sculptured stone, lifted easily upon the sky. Its mouth gaped, exposing a fence of teeth like daggers. Its eyes rolled, ostrich eggs, empty of all expression save hunger. It closed its mouth in a deadly grin. It ran, its pelvic bones crushing aside trees and bushes, its taloned feet clawing damp earth, leaving prints six inches deep wherever it settled its weight. It ran with a gliding ballet step, far too poised and balanced for its ten tons. It moved into a sunlit area warily, its beautiful reptile hands feeling the air.

"My God!" Eckels twitched his mouth. "It could reach up and grab the Moon."

"Shh!" Travis jerked angrily. "He hasn't seen us yet."

"It can't be killed." Eckels pronounced this verdict quietly, as if there could be no argument. He had weighed the evidence and this was his considered opinion. The rifle in his hands seemed a cap gun. "We were fools to come. This is impossible."

"Shut up!" hissed Travis.

"Nightmare."

"Turn around," commanded Travis. "Walk quietly to the Machine. We'll remit one-half your fee."

"I didn't realize it would be this *big*," said Eckels. "I miscalculated, that's all. And now I want out."

"It *sees* us!"

"There's the red paint on its chest!"

The Thunder Lizard raised itself. Its armored flesh glittered like a thousand green coins. The coins, crusted with slime, steamed. In the slime, tiny insects wriggled, so that the entire body seemed to twitch and undulate, even while the Monster itself did not move. It exhaled. The stink of raw flesh blew down the wilderness.

"Get me out of here," said Eckels. "It was never like this before. I was always sure I'd come through alive. I had good guides, good safaris, and safety. This time, I figured wrong. I've met my match and admit it. This is too much for me to get hold of."

"Don't run," said Lesperance. "Turn around. Hide in the Machine."

"Yes." Eckels seemed to be numb. He looked at his feet as if trying to make them move. He gave a grunt of helplessness.

"Eckels!"

He took a few steps, blinking, shuffling.

"Not *that* way!"

The Monster, at the first motion, lunged forward with a terrible scream. It covered one hundred yards in four seconds. The rifles jerked up and blazed fire. A windstorm from the beast's mouth engulfed them in the stench of slime and old blood. The Monster roared, teeth glittering with sun.

Eckels, not looking back, walked blindly to the edge of the Path, his gun limp in his arms, stepped off the Path, and walked, not knowing it, into the jungle. His feet sank into green moss. His legs moved him, and he felt alone and remote from the events behind.

The rifles cracked again. Their sound was lost in shriek and lizard thunder. The great lever of the reptile's tail swung up, lashed sideways. Trees exploded in clouds of leaf and branch. The Monster twitched its jeweler's hands down to fondle at the men, to twist them in half, to crush them like berries, to cram them into its teeth and its screaming throat. Its boulder-stone eyes leveled with the men. They saw themselves mirrored. They fired at the metallic eyelids and the blazing black iris.

Like a stone idol, like a mountain avalanche, Tyrannosaurus fell. Thundering, it clutched trees, pulled them with it. It wrenched and tore the metal Path. The men flung themselves back and away. The body hit, ten tons of cold flesh and stone. The guns fired. The Monster lashed its armored tail, twitched its snake jaws, and lay still. A fount of blood spurted from its throat. Somewhere inside, a sac of fluids burst. Sickening gushes drenched the hunters. They stood, red and glistening.

The thunder faded.

The jungle was silent. After the avalanche, a green peace. After the nightmare, morning.

Billings and Kramer sat on the pathway and threw up. Travis and Lesperance stood with smoking rifles, cursing steadily.

In the Time Machine, on his face, Eckels lay shivering. He had found his way back to the Path, climbed into the Machine.

Travis came walking, glanced at Eckels, took cotton gauze from a metal box, and returned to the others, who were sitting on the Path.

"Clean up."

They wiped the blood from their helmets. They began to curse too. The Monster lay, a hill of solid flesh. Within, you could hear the sighs and murmurs as the furthest chambers of it died, the organs malfunctioning, liquids running a final instant from pocket to sac to spleen, everything shutting off, closing up forever. It was like standing by a wrecked locomotive or a steam shovel at quitting time, all valves being released or levered light. Bones cracked; the tonnage of its own flesh, off-balance, dead weight, snapped the delicate forearms, caught underneath. The meat settled, quivering.

Another cracking sound. Overhead, a gigantic tree branch broke from its heavy mooring, fell. It crashed upon the dead beast with finality.

"There." Lesperance checked his watch. "Right on time. That's the giant tree that was scheduled to fall and kill this animal originally." He glanced at the two hunters. "You want the trophy picture?"

"What?"

"We can't take a trophy back to the Future. The body has to stay right here where it would have died originally so the insects, birds, and bacteria can get at it, as they were intended to. Everything in balance. The body stays. But we *can* take a picture of you standing near it."

The two men tried to think, but gave up, shaking their heads.

They let themselves be led along the metal Path. They sank wearily into the Machine cushions. They gazed back at the ruined Monster, the stagnating mound, where already strange reptilian birds and golden insects were busy at the steaming armor.

A sound on the floor of the Time Machine stiffened them. Eckels sat there, shivering.

"I'm sorry," he said at last.

"Get up!" cried Travis.

Eckels got up.

"Go out on that Path alone," said Travis. He had his rifle pointed. "You're not coming back in the Machine. We're leaving you here!"

Lesperance seized Travis' arm. "Wait—"

"Stay out of this!" Travis shook his hand away. "This son of a bitch nearly killed us. But it isn't *that* so much. Hell, no. It's his *shoes*! Look at them! He ran off the Path. My God, that *ruins* us! Christ knows how much we'll forfeit! Tens of thousands of dollars of insurance. We guarantee no one leaves the Path. He left it. Oh, the damn fool! I'll have to report to the government. They might revoke our license to travel. God knows *what* he's done to Time, to History!"

"Take it easy, all he did was kick up some dirt."

"How do we *know*?" cried Travis. "We don't know anything! It's all a damn mystery! Get out there, Eckels!"

Eckels fumbled at his shirt. "I'll pay anything. A hundred thousand dollars!"

Travis glared at Eckels' checkbook and spat. "Go out there. The Monster's next to the Path. Stick your arms up to your elbows in his mouth. Then you can come back with us."

"That's unreasonable!"

"The Monster's dead, you yellow bastard. The bullets! The bullets can't be left behind. They don't belong in the Past; they might change something. Here's my knife. Dig them out!"

The jungle was alive again, full of the old tremorings and bird cries. Eckels turned slowly to regard that primeval garbage dump, that hill of nightmares and terror. After a long time, like a sleepwalker, he shuffled out along the Path.

He returned, shuddering, five minutes later, his arms soaked and red to the elbows. He held out his hands. Each held a number of steel bullets. Then he fell. He lay where he fell, not moving.

"You didn't have to make him do that," said Lesperance.

"Didn't I? It's too early to tell." Travis nudged the still body. "He'll live. Next time he won't go hunting game like this. Okay." He jerked his thumb wearily at Lesperance. "Switch on. Let's go home."

1492. 1776. 1812.

They cleaned their hands and faces. They changed their caking shirts and pants. Eckels was up and around again, not speaking. Travis glared at him for a full ten minutes.

"Don't look at me," cried Eckels. "I haven't done anything."

"Who can tell?"

"Just ran off the Path, that's all, a little mud on my shoes—what do you want me to do—get down and pray?"

"We might need it. I'm warning you, Eckels, I might kill you yet. I've got my gun ready."

"I'm innocent. I've done nothing!"

1999. 2000. 2055.

The Machine stopped.

"Get out," said Travis.

The room was there as they had left it. But not the same as they had left it. The same man sat behind the same desk. But the same man did not quite sit behind the same desk.

Travis looked around swiftly. "Everything okay here?" he snapped.

"Fine. Welcome home!"

Travis did not relax. He seemed to be looking at the very atoms of the air itself, at the way the sun poured through the one high window.

"Okay, Eckels, get out. Don't ever come back."

Eckels could not move.

"You heard me," said Travis. "What're you *staring* at?"

Eckels stood smelling the air, and there was a thing to the air, a chemical taint so subtle, so slight, that only a faint cry of his subliminal senses warned him it was there. The colors, white, gray, blue, orange, in the wall, in the furniture, in the sky beyond the window, were . . . were . . . And there was a *feel*. His flesh twitched. His hands twitched. He stood drinking the oddness with the pores of his body. Somewhere, someone must have been screaming one of those whistles that only a dog can hear. His body screamed silence in return. Beyond this room, beyond this wall, beyond this man who was not quite the same man seated at this desk that was not quite the same desk . . . lay an entire world of streets and people. What sort of world was it now; there was no telling. He could feel them moving there, beyond the walls, almost, like so many chess pieces blown in a dry wind. . . .

But the immediate thing was the sign painted on the office wall, the same sign he had read earlier today on first entering.

Somehow, the sign had changed:

TYME SEFARI INC.
SEFARIS TU ANY YEER EN THE PAST.
YU NAIM THE ANIMALL.
WEE TAEK YU THAIR.
YU SHOOT ITT.

Eckels felt himself fall into a chair. He fumbled crazily at the thick slime on his boots. He held up a clod of dirt, trembling. "No, it *can't* be. Not a *little* thing like that. No!"

Embedded in the mud, glistening green and gold and black, was a butterfly, very beautiful, and very dead.

"Not a little thing like *that*! Not a butterfly!" cried Eckels.

It fell to the floor, an exquisite thing, a small thing that could upset balances and knock down a line of small dominoes and then big dominoes and then gigantic dominoes, all down the years across Time. Eckels' mind whirled. It *couldn't* change things. Killing one butterfly couldn't be *that* important! Could it?

His face was cold. His mouth trembled, asking: "Who—who won the presidential election yesterday?"

The man behind the desk laughed. "You joking? You know damn well. Deutscher, of course. Who else? Not that damn weakling Keith. We got an iron man now, a man with guts, by God!" The official stopped. "What's wrong?"

Eckels moaned. He dropped to his knees. He scrabbled at the golden butterfly with shaking fingers. "Can't we," he pleaded to the world, to himself, to the officials, to the Machine, "can't we take it *back*, can't we *make* it alive again? Can't we start over? Can't we—"

He did not move. Eyes shut, he waited, shivering. He heard Travis breathe loud in the room; he heard Travis shift his rifle, click the safety catch, and raise the weapon.

There was a sound of thunder.